CHATEAU LAUX

CHATEAU LAUX

A NOVEL

DAVID LOUX

Wire Gate Press

RENO, NV

Chateau Laux
by David Loux

© 2021 by David Loux

Although this work was inspired by an actual past event (see Historical Notes), this is a work of fiction. Names, characters, businesses, places, events, and incidents are either the products of the author's imaginations or used in a fictitious manner. Any resemblance to actual persons, living or dead, or actual events is purely coincidental.

ISBN 978-1-954065-01-7 (trade paperback original)
ISBN 978-1-954065-00-0 (Epub)

Publication Date: April 6, 2021
First edition

BISAC category code
FIC019000 FICTION/Literary
FIC014070 FICTION/Historical/Colonial America & Revolution
FIC008000 FICTION/Sagas
FIC051000 FICTION/Cultural Heritage

COVER DESIGN AND INTERIOR DESIGN:
KG Design International; kgeokat@gmail.com

Wire Gate Press
Reno, NV
wiregatepress@gmail.com

In remembrance of
Catharine Laux Kraymer and her infant son, Peter,
who lived and breathed

« *Dis-moi quel est ton amour, et je te dirai qui tu es.* »
("Tell me what you love and I will tell you who you are.")

—Jean-Paul II aux jeunes dans la basilique Saint-Pie X

CHATEAU
LAUX

CHAPTER
ONE

———•———

The year was 1710, and at twenty-two years of age, Lawrence Kraymer belonged to the class of thriving young merchants transforming the city of Philadelphia. He brewed beer from the increasing supply of malting barley and hops grown in the middle and northern colonies, and the rough and crowded waterfront taverns couldn't get enough of it. Working all day and long into the night, he heaved the heavy kegs onto the drays that lined up at the brewery's loading dock, where the horses stood in their traces and the teamsters whistled for his attention.

Lawrence owed much of his good fortune to his grandfather, who had built the brewery from the ground up and who later took Lawrence in at an early age, after the boy's mother died of the coughing disease. The old man gave him a roof over his head, taught him a trade, and in due time passed on to him a thriving and lucrative business, and for this, Lawrence was truly grateful. But there was a price to be paid. The old man was disagreeable by nature and held the boy responsible for his mother's sins. He called Lawrence a bastard, without the least bit of remorse. He worked the boy like an indentured servant, whipping him at the least sign of sloth, and these many years later, Lawrence needed a break. He sought refuge from the recriminating spirit that persisted in haunting him. Putting a trusted employee in charge of his brewery, he hired an Indian to take him on a hunting trip up along the Delaware.

They each rode a horse and shared a mule between them. Lawrence had chosen this particular mule for its good demeanor, which was no small consideration, regarding an animal that could be willful and contrary. The mule carried a cast iron cooking pot, a sack of beans, and ten pounds of bacon. It also carried the canvas tent and their sleeping blankets, two axes, three muskets, with extra gunpowder, and a leather bag of lead ball. Lawrence carried a knife on his belt, along with a pouch of flints and tinder. The Indian's name was John. He carried a knife as well, and wore a leather sack slung over his shoulder. In addition to his buckskins, he wore moccasins that laced up past his ankles. Lawrence wore a farmer's field boots.

After three days of camping, John decided to head north, where the New York colony was located, but Lawrence wasn't ready to leave the wild. He wanted to stay a while longer and hunt by himself, and that was when the stillness of the woods truly haunted him, reaching deep inside, past the clutching fingers of his grandfather's ghost, to a part of him that remained unsullied. The nights smothered him with a darkness that seemed to come from above and below, forcing its way into his eyes, his lungs, and heart. The wilderness didn't judge. In aloneness, he found peace—if only for the moment—and his veins filled with a rushing motion, like the waters of a cold mountain stream. The crackling flames of the bonfires he built sent sparks spiraling up to the pressing stars. In the mornings, he became as quiet as the woods themselves, just another creature of the forest, crawling on his belly, parting branches to peer into the clearings along the river. When he took a shot, the gun sounded like thunder, the echoes a distant reminder that, as far as he knew, he was totally alone in a world devoid of human presence.

All too soon, he had to head home, back to his yeast cultures and delivery schedules, and he packed the mule and readied his horse for travel. But then, something unexpected happened. Without John to guide him, he found himself on an unfamiliar road, and it amazed him to think how he had found his way so well in the wild places, only to lose himself on the road to civilization. The limestone ridges were covered in the same canopy of hickory and chestnut and oak he had known on his outbound journey. But they were not the same. Nor were the maples and willows and sumac that grew in the draws. The split rail fences along the way were not the same ones he had passed before. Nor were the log homes and river stone farmhouses. The cattle knew it and so did the horses in the pastures, which raised their heads to look at him in a way that said he was the one that was out of place and not anyone or anything else.

A rising breeze turned up the silver undersides of the tree leaves. Chill fingers of air began to close on the back of his neck. He smelled the coming rain and counted himself lucky when he came upon an isolated farm, so close to the wild but not quite in it. Lit by one of the last slanting rays of the sun, the farmhouse looked like an island of light in the darkening landscape. Several exceptional horses grazed in a lush meadow. As the storm neared, the scene shimmered with subtle and shifting gemstone colors that flared and glowed and ebbed from one hue to the next. A tall, angular man stood in a blacksmith's shed, gripping a horseshoe in a pair of tongs. Behind him, the fire of the forge glowed red in the failing light.

All manner of people came to the colonies. Many were of desperate circumstances, but some simply didn't fit in anywhere else and so were best avoided. Philadelphia had its own fair share of delinquents. But the frontier outback was rumored to have a much worse sort, and Lawrence approached the smithy with care. Stopping at a safe distance, he marshalled his voice.

"Hello!" he called out, squeezing the breath from his lungs. After spending several days with the untalkative John and then many more alone in the tall, dark timber, his voice sounded strangely alien.

The man in the smithy paused in his labor. In the conversation that followed, the man allowed he was called Pierre, though the rest of the name wouldn't come until much later. He had a natural reserve that suggested an innate distrust of his environment in general, and a particular distrust of the humans that occupied it. He did not seem aggressive. But Lawrence noted that he did not appear to be the sort to tolerate any foolishness, either.

"Looks like a storm on your heels," Pierre said, with a curious accent, stating the obvious, trying to be friendly, perhaps. But Lawrence wasn't fooled. Strangers were not known to engage in idle banter—not here at the edge of the wild, where your safety was a concern that you often bore alone. The man was probing him, laying out a simple statement and giving him the opportunity to respond, and Lawrence turned in his saddle and looked back the way he had come. A cloud lit up. Seconds later, thunder rumbled. Astride the horse, he felt thrust up against the sky, and exposed.

"You see my dilemma clearly," he said, turning back to the man at the forge. "At the risk of imposing some inconvenience, I was hoping I could prevail upon you to provide some shelter for the night."

Pierre's eyes drifted to Lawrence's mule, loaded down with the tent, the cooking implements, the hides of beaver and deer, and the pelt of a bear. Lawrence had the feeling that Pierre was not a hunter and that his lingering scrutiny was part of a slow, methodical judgment of Lawrence's character.

"Lived on wild meat and beans, I dare say," Pierre said.

"Wild meat and beans," Lawrence agreed, chagrined at the memory of such a limited diet. At first, he had reveled in the taste of animal flesh but quickly grew tired of wild tallow and the lack of salt. Pained at having to eat so many beans in the first place and then running out and having none to eat at all.

"Might be we can find a place for you in the barn," Pierre said, after a pause.

Lawrence had expected nothing more and was grateful for whatever kindness the man cared to bestow. Climbing down from his horse, he shook Pierre's hand and then followed him to the barn, where he was shown where to put his animals and stow his gear. One of the stalls had fresh straw on which he could spread his blanket.

"I'll leave this with you," Pierre said, handing him a lantern.

Lawrence thanked him.

"Not often we get visitors," Pierre said, shrugging. Giving Lawrence one last, lingering look, he turned and left the barn. Thunder boomed and the ground shuddered.

It was one thing to be alone in the woods, where no one had any knowledge or expectations of you, and quite another to be in a space owned and controlled by someone else, where the surrounding structures had been shaped by hands other than your own, and where human breath and blood gathered and coursed in unknowable fashion. Lawrence stood in momentary dejection, his feet planted wide and his shoulders slumped. All over again, he felt like a child with a dead mother, standing on the doorstep of an old man he had never met, a note of introduction in his hand. His mother had not spoken to her father since the unfortunate birth of her child, and the note was the only provenance Lawrence had. He sometimes felt as if he still stood on that doorstep, waiting, waiting.

The barn had darkened, and he struck his flint to light the lantern. The shadows cast by the glow loomed large. He could still hear the thudding draw of the bolt on the other side of his grandfather's door, the shudder of wood and the squeal of hinges, and as much as he appreciated the shelter of the barn, he already regretted the position he'd put himself in. He hated to feel beholden to his grandfather, to this man Pierre, or to anyone else.

Hearing a sound behind him, he whirled around, his heart in his throat. A boy of about thirteen stood there, his face glowing in the lantern light. He had sandy hair and ruddy cheeks. Another boy ranged past him, swinging wide. He looked a year or so older, with darker hair and a fuzzy lip. Both were unusually tall, lanky, and well-proportioned, with coltish insouciance, and Lawrence's surprise at their sudden arrival was soothed by their youth and the friendly curiosity in their frank gazes.

"Ma sent us," the younger brother said. "Pa told her about you and she said to invite you to supper, but that anyone who's spent time in the wild would have to take a bath before coming into any house of hers. Pa was all for sending you down to the creek, but Ma said you'd get struck by lightning for sure and she wouldn't have it. Pa said go ahead and use the horse trough. Just be sure to pull the plug when you're done and then pump in some fresh water." He held out a bundle that included a clean linen shirt and a pair of woolen breeches, in addition to a towel, a washcloth, and a big bar of soap.

The older brother appeared to be the more reserved of the two. He studied Lawrence with obvious interest but came no closer. "Come on," he finally said, tersely, to the younger boy. "Ma said we shouldn't linger."

"I'm not lingering," the younger one said, stoutly.

The older one gave Lawrence a look that begged his indulgence. "He always dillydallies," he said, as if in answer to a curiosity Lawrence may have had.

"I do not," the younger brother said.

A sudden light flickered, followed by a thunder crack. A deluge of rain hit the barn.

The brothers turned to leave, but Lawrence stopped them.

"Aren't you going to tell me who you are?" he said.

The younger face brightened.

"I'm Georgie and this here's my brother, Andrew. You haven't met Jean yet."

"Jean?" Lawrence said. But the brothers had turned again and disappeared like phantoms. Their silhouettes appeared at the doorway of the barn, and a flash of lightning revealed a third youth who appeared taller and leaner than the other two. He carried a musket, and Lawrence realized the boys had taken no chances and that he had been under a watchful eye the whole time. He shook his head with admiration.

Rain poured from the dark sky and thundered down against his shoulders and head as he took his cold bath, his bottom slick against the slippery surface of the horse trough. Scrubbing the bar of soap furiously against his hands, he then ran his fingers through his hair and down his face, startled at the extent of his beard. He had had the beard for two weeks and hardly given it a thought. But now that he was about to share a meal with people he didn't know, he wondered what they would see when they looked at him. Returning to the barn, he toweled off and dressed in the borrowed clothes, then swiped at his hair and whiskers, hoping it was enough to make him presentable.

Then, it seemed miraculously, he found himself in a kitchen banked with the smells of meat and freshly baked bread. A young woman with braided chestnut hair knelt in front of the hearth, using a wooden spoon to scrape at the browned bits that had collected in an iron pot. An older woman set a plate of scallions and radishes on the table. She hardly seemed old enough to have children nearly grown. There were eight place settings, and Lawrence saw the two boys he had already met and the third, whom he had seen only in silhouette, all seated at the table and looking at him with the quiet enthusiasm of country folk, who rarely got to spend time with someone from outside of their small community. The man who had earlier introduced himself as Pierre sat beside a little girl of about four, with blue eyes and red curls, dimpled cheeks.

Lawrence's eyes swam the length of the room, trying to take it all in.

"Welcome," Pierre said, gesturing toward an empty space at the opposite end of the table. His earlier gruffness seemed to have evaporated. "My boys you already met. That's my eldest, Catharine, over there, and this here's our little Magdalena. The stern one is Beatrice," he said, smiling.

"I'll show you stern if you're not careful," said the woman named Beatrice, digging at her husband with a look that told him he had better watch out or there would be a price to pay for such teasing. Her brown hair was braided like her daughter's and her eyes were honey-colored, her back long and straight. She wore a simple linen dress, an apron, and wooden shoes.

Lawrence felt the need to apologize, at the outset, that he was dressed in someone else's clothes, and the two youngest brothers jostled each other, as if sharing a private joke. Beatrice quickly took charge.

"Just go on now and sit yourself down," she said, with a touch of bluster. "Boys, pass our guest the radishes and salt. The bread is ready and the roast is taking a rest. Pierre, maybe you should go to the cellar and fetch some of the better wine."

"You see who gives the orders around here," Pierre grumbled, giving Lawrence a wink. He stomped out of the kitchen. A door opened and Lawrence heard heavy foot treads on wooden steps.

"He's not really mad," the little Magdalena piped up, with an authority that belied her age. She raised her cream-colored chin and gave her red curls a toss. "He acts like he is but he's not."

Pierre returned with a bottle of wine cradled in his hands. Beatrice removed the bread from its baking pan and placed it on a cutting board. She brought a platter of roasted beef to the table, and Catharine served the sauce in a cream pitcher. There were boiled potatoes with churned butter, and freshly picked green beans from the garden. Beatrice asked Pierre to say grace, and the family folded their hands and bowed their heads as he did so. Then they tucked into the meal with gusto. They were aware of the stranger in their midst—in fact, keenly so—but no one troubled Lawrence to explain himself just yet.

"Papa, tell us a story," said Magdalena, swinging her feet under her chair.

"A story?" Pierre said, as if such a notion would never have occurred to him.

"I'm sure our guest is not interested in stories," Beatrice said.

"Tell the one about the Poor Lonely Dragon," said Georgie.

"The one who makes the sky dark when it spreads its wings," added the little girl.

"Ah, the Poor Lonely Dragon . . ." Pierre said, with a mischievous twinkle. He made his hand into a claw and reached toward his daughter. She yanked her arm back, shrieking, and Lawrence's body jerked. At a time when many children did not survive to adulthood, love was often like a coin pinched tightly between the finger and thumb—present, perhaps, but not freely given—and Lawrence was not used to such open displays of affection. It was hard for him to imagine that something he had never personally experienced could exist here in such abundance.

Oblivious to his guest's disquietude, Pierre told the story of a lonely dragon that lived in the Pyrenees Mountains, where Pierre was from. It wandered the world, spreading darkness in its wake, looking for a lost love, and Lawrence could feel the dragon's pain. He could feel its suffering. And then, when the story was over and the dragon had wept itself to sleep in its poor lonely cave, it was someone else's turn to talk. All eyes turned to him. They looked at him as if what he had to say really mattered and his usual reticence crumbled. The personal reserve he wore like a coat of armor began to feel cumbersome.

The words came hesitantly at first. Then, they began to gather and spill in greater volume, building until they became a torrent of sound and intonation. He didn't know any stories like the one Pierre had told, so he talked about his brewery in Philadelphia, the commotion of life in the port city, the people coming off ships with little or nothing to their names. He liked making beer and selling it to the local taverns, but something was missing, he said. He liked the jangling of the horse harnesses and the barking of the dogs and the whistles of the men in the wagons. The music at night. The piano and the violin, the chanters who sang on street corners. But even in such a wonderful place, there was a hole in his chest that the wind blew through, and he told how he had sought the dark solitude of the timber beyond the edge of the homesteaded land. He told of rivers of wild shad and bald eagles and early morning mists dense enough to bathe you from the inside out, washing clean your lungs and eyes and between the fingers of your searching hands.

Barely touching her meal, Catharine Laux watched him devour his, and when he had finished, having done most of the talking and having had more than one helping of every dish, not to mention an abundance of wine, he pushed back from the table and their eyes met and lingered. The cheeks above his hunter's beard flushed and Catharine turned away, but too late. He had already seen her seeing him.

Eventually, good nights were said, and Lawrence found himself outside the house, deeply roused, lonely in a way he had never been before. Even the barn held a certain magic, and he lay awake most of the night listening to a rain that fell through the darkness, washing the buildings and the landscape, running in rivulets to the meadow where it flushed into the creek, which grew swollen, thickening as it roped off into the night. He felt as if the rain pummeled his body, washing him clean, and in the gray light of dawn he rose, packed his mule and left the homestead, still in awe of the night before—the food, the company of a close-knit family, and a young woman so abundant in beauty.

TWO

Catharine remembered every detail about the night the stranger showed up at the farm. She remembered the excitement of his arrival and the anticipation of his entrance into the house. She remembered the young man himself, his dark, wavy hair and intense eyes, the broad shoulders and muscled arms, the soapy smell of him. More than anything, she remembered the words that spilled from him like poetry, as he spoke of places she had never been and things she had neither done nor seen. She remembered the looks they had exchanged, when he seemed to see into her heart.

But life goes on in the country, and she had no reason to think she would ever see him again. The sky rains and the land dries out, and there's always work to be done—the washing and ironing, the cleaning, the endless preparation of food. An autumn passed into winter, the dark months of rain and snow, the days of frozen, cracking earth, when even the windows iced over. The dark months passed, too, and then, when the sun turned to butter again and the land hummed with new life, the rumors began to fly. A young merchant from Philadelphia was poking around in the community, looking at forested acreage and asking about prices. He asked about land and he asked about Pierre, the reticent French farmer that everyone knew but none very well.

Catharine had little interest in such idle gossip and tried not to pay it much heed. At eighteen, she was already past the age when some girls married. She could have blamed her father, for the few boys who had dared show up at the farm with fistfuls of wildflowers could not even muster the courage to speak to him, let alone make their intentions known. But she knew the fault was not Pierre's alone. The last boy had left the farm in tears, and Catharine had determined she would not encourage such things in the future. It was simply too distressing to witness the humiliation of these would-be suitors, and she already fancied herself along the lines of her Great-Aunt Esclarmonde, whom her father described as a rare beauty who had chosen never to wed.

As a child, Catharine had loved to hear stories of this exotic aunt.

"Tell me about Aunt Claire," she used to beg, and her father would take her onto his knee and appear, for a moment, lost in thought.

"Ah, the beautiful Esclarmonde," he would finally say, beginning the story the same way each time, making little Catharine catch her breath. "She was a countess, you know, from a very special family." Invariably, he would then pause. "She was your grandmother's sister and such a rare beauty that men came from all over the world just to look at her. Her beauty was said to turn a man to stone, and to this day—" he would hold up a finger, "—there is said to be a forest of stone, somewhere in the ancient County of Foix, filled with tall rocks that used to be kings and princes."

The little girl clapped her hands in delight.

"But why didn't she marry?" she asked and then waited for the answer she knew would come, her little body rigid with anticipation, her heart beating hard.

"Because," her father said, pausing for effect. When the silence became excruciating and she couldn't stand it another second, he would finally go on. "Because she was *perfect*, just the way she was," he said, and now, even as a young adult, Catharine felt as if she were still the child she had once been, in a boat on a quiet pond, drifting slowly toward an island of happiness.

◆　◆　◆

RUMORS OF THE MYSTERIOUS STRANGER persisted and then, one day, a visitor showed up at the farm. It was the same young man who had spent the night in the barn the previous fall. But instead of borrowed clothes, he now wore a russet jacket over a yellow waist-coat, an ascot of ruffled silk, and cream-colored breeches. He had ridden in an open carriage and brought gifts—a fowling piece with a curly maple stock for Pierre, hunting knives for the boys, and chocolates for the women. As an extra gift, he gave Catharine a silver spoon that was polished to a shine, in its own wooden box. The gifts caused quite a stir and Pierre was reluctant to receive them, but Lawrence insisted with such sincerity that Pierre relented. Lawrence then asked Beatrice if he could sit on the porch with Catharine, alone, and Beatrice allowed it, with the provision that the kitchen door remain open.

Catharine still wore her apron and hardly thought she was dressed to receive anyone. But pushing a few stray hairs into place, she went out onto the porch, where she and Lawrence sat in two of the many empty chairs. Lawrence perched on the edge of his seat and stared down at his hands, which he folded together and then unfolded. He stood up and paced to the edge of the porch, before returning to his chair and sitting down awkwardly. The last time Catharine had seen him, he'd worn a hunter's beard. Now he was clean-shaven and sunburned. His dark hair stuck to his glistening neck.

Haltingly at first, he said the night he had stayed at the farm those several months ago had changed his life. He'd had a good life and offered no complaints, he said. But he had never known what it was like to belong to a family until his evening with the Lauxes, and when he got back to Philadelphia, something was different. Something was wrong. He breathed and slept and did the things that all living people do, but everything seemed different and would never again be the same. All he could think of was her, and he thought of her day and night.

Looking at her in earnest, he said he had come to a decision that he prayed she might find agreeable. He had found an acreage of virgin timber with high ground for a house and a good stream of water for pasturage. The land would have to be cleared, of course, but it was just what he was looking for and he had taken the leap of faith such a purchase required.

"But you live in Philadelphia," Catharine said in astonishment. Lawrence admitted there were incumbent challenges, logistical issues, things that would need to be worked out if he were to leave the city and move to Watertown.

"But, sir, what about your business?" she asked, and he admitted that the business was, indeed, a complication. But he hastened to add that while the business had flourished and blessed him in many ways, he wanted something else, something more. He wanted something uniquely his own, he said, something that made him feel whole and no longer like half a person.

"Why would you feel like half a person?" she said, and he responded that she simply couldn't understand, coming from a family like hers. She would just have to accept that what he was trying to say was a true thing. And looking at him, she finally asked the question that was foremost on her mind.

"Mr. Kraymer, pardon my asking, but why would you do all of this?"

His response was not anything she could have expected. He stood, as if to distance himself from her, and the color drained from his face. Feeling suddenly very awkward, seated in her chair with Lawrence towering over her, Catharine extended her hand, expecting him to help her rise. But that is not what he did. Taking her hand, he dropped to his knee, so that he looked up at her.

"Miss Laux, if you're not already promised, would you consider me as a suitor?" he said, his face still deathly pale.

Catharine gave her hand a convulsive tug, but he held onto it and she relaxed. The pain of his earnestness was so obvious that she felt sorry for him, and she glanced over her shoulder to see if, perchance, her father had come to the open kitchen door. It wasn't exactly a marriage proposal, but pleasing nonetheless, and the thrill that began to uncoil and work its way through her could not be denied.

"Yes," she said, her heart hammering, her face heating up, astonished at what seemed to be happening.

CHAPTER

THREE

———————●———————

Pierre could not have anticipated the impact Lawrence would have on his life. Up to that point, he had never had to explain to anyone outside the family how he had ended up in one of the middle colonies, where social refinements were rudimentary at best. Far from anything extraordinary, the fact that his father was a nobleman in southern France was just another fact of life as he knew it. He didn't care one jot that others might struggle to understand how a French aristocrat had become a colonial farmer.

Catharine's relationship with the young entrepreneur changed everything. The reclusive farmer now had to face inquiries as to who he was and where he was from. For Pierre, the storied past of a noble family had the feel of a worn shoe, but to Lawrence it was altogether different. Born amid questionable circumstances into the turmoil and uncertainties of a youthful colony, Lawrence listened raptly. At first, he appeared overwhelmed, then his eyes began to glow. He looked at Catharine as if seeing her anew. He said he was going to build her a house that would make her proud, though he stopped short of actually explaining what he had in mind.

"Papa, aren't you the least curious?" Catharine asked, sometime later, imploring Pierre to visit the construction site. To be honest, he had avoided the site. Catharine pointed this out. She pouted, which was so unlike her, and that was how Pierre finally found himself at the patch of torn earth, where the primal forest had been reduced to a field of stumps. Horses nickered and chains rattled, as men busily unloaded wagonloads of rock. Lawrence stood next to a smaller man, near an expansive area where wooden stakes had been driven into the ground and lengths of rope stretched between them. The smaller man had a roll of parchment clamped under his arm. He took notes in a small leather book, stopping now and then to swat at a cloud of insects.

Pierre found Lawrence perplexing at times. The young man seemed extraordinarily sure of himself. But there was a cautious edge to his posturing, as if he lay in wait for an unkind remark or a mean-spirited observation. He seemed drawn to Pierre and to genuinely desire the older man's goodwill. At the same time, however, there was a hesitation, as if he had a fundamental distrust of another man's benevolence.

"I heard you were building something special," Pierre said, as they shook hands. The strength of Lawrence's grip was not lost on him. It disturbed him, reminding him that his daughter was a young woman now, with a mind of her own, and that she was bound to make decisions that didn't take her father into consideration.

Lawrence tilted his head to the side.

"I don't suppose . . . Miss Laux . . . told you?"

"Told me what?" Pierre said.

Lawrence looked embarrassed. He beckoned to the man with the parchment, who folded his notebook closed and tucked it inside the wing of his leather vest. Nearing where they stood, he composed a smile. He had dark hair and narrow eyes, a narrow face with a long chin. "You wish to speak to me?" he said in a voice that rose in a solicitous manner.

"Aye, this is Mr. Laux—the gentleman I was telling you about," Lawrence said.

"Ah, yes, the father of your *belle fleur*," the man said, holding out a hand that drooped from the wrist. His dark bud of a mouth twisted into a smile.

"This is Guy LeBlanc," Lawrence said to Pierre, before glancing back to the man and his parchment. "Why don't you explain to Mr. Laux here what we're building?"

"Why, we're building a château, *monsieur*," LeBlanc said, as if some things were obvious.

Pierre blinked, two things impacting him at once. First of all, he had no idea that Lawrence was building a château, and a cascade of emotions surged through him. He well remembered the château of his youth, which his father, the *seigneur*, had called a *manoir*. It was their family home, an estate that had been handed down over many generations. Unlike the nearby villagers, the manoir people wore fine clothes and leather shoes. But it was the manoir, itself, more than anything, that set them apart, rising from the ground like a fortress, with its tiled roofs and surrounding wall, and some might have thought it grand. No one could have known how such an apparent blessing could turn into such a terrible curse.

Secondly, but just as instantaneous, was the realization, from his accent, that LeBlanc was Parisian. The France that Pierre had known was a divided country, filled with many hatreds that went all the way back to the earliest of times. The language of the south was a mélange of Occitan tongues—often little more than patois—which used the word *oc* to signify yes. As far back as the Middle Ages, the region as a whole was often called the *Langue d'oc*, or Languedoc. The north, on the other hand, where Paris was located, spoke a different language, a harsher one to the southern ear. The northerners used the word *oui* for yes and Pierre's father had often referred to the northerners as the *Langue oui*. He said this spitefully and only in private, of course.

"LeBlanc has been a godsend," Lawrence was saying, visibly relieved that the secret was finally out. "I couldn't believe my good luck. Do you know how hard it was to find anyone who knew anything about building a château? I thought I was going to have to cross the ocean to find an architect for a project like this, and here he was, right under my nose, sitting in a tavern in Philadelphia like any other fellow."

"The good fortune was mine, most certainly," LeBlanc said, shifting his eyes to Lawrence and then back to Pierre in his disarming fashion. "In your colonies, there was much work to be had, and I came to seek the fortune, as you might say. But they were building in wood and the common brick, and I despaired of meeting a man of Mr. Kraymer's discriminating taste. To build a château in this New World of yours—how could I say no to such a rare proposition? I am most honored to be of humble service."

He paused, giving Pierre a prying look.

"The monsieur is not pleased?" he said.

"What Mr. Kraymer decides to build is his own concern," Pierre said, trying to sound dispassionate.

But the discovery of this château in the making *had* affected him, and very deeply. His gaze drifted to the far edge of the clearing, where the uncut trees still rose from the ground like blackened, tortured hands with twisted fingers, and a chill crept down his spine. He couldn't shake the notion that the New World and the Old were not so different after all, and that the scarring of the land could rouse something that should have been left unmolested.

◆ ◆ ◆

PIERRE FELT UNSETTLED AS HE left the construction site. He was sensible to the fact that, in all likelihood, Lawrence was trying

to please him. But the young man's seemingly rash decision to recon-
struct one of the relics of Pierre's own past only served to remind him
of the boy he, himself, had once been, playing with swords made of
wooden sticks and happily unaware that there were monsters in the
world far worse than anything he could have imagined. The time was
long gone when Pierre had been able to take for granted the smells of
cassoulets and baking bread. As a child, he could never have foreseen
that the mother who seemed so fierce in her intellect and so unwavering in her love could abandon him with such thoughtless ease.

Remembering his mother, with her Magdalena hair and milky
skin, was just too painful, and Pierre stood up on the trundling wagon,
because sometimes the simple act of standing was all that you could do.
To escape your past, you had to rise. If he were a bird, he would have
flown and flown higher and higher, never once looking at the ground.

But you can't stand forever, and in his present mood, nothing
seemed to please. The road home seemed interminable. Then, when
he finally got to the storage shed and had to unload the wagon, the
dust from the flour sacks itched his neck. Coming out of the shed, the
sunlight blinded him, and by then, the three dogs had found him—a
pair of mastiffs and their full-grown offspring, rounding the barn and
bounding in his direction. They were big dogs, big enough to bowl
him over in an unbridled moment of jubilation, and he had no patience
for their frolicking display. He made a gesture with his hand, and they
sat on their haunches, their eyes sharp and attentive, their massive
heads with the fleshy jowls rooted to the broad, muscular shoulders.

And then, still weighted down by his thoughts, Pierre glanced
toward the house and saw them. Catharine carried the wooden
chicken bucket on her arm as she headed toward the barn to collect
eggs, and little Magdalena skipped on ahead, leaping into the air in
an effort to catch butterflies. What a wonder it was to have children,

he thought. You prayed for boys, for the heavy lifting and the defense of all that a family held dear. But you hoped for girls, for the joy they brought to a father's heart and for the gift of flight they gave you.

◆　◆　◆

PIERRE CLOSED THE GATE AND headed toward the house, the dogs loping around him. The house was cool and gloomy, the kitchen empty, the living room with its rocking chairs and large fireplace quiet and undisturbed in its solitude. He didn't even try the upstairs, because he knew no one would be there, not in the middle of the day, and he went back outside and circled to the garden, where he found Beatrice wearing a floppy hat of woven straw and holding a hoe that she worked back and forth where the corn grew and the squash spread green splashes of leaves.

"Hello, wife," he said.

"Hello yourself," she retorted, straightening her back and eyeing him.

She was a fine-looking woman, he thought, his mouth pulling into a grin. He thought of her hair, which smelled like alfalfa, her sunburned face and the whiteness of the skin under her clothes. As he looked at her, her eyes narrowed.

"You've got nothing to do?" she said, suspiciously.

"Don't worry yourself, woman. I'm not here to ill-treat you."

"I'll be the judge of that," she muttered, and his grin broadened.

"Not that I ever have."

"I wouldn't think too highly of yourself—it's unbecoming."

She chopped at a weed that crowded a cornstalk.

"I dropped in on Lawrence on the way back from Watertown."

"Oh?" Beatrice said, concentrating on her work.

"Did you know he was building a château?" Pierre asked, suspiciously.

Beatrice sighed, placing the head of the hoe on the ground and leaning on the long handle. She gave him the kind of look she reserved for the times when there was something difficult to discuss.

"Catharine has been wanting to tell you, and I dare say Lawrence has, too. But you're not always an easy man, Mr. Laux. To your wife, you are like the blessed sunshine and to your children . . . well, I don't have to tell you. They think you walk on water. But we are your family. We know you for the man you are. Can you imagine what it must be like to be someone like Lawrence Kraymer, who never had a father? Who never had a family to speak of? Can you imagine what someone like him must think of you?"

Pierre struggled to find a response.

"Mr. Kraymer is not just anybody, you know," Beatrice said, more gently. "He will very likely become part of our family, and is already part of our lives. He has been calling on our Catharine, now, for several months, and I think he is just waiting for the right moment to fully reveal himself with a formal entreaty."

"But why a château?" Pierre said, letting his exasperation leak out a little.

"I'm not sure that even he knows the answer," Beatrice said. "He has the means, certainly, and judging by the amount of time he is spending here, he's got that, too. Beyond that, I can only guess. But look at it this way. You ask any of your children who they are, and they wouldn't give it a moment's thought before telling you straight out they are Lauxes. To them, the name says it all, and where does that leave someone like Lawrence? How does it make him feel? You may have awakened something in him, but before you go thinking the château is about you, I would suggest it's very much something else. It's about him and that's all, pure and simple—him and the man that he wants to be."

Pierre looked at her a long time as her words sank in. It made him ill at ease that Lawrence presumed to think he would be impressed by a château. He didn't like it that his daughter appeared to be complicit, and that even his wife was taking sides. In fact, there were a lot of things he didn't like that he couldn't seem to do anything about. Finally, he relaxed and nodded.

"You give wise counsel," he said, with grudging recognition.

"Oh, go on now," she said, blushing at the unexpected compliment.

"I'm serious," he said.

Beatrice paused.

"If you've got nothing to do, I can find something for you," she said, twitching with a smile under her hat.

"What are you suggesting?"

She looked at him askance.

"Ah . . ." he said, grasping her meaning. Even here, life had its pleasures, the little things that made drawing breath worthwhile. It took an unusual person to live so close to the rough and wild, with few neighbors and none of them close enough to make a difference if misfortune struck. It took a brave woman to live in such isolation and to trust Pierre with her safety, which was no small concern, so far from even a modicum of civilization. Pierre had his reasons for choosing to live at the edge of the known world, but it took a bold person to want to share such a life with him. He normally shied away from tempting fate too much. But for a daring, precious moment, he felt like the luckiest man alive.

CHAPTER
FOUR

———————•———————

The construction of Lawrence's château created the opportunity
that Pierre's second son, Andrew, had been waiting for. At first,
the youth's participation in the project was on the order of holding
a piece of scaffolding while someone else drove the nail, or fetch-
ing a bucket of mortar for the masons. But something had been
awakened in him. For the first time in his young life, he realized
that the act of living was not just trying to fit into the whole cloth
of the family he had been born into. He saw that an environment
could be altered. Like a jumble of granite blocks, it could be ordered
in a manner that might yield something new and unexpected, and
he rose to the sun each morning with the feeling that something
extraordinary was about to happen.

When he got to the building site, he found Lawrence squared
off with LeBlanc, the architect, who stood with his high, cuffed
boots planted wide and his ruffled sleeves folded against his chest.
Lawrence paced back and forth in front of the smaller man, clearly
perturbed.

"How do you expect me to get the place done?" Lawrence
demanded.

Andrew sidled up to his older brother Jean, who stood a short
distance away. Like Andrew, Jean had been doing odd jobs at the
site. He wore a leather apron, similar to the ones the masons wore.

"What's going on?" Andrew said.

"I'm not sure. I think LeBlanc dismissed somebody," Jean said.

Andrew gave a quick look around, wondering how he hadn't noticed that something was amiss. A lot of work had been accomplished at the site, but now things were most definitely at a standstill. The rock walls outlining the structure were barely five feet tall and the fire had gone out in the kiln where limestone was burned for the mortar. Men sat idly in whatever shade they could find, smoking their pipes.

"You expect much from me and I, in turn, have expectations of others," LeBlanc said, with barely concealed disdain for the men he had to work with.

"What does that have to do with what we're talking about?" Lawrence said, impatiently.

"Without the rock, I can do nothing—*rien!* All I ask is to have the rock. Is that too much to ask for?"

"If you have any more problems, just tell me," Lawrence said. "Don't take matters into your own hands, okay?"

Shaking his head, Lawrence turned his back on the architect and stalked over to the Laux brothers. His face was flushed. He stood in front of them, glowering, and Andrew felt a small flutter of excitement.

"Is there a problem with the rock?" Andrew asked, solicitously.

"If it's not one thing it's another, and yes, to answer your question," Lawrence said. "The shipments have slowed and the masons have nothing to do. LeBlanc claims it's not his fault. He always has to blame somebody else when something goes wrong."

"So . . . what will you do about it?" Andrew said, making his play.

Lawrence blinked.

"Who? LeBlanc?" he said.

"No, the rock. If we leave right now, we can get to the quarry by tomorrow morning. It's just a thought. Maybe you have a different plan."

Lawrence gave him a startled look and even Jean seemed surprised.

"We?" Lawrence said. "*You?*"

Andrew shrugged.

"Someone's got to find out what's going on."

"You've never been away from home before, have you?" Lawrence said, dubiously.

"Pa's my problem, if that's what you're worried about," Andrew replied.

◆　◆　◆

LAWRENCE SAT ON THE FARMHOUSE porch, alone among the many chairs, while Andrew went inside. Already, he was wondering if bringing the youth along was a good idea. The boy's initiative had caught him by surprise, and he wondered if he had agreed too quickly.

Lawrence had been extraordinarily lucky to inherit a fully formed brewery business, with a product in such high demand that hard work alone sufficed to make him a wealthy man. The château, on the other hand, was in a process of birthing that seemed to have an endless capacity for complications. Problems arose and decisions had to be made, and each decision had its own challenges. Granite, for instance, was not so common in a countryside of limestone and sedimentary rock. In a land still largely untouched by human endeavor, he had to find it and then quarry it himself.

But running a quarry meant having to hire and manage the men who worked it, and Lawrence felt a growing appreciation for what his grandfather must have gone through when he established the brewery in the first place. To create something out of nothing was an accomplishment—to have an idea and then to flesh it into reality. To know what to do and puzzle out how to do it. To solve one problem without creating another. Lawrence had the uneasy notion that the ornery old man and Andrew Laux might have a lot in common.

His right knee jiggled up and down as he listened to the ebb and flow of voices from inside, the determined tenor of the boy, the softer but firm notes of Beatrice's voice, and the deeper tones of the words spoken by Pierre.

"He's still a child," Beatrice said.

"He'll be whatever we let him be," Pierre said.

"Why rush things? Won't he grow up soon enough?"

"Is it right to hold him back?"

"But what if something happens to him?" Beatrice said, and outside, Lawrence found himself swayed. He wondered what he could have been thinking when he agreed that Andrew should come. He must've been out of his mind, he thought.

"I have to hand it to you," Lawrence said, when he and Andrew finally took to the road, leaving the farmhouse behind. "Your ma's a formidable person, and she sounded none too happy about this trip. I'm not quite sure how you got her consent, to tell you the truth."

"I told you to leave my parents to me," Andrew said, as if he, for one, had never had any doubts that he would get what he wanted.

"Even your pa . . ." Lawrence said, giving his head a shake.

But Andrew had other things to worry about than what Lawrence thought or had to say. The youth's horse was the more spirited of the two, and it made one of its little dashes, surging forward and then prancing with high steps, as if planning its next outbreak. At first, Andrew calmed the horse, patting the arching neck and murmuring with a gentle voice reserved for high-strung creatures. But the horse wasn't the only one feeling its oats, apparently, and Andrew loosened the reins. Throwing an unprovoked, challenging glance at Lawrence, he took off at a gallop, leaving Lawrence to plod along with only his thoughts for company, wondering what he had gotten himself into.

◆　◆　◆

BY THE TIME THEY ARRIVED at the roadside inn, Lawrence was good and ready for a drink. A wall of aromas met them, greasy meat and yeasty beer, the bite of wood ash and tobacco smoke, and then there was the guttural murmur of muted conversation. Lawrence paid for the night and they took their bedrolls to the room before returning below for their meal.

The innkeeper brought them a trencher of pork ribs and wooden mugs of warm beer. Two men stared across at them from another table. One wore a tattered British officer's coat, with rips and gaps in the cloth that looked like bullet holes. The other wore a leather hunting shirt and striped pants. He had a tomahawk stuck in his belt.

"Pa warned me to be careful," Andrew said, eyeing them. "He said the thing you have to understand about inns is that people are tired from traveling and when they stop for the night, with nothing else to do, they start drinking. He said that when a man imbibes too much, he can change, and it's not always for the best."

Lawrence was still annoyed by Andrew's antics earlier in the day, and the comment irritated him. As a brewmaster, he had spent many an evening in taverns and hardly considered himself the worse off for it. He was loath to contradict Andrew outright, however, and eyed him grudgingly.

"Your pa keeps a wine cellar, as I recall," he said, but Andrew ignored him.

"He said you don't always really know a man until he drinks too much," the youth went on.

Andrew kept a wary eye on the rough-looking men on the far side of the room, and Lawrence wondered if the boy doubted Lawrence's ability to protect him, should the need arise. This in turn made him wonder what had been said back at the farmhouse— what Pierre might have told his son that an outsider like Lawrence couldn't hear. Lawrence had to allow that he was tired from the several hours on horseback and shouldn't presume to pass judgment. But he was well on his way to becoming his own man, now, and he reminded himself that he was the one in charge. This was his trip and Andrew was his responsibility. What Pierre had to say shouldn't have to matter so much.

"You have nothing to worry about. Not when you're with me," he said, raising his mug to catch the innkeeper's eye. The beer had a tang of bitterness that Lawrence liked, and he quaffed the draft the innkeeper brought and then had a third. All the while, he felt a certainty rising in him. However unreasonable it might seem in the light of a new day, he became convinced Pierre must only have allowed Andrew on the trip in order to test him, Lawrence, in some way. And along with the certainty came anger. Pierre might have been the aristocrat, but Lawrence was the one building the château. Surely, he was entitled to far more respect and consideration than he was getting.

A fog entered his mind. His voice got louder and Andrew suggested they go up to the room. "We just got here," Lawrence said, adamantly, and several rounds later, when he finally stood up, his chair toppled over backwards. Andrew led the way. The boy took one last glance at the man in the officer's coat, and when they got to the room, he went straight to the chair that sat next to the washstand and used it to brace the door.

"What are you doing?" Lawrence said, in drunken astonishment.

"Pa said not to take any chances," Andrew said.

He spread his bedroll on the floor, then reached into his pack and removed a pistol and powder horn. Crouching in the dim light of the oil lamp, he tapped a little bit of powder into the flash pan. Evidently satisfied that all was ready, he placed the pack next to the bedroll and rested the pistol on top of it. "Pa doesn't like inns," he explained. "He says they're good places to run into bad people."

"So he gave you a pistol?"

Andrew pulled off his boots and lay on top of the bedroll, still dressed in his shirt and pants. He placed his hands behind his head and stared briefly at the ceiling before closing his eyes.

"He said anybody who forces his way into the room is not a friend, and that I should put a ball into the middle of 'im."

"And then what, get hanged for it?" Lawrence said.

"Pa said getting into trouble for protecting yourself is better than getting into trouble for not," Andrew replied, unperturbed, his eyes still closed.

Lawrence glared at him for several moments, then blew out the lamp and slumped heavily onto the bed. Without knowing he had fallen asleep, he began to dream. He and Catharine were in the meadow below the Laux farmhouse. Surrounded by sunflowers as tall as their heads, they had beaten a flat area to lay down a blanket. Catharine had a picnic basket of cold chicken and jars of tea made from the wild mint that grew along the nearby creek. She took off her bonnet and her hair glinted an auburn mix of chestnut and reds in the sun, her laughter melodious as the music of water over stones. He wanted her so badly he thought his belly would split open, but then Pierre was there, sitting on the blanket beside them, chewing on a piece of chicken and talking about the crop of alfalfa they would have to harvest soon. Pierre ate with his fingers and Beatrice was there, too, wanting to know if anyone wanted more tea. Lawrence looked for Catharine but she wasn't on the blanket and she wasn't in the sunflowers. He searched the farmhouse, and it was dark and empty.

◆　◆　◆

LAWRENCE SPENT THE MORNING IN brooding silence. His eyes burned and his throat scratched, and when they got to the quarry, he found the men dozing in the shade of a small shack. He blinked and shook his head. His wounded pride balled up inside of him. His face darkened.

"What's going on here?" he snarled, jerking the horse to a halt in front of the sleeping men. He jumped down from the saddle and flung the reins against the ground. "We run out of rock, and I make the trip all the way up here to find out what the problem is, and what I find is that nobody's doing anything. What do you think I'm paying you for? Where's my rock?"

The men stumbled to their feet.

The foreman stepped forward to try to explain. His gaze darted back over his shoulder to a hillside, where the ground had been laid open and the rock exposed.

"We ran out of powder," he said. "We can't blast without powder and we ran out."

"You ran out?"

"We're waiting for more."

"You ran out of blasting powder?" Lawrence repeated, his voice rising with incredulity.

He plucked a chisel from the leather girdle the foreman wore. From another man, he took a rock hammer and strode over to the exposed rock of the quarry site. Bending, he searched intently for a seam, and finding one, placed the bit of the chisel against it. Holding the chisel steady, he struck it with the hammer. He struck several blows and the hammer and chisel rang against the rock.

"Bring me a sledgehammer!" he shouted over his shoulder. Several men stood around, watching him, and one held out a sledgehammer. Lawrence grabbed it and gave the chisel to Andrew. "Here," he said, "hold this against the crack in the rock."

Andrew knelt and held the chisel at arm's length. Lawrence swung the hammer in a big arc and Andrew didn't flinch. He held the chisel steady. After several blows, the rock split and Lawrence tossed the hammer aside. He was breathing heavily.

"That's how you split a rock," he said. He gestured toward a horse and wagon parked next to the shed. "I'm going to take the wagon and go get you some powder, and when I get back, I expect a pile of rock to take home with me. Am I clear on this?"

The men shuffled uncomfortably, avoiding his probing gaze.

"Do you want me to go with you?" Andrew asked.

"I want you to stay right here and make sure we get some rock to take back with us."

The quarrymen eyed each other with dubious reluctance. They were used to blasting, not hammering out splits. But they wouldn't have been there in the first place if they didn't need the money.

"How'm I supposed to do that?" Andrew said.

"How should I know? Your father gave you a pistol, didn't he?" Lawrence said, stomping off toward the horse and wagon.

FIVE

———•———

The southern France of Pierre's youth had been a crossroads for a very long time and had learned to hide its secrets well. Pierre's father was a Protestant, following a Calvinist tradition that reflected his roots in the region once known as Navarre. But in this part of the world, religion was sometimes like a new coat of paint on a very old house, and Pierre's mother was a Cathar—a group of mystical worshippers that elevated women as well as men to the highest level. None of this would have mattered to young Pierre, except that Louis XIV, then king of France, was a northerner with little appreciation for the complexities of the south. He was a Catholic, and as such, took the extraordinary step of billeting northern troops in the homes of southern Protestants in an attempt to force their conversion.

In retrospect, Pierre was glad his father had not been at the manoir when the soldiers pounded on their door. Weeks earlier, the seigneur and his bodyguards had ridden out of the courtyard, with all of their usual pomp and urgency, promising a speedy return. Faced with the news that the king's troops were advancing, Seigneur du Laux had said he would petition the king, personally, for a reprieve for his family. He was counting on his position as a courtier to grant him the Sun King's ear.

These many years later, Pierre could still see his mother struggling to sit up in bed, lowering her legs over the edge of the mattress and testing the floor with her naked feet. Pierre had helped her up and she put on a white robe, tying it with a sash around the waist. Her knees kept buckling and she couldn't stand on her own. But at the age of thirteen, Pierre was already as tall as most men. He had an erect posture and a strong, lean frame, and was able to support her with ease.

"Take a walk with me," she said, leaning on his arm, her body long and thin and nearly weightless. "I must show you something."

"*Mamà*, it's not too late to reconsider," he said, referring to what Cathars called the *endura*, a willful act of starvation. To Cathars, the endura was not suicide so much as a cleansing of the spirit, but Pierre couldn't accept why his mother would do such a thing—for in spite of their present difficulties, they still had each other. He couldn't understand why she would choose to leave him in this way.

"I am doing what I must," she murmured, imploring him with her eyes. "We have talked about it and you know it is true. Now help me, please."

"Maybe we should just sit here on the bed. I worry a walk will be too much for you."

"Too much?" she said, her eyes softening as she gazed at him, and in retrospect, he knew how silly his statement must have seemed. Was it too much to have the *Langue oui* billeted in your home, just because some of you were Protestant? Was it too much for the soldiers to climb into the beds of noblewomen—their daughters and housemaids? His mother had at least been spared this atrocity. "She's just skin and bones," one of the soldiers had spat. But it wasn't entirely her emaciation, either, that saved her. The soldiers sensed she was different, even though they couldn't have named the reason. They looked at her with caution and maybe even fear, thinking, perhaps, that the Languedoc was known to have witches and maybe she was one. What else would explain her complete indifference to them?

"Hush now, and do as I ask," she said, her mouth turning into a wan smile.

Slipping an arm around her waist, he supported her body with his own, feeling her bones against his side. Slowly, they shuffled from the bedroom and across the great room, where three of the soldiers played cards. The soldiers looked at them with eyes that were bloodshot from drinking the manoir's finest wines. The stink of these men filled the room.

Out in the courtyard, his mother leaned on his arm with the weight of a wilted flower. She gestured toward the garden.

"This is where you must bury me," she said, pointing toward the patch of ground where her beloved roses grew.

"Don't talk that way, Mamà. I can't even think of such a thing."

"Someone must think of it, and it is only you and me, now," she said, her voice hardly a whisper. "Your father would have returned by now if he could have and we must assume he has been arrested . . . or worse. Being a Protestant is not good for anybody right now—even in the king's court. Do you understand fully what I am saying? We must fend for ourselves and I must tell you my wishes. You must know what to do."

She gestured again, and he helped her to the stone bench where she had sat so often for her prayers. Lowering her to the bench, he helped cover her pale, thin legs with the skirts of her robe. He sat next to her, his arm still around her, and the sunlight shone on their faces. In the near distance, a field of lavender sloped toward the river that had run through his childhood, where he fished and swam and dreamed.

"I am nearing my end," she said. "Soon I will be gone and you will be on your own."

"You mustn't talk that way. Don't abandon me, please."

"Darling boy, listen to me. I'm not abandoning you. I am setting you free, and you must leave while you can. You are as tall as your father and the soldiers will not forgive you for this. When I am gone, I fear they will provoke you. I fear they will provoke you to harm."

"I won't leave you," he said, resolutely.

"No, of course not," she said. "Don't you see? That is why I am doing what I must."

Her hand slipped into her robe, and then she was pressing a heavy leather pouch into his hand.

"This is all I have left and you must take it," she said. "It is not much, but it should get you to Lausanne, where we have relatives. Just introduce yourself and they will know who you are. They will protect you, because they are family and that is what family does."

"Mamà, I can't leave the manoir. I won't!"

"Of course you can, and you will."

"Mamà . . ."

"Hush now," she murmured. Her hand searched for his and she pressed her head against his shoulder. "Let's just sit together for a while," she said, the warm fragrance of her hair wafting down over the years.

◆　◆　◆

THE SENSE OF HELPLESSNESS PIERRE had endured during those final days of his mother's life was a hard burden to shed, and even now, these many years later, he struggled. He leaned the long-handled saw against the apple tree he had been pruning. How he liked these trees. They were cultivated yet resilient, gripping the earth with their roots and reaching their hardwood branches into the air, standing against sun and wind and rain, holding on through a winter's cold and offering their fruit when the time was right. There was a lot an apple tree could teach a person who had the patience to learn, he thought. But the dogs were barking in a frenzied manner and he needed to find out why.

Rounding the barn, he saw that the wire gate to the yard was open and three people stood at the bend in the flagstone path. One appeared to be a woman and the two others had the beards of men. All wore dark woolen cloaks, in spite of the heat. The men carried staffs and bundles of bedding, and the dogs circled them, backsides in the air and shoulders crouched low to the ground, their massive heads extended, jowls quivering with each throaty bellow. The strangers held their hands high against their chests as they stood and patiently waited.

Pierre's initial concern turned to disbelief. A leap of intuition told him who they must be, while at the same time denying such a thing could even be possible. Aside from his mother, he had met very few others—those ghosts of the past who called themselves *Bons Hommes* and *Bonnes Femmes* and who were otherwise known as Cathars. His mother had kept to the manoir, where she worshipped in secret and received guests in private, and he had accepted her peculiarities in the same way most children accept the nature of a nurturing parent.

Walking through the gate, Pierre quieted the dogs, and the woman raised her hand in greeting. Her companions raised theirs. Beatrice had come to peer from the door of the house, and Pierre motioned to her that all was well.

"Peace," he said in his native Occitan, the word sounding hollow after so many years of disuse. He waited, wondering if he had thought wrong. Perhaps they were not Cathars after all and would not understand his Occitan patois. The colonies had a mishmash of all kinds of people and perhaps these were just some kind of New World pilgrims.

"*Patz*," they murmured in return, stirring among themselves, glancing at each other as if for reassurance.

Pierre's tongue failed and Beatrice came to his rescue. Stepping out onto the porch, she invited the visitors to be seated on the chairs that were clustered there. She asked if they would like refreshment—some water, perhaps, or mint tea.

"Oh, some water would do a body good and be much appreciated," the woman said, in the same quaint accent as Pierre's.

The woman had white hair and dark eyes that were faded around the edges, a face that sagged around the mouth. Beatrice returned to the porch with a tray holding glasses and a pitcher of water. She placed the tray on a small table and excused herself to go back into the kitchen.

Pierre sat down, tentatively.

"You are no doubt surprised to see us," the woman said.

"I am rarely surprised by very much, but yes," Pierre admitted. He tried not to stare but his efforts were in vain. One of the men coughed. He had long, thinning hair and a wiry beard. His cheekbones and jaws were like fine little twigs that supported the hollowed-out structure of his face, and the cough made his Adam's apple jolt along the reedy stretch of his neck.

"Perhaps you thought there were no more of us left," the woman said.

"No," he said. But she had not missed the mark by much. Having escaped from the jaws of his Pyrenean past, it had been all too easy for Pierre to think he had left the Old World behind for good, and that he was safe at last.

"We persist in spite of the onslaughts of the Evil One," she assured him.

One of the men murmured.

"And here you are," Pierre said. Again, he couldn't help himself, and his eyes drifted to the wire gate at the edge of the yard, which still stood open.

"You're wondering if there are more of us here, scattered among you, hiding out in this new land of yours," the woman said.

He raised his eyebrows, embarrassed once again to have his thoughts so easily discovered.

"Madame Eleanor always said you were a special child. She and her sister Esclarmonde would have taken the *consolamentum* together, but your father wanted an heir and it was your mother's wish to make him happy. That is why she waited. And she never regretted the decision. She always said you were the best thing that ever happened to her, aside from the blessing of the Holy Spirit, of course."

The consolamentum was a Cathar sacrament, wherein the individual vowed to forego the material things in life and lead a holy, ascetic existence, abstaining from earthly passions such as gluttony and sex. Most people who took such vows waited until their death-beds, because the vows were so difficult to honor. Pierre's aunt, Esclarmonde, had taken the vows when she was still a teenager.

"Your parents had an agreement that resulted in your birth, and Madame Eleanor never regretted it. Not once. It is important that you know that."

"An agreement?"

"Why, yes. It would have been very difficult for your mother to take her vows without your father's support. It has been done, of course, but your mother was not inconsiderate."

Pierre felt numbed.

"And you came all this way to tell me this?"

"Goodness no, dear," the woman said, with a ripple of laughter. "We did promise your mother to keep a watch on you in case anything ever happened to her. But who would've thought you'd end up here? Who would've thought we'd be here as well? The True God is full of surprises, that one. His ways are beyond our knowing."

"So why *are* you here?" Pierre said.

"Where the True God leads, we follow," the woman murmured, evasively.

But while she spoke, her eyes had drifted and her face froze. She blanched, and Pierre turned to follow her line of vision. It was just little Magdalena, standing in the open kitchen doorway. Just his little girl, her red hair wreathing her face in a flame of curls and those eyes like circles of blue sky.

"Madame Eleanor!" the woman gasped, her voice a breathy rush of astonishment and maybe even fear. Pierre had always said the girl was the image of her grandmother, and here was the proof. A woman who had once known his mother thought she was seeing her again, and in a most unexpected place.

The Cathars stayed a while longer. Pierre sent Magdalena back into the house and the Cathars kept stealing glances at the empty doorway, as if magnetically drawn. Pierre offered them shelter for the night and they declined, saying they still had miles to go, and Pierre was glad. As happily surprised as he had been to see them and speak to them of times past, he would rather they hadn't shown up in the first place and was well satisfied to see them on their way.

SIX

Not long after the Cathars' visit, Pierre sat with the rest of his family on the front porch as another twilight slowly gathered. All except Andrew, that is, who had developed strong notions. He came back from his trip with Lawrence a changed person, not in a bad way, but rather in the manner of a young man growing up and hitting his stride. The suddenness may have caught Pierre off guard. But changes were inevitable, Pierre consoled himself, and he shouldn't be surprised that a son now thought he had better things to do than spend time with his family.

Beatrice sat in the fading light with a bowl of bush beans in her lap. Never one to be idle, she snipped the ends off the beans with her fingernails. Georgie fidgeted. He lurched off his chair and dashed out into the yard, where he plucked a feather off the grass. Returning to his chair, he used the feather to tickle Magdalena's arm, and she jerked away, making a face.

"*Stop it!*" she said.

"You're such a baby," he said.

"I'm not a baby."

"Are too," he teased.

"You're the one who's a baby."

"Am not!" he said.

Pierre stood up.

"Where are you going?" Beatrice asked him.

For some reason, the question struck Pierre and he paused. Odd as it might sound, he couldn't recall anyone ever asking where he was going before. For a moment, he felt a little adrift, wondering if anyone ever really knew where they were headed. We just get shuffled one way or another, as the container of life that holds us shifts, until one day we find ourselves on a darkening porch on a farm in Penn's colony, with cicadas buzzing in the trees and frogs chorusing in the meadow, and squabbling children in the yard.

"I'm going into the house," he said at last.

"You're still thinking about those strange people who visited, aren't you?" Beatrice said, in a tone that was at once inquisitive and dismissive. "You just have to forget about them," she called after him, as he left the porch.

But Pierre was beyond admonitions. The house lamps had not been lit and he carried his thoughts through the dark, empty kitchen and on into the living room, where he sat in a rocking chair in front of the cold, dark fireplace. The air smelled of soot. The house was made of plastered river stone, and it enclosed him like a cave, cool and remote and empty, reminding him that there had been a time when itinerant Cathars sojourned in caves, away from prying eyes and the loose tongues that might give them away. They had to be cautious. Having been hunted over the centuries, their safety lay in the fact that few people knew of their continued existence.

"Ah . . ." The sound burst from him unexpectedly.

Now that they had been provoked, his memories spilled and ran rampant. He chased them, clumsily, and to little avail, thinking of a mother who said she loved him and called him special, only to abandon him through her death. Of his iconic aunt, Esclarmonde, beautiful enough to stab even a child's heart with one of her looks.

A daughter who was so much like her grandmother that he feared the Cathars might try to spirit her away. He wanted to believe that love was stronger than death and that beauty could tame even the cruelest hearts. More than anything, he wanted to believe that his children were safe and secure in his care.

◆　◆　◆

WHEN HE AWOKE, THE HOUSE had grown much darker. The fireplace was a shadow within the gloom. In the stillness that surrounded him, he could smell human perspiration, the residue of lye soap on cotton clothing, and he could feel a pent-up sense of urgency that was not his own.

"Pa, it's me—Jean," said the voice of his eldest son.

Ah, yes, Pierre thought. First Andrew and now Jean.

"Ma said not to bother you, but I thought you might not mind. You don't mind, do you?"

"Of course not," Pierre said, quietly. "You never bother me. Without you, I'd just be a poor soul sitting by himself in the dark, and how sad is that?"

"Aw, come on, Pa—you're not that way," Jean said.

Pierre appreciated his son's sentiment, but felt as if he might indeed be "that way," and the thought gave him pause. Finally, he asked, "What can I do for you?"

"Pa . . ."

His son had something to say, and he thought he knew what it was. You couldn't have one son heading off in his own direction without the other one feeling left behind. Georgie was too young, but his day would come soon as well. "I'm right here," he said, reassuringly.

"I've been thinking, that's all. I'm not complaining about anything and don't want you to think I am. But I've been thinking I'd like to do something different with my life."

"What do you have in mind?" Pierre said, quietly.

"What do you think about me joining the Royal Marines?"

The question gave Pierre a jolt. It was no surprise that Jean didn't want to be a farmer. It just wasn't in the youth's nature. But the marines? Where did that idea come from? The Crown was well-known for its disrespect of the colonials. The British thought the colonials were cowards for fighting like the Indians, hiding behind trees and rocks and other points of concealment. They loathed their homegrown brethren.

"Pa?" Jean said.

"I'm sorry. Yes . . ."

"You're the one who taught us to shoot and defend ourselves. You always said to think with our heads, stand with our hearts, and fight for what's right."

"I taught you to take care of yourself," Pierre agreed. "I taught you to be strong and to stand up for your family. I taught you to protect what you love."

"And that's what I want to do," Jean said, his voice cracking. "I want my life to count for something. I want to do something important."

"You already count for something."

"Pa, I want to be an officer," Jean said, and Pierre's mind drifted to the stories of his father's much older brother, Raymond, who had been the rightful heir to the family manoir. Like Jean, Raymond had wanted to be an officer, and Raymond's father, the seigneur at the time, had forbidden it, fearing the untimely death of his oldest son. But fear never slowed the pace of misfortune and all the seigneur got for his disapproval was a son who went to war anyway, at that much earlier time, before the so-called peace, when families were divided and Catholics and Protestants actually leveled muskets at each other. Some families lost all their sons when one side pointed a gun at the other and both sides pulled the trigger.

"Pa?" It was Jean who spoke, but Pierre heard another voice—that of his uncle Raymond, who lay buried in a small village near Bèziers. The spirit of the man lived on. According to family lore, Pierre's uncle was the kind of person who could not be deterred once his heart was set on something. He would have joined the military even if he had known he would die. That's the heartbreak kind of man he was.

"Aye," Pierre said, lowering his chin until it rested on his chest. First the Cathars and now this, he thought, struggling with a past that seemed stubbornly resilient, still alive in its own way, like a wheel that goes round and round, creating the illusion of time, the same old wheel regardless of the distance traveled. He didn't blame the Cathars for persisting to survive or Jean for wanting to be a soldier. He just needed a little time, now and then, to catch his breath in the face of apparent inevitability.

CHAPTER
SEVEN

———●———

Jean was invigorated after the talk with his father. He performed his chores at the farm and pursued his work at the château with a sense of purpose, buoyed with the knowledge that mere drudgery had an end for him and that meaning was on the march. Like a hawk high in one of the towering oaks, he looked down on a world of mortal men but felt the sun on his back and knew that he could fly if he wanted to. The time was coming when all he had to do was open his wings and a stout breeze would carry him away.

The other workers at the construction site seemed to sense this change in him. Their eyes crinkled in the corners when they looked at him, and they were more likely to strike up a conversation and ask his advice on things he had no reason to know about. The way people were when they felt at ease. The man named McDonall was the exception. He always had to stop and glare, as if resenting the very air Jean breathed. This time, McDonall was at the limekiln, and he straightened to watch the wagon pass. He stood in the acrid smoke, his gray jowls sagging, his eyes red-rimmed. Jean raised a hand to wave but the man just stared, and Jean abandoned the gesture, giving a curt nod, as if he had not expected the other man to acknowledge him in the first place.

He'd heard the rumors, of course. The men said McDonall was a little bit off. That was the way they put it. There were stories he had a wife whom he had put with child back when she was hardly old enough to be called a woman, though no one had ever actually seen her or cared to, for that matter. For the most part, the men were all too willing to avoid the reminder that lesser beings walked among them.

"What do you think about McDonall?" Jean finally asked Lawrence, deciding to voice his concerns. Lawrence stood next to the château with his hand on his chin, scratching against his whiskers as he contemplated a ragged patch of ground where more trees had recently been cleared. The stumps had not yet been removed and the trees at the far edge of the clearing looked startled, as if caught off guard to be so newly exposed. A cold, damp draft of air seemed to snake along the ground.

"Who?" Lawrence said.

"McDonall. You know, the man on the kilns?"

Lawrence gave him an inquiring look, his hand lingering on his chin, as if he needed something to hold on to while piecing his thoughts together.

"McDonall?" he said.

"You know—the one who's always complaining about everything."

But Lawrence had turned away again, once more considering the stump-stubbled ground. He held up a hand, then raised the other as well, in a framing fashion.

"What do you think about a vineyard?" he asked.

"A what?"

"It's something LeBlanc said and it's sticking in my mind. He said a proper château ought to have a vineyard, and I'm thinking why not? We could raise our own grapes and have all the wine we want."

Jean didn't know what to say. He was unprepared to think about anything besides McDonall, and Lawrence leaped at his silence, no doubt seeing it as reproof.

"I know," Lawrence said, nodding dismissively as if shrugging off criticism. "They say we can't make good wine in the colonies, right? But why not? Plenty of sunshine and good dirt—we should be able to grow anything."

"Look, I'm sorry I even brought it up," Jean said, referring to McDonall.

"What?" Lawrence asked, as if he had no idea what Jean was talking about.

"Just forget it," Jean said, feeling foolish. But his concerns remained. They circled and came back at him like biting insects, and he wondered why Lawrence couldn't see what he, himself, found so obvious. McDonall had done nothing wrong—not yet. But he had a darkness that seemed to spread to those he looked at and the things he touched, and Jean felt a growing certainty that some men could not be trusted. Some men had lesser lights and you ignored them at your peril.

◆ ◆ ◆

JEAN SAT ON THE BENCH of the large flatbed wagon. Two horses pulled this time, in anticipation of a heavy load, beasts with big shoulders and powerfully muscled haunches, hooves as big as supper platters. Jean's father had loaned them to Lawrence for the type of work that required extraordinary effort. They also took more skill with the reins, making Jean the logical choice to handle them.

From up ahead, he heard the cheers and guffaws of men at play, and entering the clearing where the new sawmill stood, he found the men standing in front of one of the drying sheds, where the fresh green wood was stacked. Three rounds of a log had been arranged in a pyramid fashion, with one propped up by the other two. The round on top had a dark center, as if the sapling had been blackened with fire before the rest of the tree had grown around it, maturing but leaving the scar, and Jean watched Andrew raise a tomahawk above his right shoulder and send it forward in a long, spinning loop that stuck the blade into the wood with a thud. The men broke out in cheers and Andrew took a bow.

"I see you're working on your bossing skills," Jean said, setting the brake and swinging down off the wagon.

Andrew squinted at him. It was one of the new mannerisms that seemed to go along with the new job Lawrence had given him. The sawmill had been Andrew's idea, after all. Lumber was as big an issue for the château as rock, and Andrew took the position that they wasted good money buying from the existing mills. While only sixteen, the youth displayed unusual entrepreneurial talent, and Lawrence put him in charge of the new operation.

"Yeah, well, I'm a businessman now, and we have to think about things like morale," Andrew said, eyeing his brother critically. "I keep telling Lawrence that the men need a break every now and then, but you know what it's like trying to tell him anything. The way I see it, with him gone back to Philadelphia and me being the one that's here, what I do and how I do it is my call."

Jean shook his head, amazed to hear his brother speak so dismissively of their employer.

"Did he say how long he'd be gone this time?"

Andrew shrugged.

"I'd get tired of going back and forth between here and Philadelphia like he does. But that's his business. I've got my hands full with the sawmill."

Jean continued to shake his head in wonder. The boy he had known was still in there. Jean could see him peeking out of those increasingly cynical eyes during moments when Andrew's guard was down. But such moments were becoming rare indeed.

"Walk with me?" Andrew said.

He led the way to the milling platform, where he stood with his feet planted wide, much like Lawrence liked to do, surveying the operation with a critical eye. The platform had a roof to keep off the rain, and a wooden frame inside, that had three levels. The upper and lower levels were spacious enough for a man to stand and the middle one was just tall enough for a good-sized log to slide through. A man stood on the top level, holding the upper handle of a long saw. The man was built like a block of granite, short and wide, with big neck and powerful arms. He pushed and pulled on the handle of the saw, which extended down through a squared-off log to the lower level, where another man gripped the handle of the other end, pulling and pushing in coordinated fashion with the man above. A wooden brace guided the saw blade against the log, and as the men labored, a long, thin board took shape from the barked, squared log.

"So tell me—what do you see?" Andrew said.

"I see a couple of men sawing logs," Jean said.

"Is that all?"

"Who cares," Jean said, irritably. "Does everything have to be a game with you, now that you're so important?"

But Andrew was unfazed.

"What I see is limitation," he said. "I see a board that will take much too long to produce. At the rate the sawyers are going, how many boards can we make? A dozen a day? Don't get me wrong, the men're doing a great job. But a fellow can only saw so much wood and that's my point. It limits us. Even if we built new platforms and hired additional men on the saws, there's still only so much a man can do. We'd never be able to expand very much."

"Maybe you're sawing all the lumber that we need."

"Are we? Lawrence doesn't seem to think so. He wants the château to get done faster, and that's why he started the sawmill in the first place and put me in charge. He says to build another platform and hire more men. But I have to make decisions, too, and I have to ask myself if that's the best approach to producing more lumber. Should we build more platforms? Is that really the best way to get the result we want?"

They were interrupted by a sudden silence as the ripping of the saw blade stopped and the two sawyers abandoned the platform, walking like crabs, shifting from one hip to the other, arms held out like giant pincers. Their hair glistened and their homespun shirts stuck to their barrel chests. The man from the lower platform was caked with sawdust from the chin down, and he raised his hand in a cheerful wave as he headed toward a shade tree, where several brown gourds of water sat on the ground.

It was one of the first times Jean had seen his younger brother treated as an equal by someone who was of no relation and unbound by the mercies of love, and it gave him one of those moments of pause. The two brothers were changing, each in his own way, and in one of those rare moments of clarity, Jean could see the gulf widening between them. He had a choice. He could view the gulf as a personal threat or allow that different paths were equal in more ways than not. The decision came easy for one with a heart the size of Jean's. The future had enough bounty to bless them all, he reasoned.

◆ ◆ ◆

EVER QUIET AS IT SLIPPED into late afternoon, the day had the eerie apprehension of one thing ending and another not yet begun. The farmhouse and its outbuildings seemed to huddle together, as if taking refuge among themselves, the way cattle do when a predator is near, and as Jean drew closer, he saw a horse and cart that he did not recognize. The horse was brown, with drooping head and black mane that needed combing. The cart sat empty.

Jean walked his horse to the barn and gave it a quick rubdown, turning frequently to look toward the house, hoping to catch sight of the visitor or some hint of what was going on. The dogs milled nervously on the lawn in front of the porch. A man came out through the open kitchen door and Jean recognized the doctor from nearby Watertown. He was not a man who made house calls without serious cause for concern.

"Thank you, doctor," Beatrice said, from the open doorway.

"It's a nasty bite, but I wouldn't worry too much. She's young and strong like we were once," the doctor said.

"What's wrong?" Jean asked, drawing near.

"Just a little dog bite," the doctor said, shrugging as if he had seen far worse, but the nonchalance did not quite sap the concern from his face. The three mastiffs followed after the humans at some distance, alert and not entirely trusting, ranging from one side to the other and looking to Pierre for any signal he might give them. The one named Romulus looked particularly forlorn. "You tell your sister to take the powder I gave her and in three or four days she'll feel better—you can count on it."

The doctor climbed aboard the cart and took up the reins. Twilight was moving in and he glanced up, as if noticing for the first time. Nodding a final farewell, he shook the reins and the horse leaned into the harness. The cart budged. The doctor gave another shake and the cart creaked. It started to roll.

The dogs stood just outside the gate, panting.

"Who got bit?" Jean wanted to know.

"Catharine was feeding the dogs and one of them took her by the arm," Pierre said. "Your brother Georgie rode to town for the doctor."

"Is it bad?" Jean asked, hurrying to keep up with his father.

"It's bad enough," Pierre said. The dogs skulked behind them, seeking some kind of reassurance that all was well. Pierre ignored them, and not in a good way. He ignored them in the manner of a man struggling with dark and unpleasant thoughts.

Catharine sat on a kitchen chair, resting her arm on the table. It was wrapped in cotton cloth from the wrist to the elbow, and already the red was seeping through. Her hair was disheveled, her face white. She looked distracted and confused. Georgie sat on another chair, explaining what she had done wrong and why she had ended up getting bitten.

"You just leave your sister alone now," Beatrice said, moving a steaming teakettle from the hearth. She poured water into a porcelain teapot.

"I'm just saying that Romulus was hungry. He probably thought she was taking the dish away, that's all. He gets aggravated that way—that's all I'm saying."

"Well, you've said enough. Now go on and make yourself scarce. I've got supper to get ready and you're no help upsetting your sister more than she already is. See how you like it, getting bit by a dog as big as you are."

Pierre stood at the kitchen counter, mashing some green herbs in a kitchen mortar. By then, little Magdalena had come to sit at the kitchen table. She watched intently as Pierre gently untied

Catharine's bandage to lay open the wound. A nasty set of punctures oozed dark red, and Magdalena's eyes got big. Pierre cleaned the wound with soapy water and then used a butter knife to apply the green paste made from the mashed herbs.

"I'm not naysaying the doctor's medicine," Pierre said. "But this here's something a shepherd boy once taught me. There wasn't anything he couldn't cure. He fixed me up many a time, and I wouldn't mind it a bit if he was here right now."

The kitchen door stood open. Romulus had sneaked into the house and lay on the kitchen floor, his gigantic head on his forepaws. His eyes rolled up to watch what Pierre was doing.

"Kindly get that dog out of my kitchen," Beatrice snapped, without so much as a glance in its direction.

◆　◆　◆

THE NEXT COUPLE OF DAYS were the kind of quiet where even the shadows seemed to slip around on tiptoes. Romulus was fed but otherwise ignored. He stayed out of everyone's way and his eyes took on a mournful quality as Catharine took a fever. Pierre continued to treat his daughter with the herbal concoction he had prepared, but her fever persisted. On the second day of her fever, a commotion filled the kitchen. The door burst open and Lawrence Kraymer stood there with his boots on, his feet splayed wide, his elbows akimbo. His eyes were wild.

"Where is she?" he demanded.

Beatrice was at the hearth boiling water for a tea of willow leaves Pierre had gathered. Her hair was braided and she wore her apron. She gave Lawrence the concerned and somewhat disapproving look of a mother with a troubled son.

"If it's Catharine you're referring to, she's upstairs in her bed."

Lawrence glanced sharply toward the doorway leading to the stairs.

"Why wasn't I told?" he said.

"You were in Philadelphia, Mr. Kraymer," Beatrice said, firmly.

"I know where I was," Lawrence said.

"Of course you do," Beatrice said, placing her hand on his arm, adopting a more comforting manner. "She's right here with her family. We're taking the best care of her we can and praying to God to make up for our shortcomings."

"Shortcomings?" Lawrence said.

His chest rose and fell as if he had run a great distance, and his eyes rose toward the upper floor, gaping with concern.

"Go on," Beatrice said, nodding.

Lawrence climbed the stairs in great leaps, and Beatrice followed with a washcloth and a basin of hot water. Catharine lay in the bed with her eyes closed. Her face was gray and she looked feverish. Lawrence pulled up a straight-backed chair and sat in it, holding her hand.

"Hello, Lawrence," Catharine said, weakly, opening her eyes with the struggle of a child fighting sleep. She labored to breathe. "Please don't be alarmed. I'll be okay, I promise. It was all my fault, you know. I have to learn to be more careful."

"Dear God in Heaven," Lawrence said.

His face sagged. He struggled for words.

"I'll be fine," Catharine said, her voice fading.

Beatrice went around to the opposite side of the bed and set the basin on a small table. Bending over, she gingerly raised Catharine's arm and began to unwind the bandage.

"I have to change the dressing," she said, apologetically.

Lawrence gasped as the now-gaping wounds came into view. Setting the soiled bandage aside, Beatrice took a clean cloth and dipped it in the steaming water. She held the washcloth suspended until it had cooled somewhat, then gently pushed it against Catharine's arm, dabbing up the green smear of the poultice that Pierre had prepared. Taking a small bowl from the bedside table, she applied a new dressing with a kitchen spoon, spreading the paste into the wounds.

"You don't need to see this," Catharine murmured to Lawrence. "I'll get better, I promise, and you can see me then. It won't be so bad, you'll see."

"I won't leave you ever again," Lawrence said.

"Goodness, Mr. Kraymer, are you finally proposing to me?" Catharine said, with a weak smile.

"I don't know how I could ever live without you."

"You do go on, sir," Catharine said, faintly.

The effort of speaking seemed to take all the strength she had left, and she lapsed into silence. Her eyes closed. Her chest rose and fell, but ever so slightly. Lawrence lowered his head. With one hand still holding hers, he used the other to hide his face, his shoulders spasming.

EIGHT

O ver the course of many years, Pierre had accumulated a lot of *savoir faire*. It was an important skill that had helped him to remain balanced in difficult situations. One could argue that it had even helped him to survive. But in his experience, a disparity of force, whether in the form of a massive dog or brutish humans, had to be taken seriously. His mother had foreseen correctly how the soldiers would treat him after her death. Their official mission was to convert Protestants to Catholicism. But in the face of what appeared to be an uncommon display of wealth, the lingering presence of a mere boy was not enough to check the soldiers' baser instincts. They set upon him with a vengeance until he had to fight and flee, clinging to the back of the beast his father had called his warhorse, holding on for dear life as the animal drove its hooves into the ground and propelled them both along.

After all these years, he could still feel the horse between his knees. He'd traveled by night to avoid detection, past other maniors standing ghostly in the moonlight, and he wondered if they harbored soldiers as well. Some of them had been burned during one of the many past years of conflict, and stood still blackened and torn open by the fires that had consumed them. Once, taking shelter under a tree during a sudden storm, Pierre found an old, frayed piece of rope hanging from a limb and bones scattered on the ground below, ribs and a pelvis, the fan-shaped bones of a foot. Traveling at night, he didn't see many people, but when he did, they huddled away and said nothing. Even in so-called peaceful times, people were afraid of strangers, and they hid their faces from him.

After two weeks on the road, he reached a town with a little auberge and resolved to spend the night in a proper bed. Even his horse seemed to look forward to a bed of straw and the prospect of some oats, because it quickened its gait, flaring its nostrils and arching its neck.

The inn was a two-story house on the edge of town, the lower level of stone and the upper of wood, with yellow light glowing through sooty windows. Lamplight illuminated the open doorway of a small barn behind the inn, and a man with a single black tooth in his upper gum ambled to the opening.

"I thought I'd get a room for the night," Pierre said.

The man looked at the horse with open admiration. They were not so common, these unusually large, archaic beasts that *chevaliers* used to ride into battle in medieval times. They were far more difficult to handle than the average saddle horse, and not very useful for everyday purposes. Shifting his attention to Pierre, the man frowned, and Pierre cleared his throat, trying again.

"I would like a room," he said, hoping he did not sound like a common fugitive.

Pierre had never traveled far from home before, but he remembered his father talking of the different dialects that people spoke, even in neighboring valleys, and he patted himself on the chest and gestured toward the inn, placing his hands together and leaning his head against them as if they were a pillow. The man nodded with sudden understanding. He reached for the horse's bridle, and Pierre dismounted, swinging a leg down to the ground and pulling his bedroll and pack from behind the saddle. His saber was wrapped in the bedroll, with the hilt sticking out, and the man's eyes lingered on it. He gave Pierre an appraising look but said nothing, then turned to lead the horse into the barn.

Pierre tucked the bedroll under his arm and slung the pack over his opposite shoulder. Limping a little from so many days in the saddle, he made his way to the house and gave a pull on the front door's wooden latch, pausing in the sudden glow of lamplight, the smell of charred meat and spilled wine.

There were two men in the dining room and they eyed him suspiciously. An open stairway climbed to the second level, where he could see a small landing and the doors to three rooms. A girl who looked to be a year or two younger than he was pushed a wet rag against an empty table. She wore a blouse with strings that tied at the throat and a dark skirt that hung limply down. Her arms were thin and white. She didn't look at him as he strode to the empty table and threw down his bedroll and pack.

"I was hoping for a meal," he said, trying to keep his voice low and looking around.

Hearing his words, she looked up at his face, frowning, rather like the man outside had done. She said something he didn't understand, words that sounded familiar but with meaning that eluded him—a short burst of sound that ended on the up note of a question. And then her face transformed. Having gotten a good look at him, she seemed frightened. Her gaze dropped to his bedroll, at the protruding hilt of his saber. Wood scraped against the floor as the other two men stood up. They left the building in a hurry.

Pierre considered his options.

"*Parlez-vous la langue au nord?*" he said, setting aside his native patois in favor of the language of the invaders.

Her eyes brightened and she nodded with understanding.

"We speak the French," she said, cabbaging together the language of the north.

Pierre lowered himself to the chair that faced the table.

"You're him, aren't you?" she said.

"I'm who?"

She backed away, bumping into a chair, then turned and hurried from the room. Pierre got up and followed her into the kitchen. She held a wooden spoon, stirring a pot of cassoulet that sat on a grate in front of a firepit. Shoveling a couple of spoonfuls into a wooden bowl, she turned around and started at the unexpected sight of him, then shoved the bowl at him. He took it, gratefully. He had not eaten anything for several days, and he didn't wait for a spoon, using his fingers to scoop up the beans and shove them into his mouth.

"Here." The girl thrust a loaf of bread at him.

Pierre set the bowl down so that he could tear open the bread. He used the crust as a spoon.

"Why did you say, 'You're him'?" he asked, his mouth full.

"You're him that the soldiers are looking for," she said. "They've been to all the towns, searching for you."

"They've been here?"

"They say you murdered one of them and that when they tried to shoot you for it the bullets went right through you without leaving a mark."

"I didn't murder anyone," he said, hotly. He had been as surprised as the luckless soldier to find his saber sticking into the man's body. The soldier had no doubt supposed Pierre would be easy prey. Even with his martial training, there was no way in the world that a thirteen-year-old boy should have survived the assault by three grown men.

She brushed past him and he followed after her into the dining room. The windows were open and she went to one and reached outside, pulling the shutters closed.

"They attacked me and I defended myself," he said.

"You can't stay here," she said. "The soldiers will come. They will find you."

She hurried to the other window and pulled those shutters closed as well.

"Where are they now?" he asked, peering through the crack where the shutters came together.

"They're here. They're everywhere. They said they intend to kill you and you know that they will. If I help you, they will kill me too."

"I'm not asking for your help. All I want is food and a bed."

The girl shook her head. She started to cry.

Outside, a dog began to bark and then yelped. Pierre ran to the door and cracked it open. Handheld lanterns bobbed in the dark, and he pushed the door shut and threw the bolt. A sudden clatter came from the kitchen and the figure of a man loomed in the entry-way to the dining room. He carried a musket, and Pierre lunged for the open stairs that went up to the bedrooms.

What happened next became very unclear to him, a collision of sudden and immediate, yet complex and unfathomable events. The discharge of the musket sent a thunderclap through the room, ending with the dull roar of stunned senses. The girl screamed but the sound of her voice was small and distant in the pillowing deafness. The hair at the back of Pierre's head gave a sudden tug as the ball passed by and he continued to scramble up the stairs. He felt cut loose from his body. His arms and legs worked as if on their own, dragging his consciousness along behind like the flailing, flapping wings of a wounded bird. The billowing cloud of burnt gunpowder filled the room with a dense, acrid smoke, and there were noises at the door—men shouting, wood splintering.

At the top of the stairs, Pierre dove into the first open room and collided with the bed. Careening from it, he knocked into a wooden table and sent a masonry pitcher crashing to the floor. Given any chance of forethought, he would not have chosen this room as his refuge, because it was no refuge at all. The soldiers would be on the stairs behind him. There was nowhere to hide, no means of defending himself. Throwing open the room's sole window, he swung a leg outside, then followed with the other and leaped.

He didn't know there was a woodshed below the window, only that he struck something solid and then went through it, with an abrupt but only momentary pause in his fall. He knew the crash must have made a racket, but he just felt the jolt and give of the roof, the tearing of the firewood against his clothing and skin. Tumbling down the woodpile, covered with woodchips and spider webs, he landed on his back on the ground in front of the shed, the inn looming above him, a faint glow of light at the window he had jumped from.

He got to his feet and lost his balance, lurching against the outer wall of the inn. He peered around the corner, hoping to get to his horse. But a soldier stood in front of the barn, holding a musket. Fully expecting another blast and the tearing impact of a ball, Pierre took off, lurching and running, off balance and falling down, pushing back up and forward, staggering off into the covering darkness.

◆ ◆ ◆

ROMULUS HAD BEEN ON PIERRE'S mind ever since the incident. For a while, there had been more important things to worry about than what to do with a dog that could no longer be trusted. But as

Catharine improved, something persisted and festered in Pierre. It grew in substance and momentum, as if he, in his rational faculties, had become little more than a bystander. It grew until the future became inevitable, looming behind the betrayal and anger and the growing revulsion that the dog triggered in him.

"Do you want to sit on my lap?" Pierre whispered in Magdalena's ear as they sat on one of the wooden benches of the Reformed Church in Watertown. Beatrice sat next to him. Catharine sat next to Lawrence, whom she now openly called her fiancé. The minister spoke in a thundering voice of a lake of fire that awaited the unholy on Judgment Day, and Magdalena had gotten up and moved past her mother's knees to squeeze in between Beatrice and Pierre, where she stuck her soft little hand into her father's big, calloused one and hid her face in his side. In response to his question, she nodded, bumping her forehead gently against his ribs.

Once in his lap, she poked her mouth up toward his ear and whispered, "Momma said we don't have to go to hell."

"Of course we don't. There is no such thing, not for you," he said.

"But what if there is a hell and we have to go there?"

"Trust me, dear girl, there's no such thing as hell, not for any of us."

"But what if you're wrong?"

"Just close your eyes—be at ease," he said, squeezing her.

After the service concluded, he carried her as they got up from the pew, her legs dangling at his side. The minister was shaking hands at the church door, his face round and soft as a white mushroom, his eyes twinkling in spite of the heavy serving of damnation he had just dished out. Now he was the small-town politician, pressing the flesh, asking after the sick and homebound. He caught sight of Catharine's arm and praised God for her deliverance. He looked up at Pierre and extended his hand and Pierre took it, more for his wife's sake than anything else, and the minister wore a look of triumph, as if he had scored another small victory in the war against darkness.

"Good to see you, Brother Laux," he said.

"Good to see you as well."

"Maybe we can count on this becoming a weekly occurrence?"

"You're a man of faith to even think such a thing, I'll warrant you that."

"It was Pierre who wanted to come and who insisted," Beatrice hastened to say, giving her husband's elbow a pinch.

"I'll count my blessings, then," the minister said, giving Pierre's hand a final squeeze and patting him on the shoulder. Magdalena turned her face away, pressing it against Pierre's opposite shoulder in her attempt to avoid the minister's searching gaze.

"That wasn't so hard, was it?" Beatrice said, as they climbed onto the wagon, with the children in the back. Pierre shrugged, but mostly he ignored her. He hadn't spoken much over the past several days, and he remained silent most of the ride home, slumped on the wagon seat, long legs bent and elbows resting on his knees.

Lawrence rode his own horse alongside the wagon and quickly dismounted when they got to the farm. He hastened to Beatrice's side of the wagon and held his hand out to her.

"Goodness!" she said, glancing at her husband as Lawrence helped her descend. A little frown flickered across her face and she seemed to hold her breath, that proud, stubborn, caring woman. Not much missed her notice and it would have been hard to imagine she had not observed the coolness between her husband and future son-in-law.

Lawrence stepped up to the wagon again and thrust out his hand a second time, for Catharine, who blushed until she was the color of sunset. She stepped down without looking at anyone, certainly not her father. Her brother Georgie let out a hoot and jumped to the ground, dashing to the house. Jean climbed out with as much decorum as he could muster. Andrew was missing, of course. Even when Lawrence found time to spend with the family, Andrew now usually had other things to do.

Out in the yard, the dogs chased each other, barking. One rolled on its back, its feet in the air, and the other two ran around it in circles. Before leaving for church that morning, Beatrice had banked enough hardwood coals in the hearth to make a low, sustained heat, and placed a beef roast on the tripod to cook while they were gone. Now, upon their return, a meaty aroma filled the kitchen. Pierre went to the dry sink and dipped his hands into the washbowl, turning a bar of soap around and around.

"You're thinking about the dog, aren't you?" Beatrice said, sadly.

He avoided her searching gaze.

"It was an accident, you know," she said.

"Was it?" he said, reprovingly.

Shaking his head, he dried his hands on a towel and then set it aside on the edge of the sink. He found his carving knife and steel. Slowly, resignedly, he slid the knife against the steel. There was the question and an answer, and the answer was already there, leaning against him from some unseen quarter, pushing against him as he sharpened the blade.

"A dog like that is no little barn terrier, with a snap that you don't have to worry about," he said, quietly. "A little dog that bites is a nuisance that can be lived with, but one of ours?" He shook his head, grimly, thinking how things could have gone. "We got lucky this time," he said, looking at her.

"Will you put it down?"

Pierre gazed at his wife for a long time, letting the question sink in. He had, in fact, concluded that putting the dog down was his only option, much as he hated to even think of it. Pierre wasn't afraid of the dog, personally. But Romulus had revealed a nature that couldn't be trusted with the safety of his children, and Pierre shuddered at the thought that it might have been the impulsive Magdalena that got too close at the wrong moment in time. Beatrice was looking at him. The eyes of the children upon him. Everyone was waiting for his answer.

"Might be there's another way," he said, at last.

Beatrice retreated from his gaze and busied herself in the kitchen. She soon had potatoes boiling. Catharine tried to set the table and Lawrence jostled her in his attempts to help, taking the plates from her and insisting on placing them on the table himself, distributing napkins and spreading the utensils. Since his return from Philadelphia, he had hardly left her side, and he now reached across her plate to cut her meat for her, as if she were a child. Setting down the knife, he spooned gravy over her mashed potatoes. Catharine's face wore rose as if it were her natural color, her eyes shining at the pleasure of being pampered.

Heavy with thoughts about the dog, Pierre hardly touched his food, and after the meal was over, he got up from the table and left the house. Still wearing his white shirt and dark trousers from church, he put a rope around the dog's neck and led the mastiff down the walkway, tying him at the gate. After hitching the horse, he tied the dog's rope to the back of the wagon and then climbed aboard. Already, his heart had begun to lighten. The fact of Romulus's nature couldn't be changed. But a dog like that could still be useful to someone who was aware of its shortcomings and was willing to restrain it accordingly. Someone who didn't have children to put at risk. Rather than destroying Romulus, Pierre had decided to find him a new home, and the rattle of the wagon and the squeak of its axles followed him out of the lane.

NINE

B y the following winter, the château was still little more than a cold, rocky edifice, with holes for windows and a roof that was still open to the sky. But the fireplaces in the great room and the second story bedrooms had been finished, giving the roofers a place to stand in their work boots and warm their numbed fingers, before climbing the ladders once again to heft the slate tiles that were cold as sheets of ice. With fire came warmth and with warmth the first true intimations of life. But with life came risk, as Catharine's encounter with Romulus had so starkly revealed. Every time Lawrence looked at the scars on his fiancée's arm, he thought of how close he had come to losing her.

Such thoughts were like the wolf that came sniffing and he tried his best to avoid them by focusing harder than ever on the work at hand. At the moment, he stood next to Andrew, who steadied the horse. Andrew wore a wool hat pulled down over his ears, a heavy coat, and sheepskins wrapped and tied around his legs. He had wool mittens as well, but they didn't do him much good, as he had to remove them to handle the horse, and the cold had turned his hands as red as mud bricks. The men on the roof suffered the most. Hunching with their hands under their armpits, they waited while the horse pulled and the elevator platform with the stack of slate shingles slowly rose up along the granite wall. The rope creaked and the horse's nostrils flared, blowing out clouds of vapor.

"You handle the horse real smart," Lawrence observed.

"Jean's the one who's good with horses," Andrew retorted. "My place is back at the sawmill. I'm wasting my time here and you know it."

Lawrence nodded. There hadn't been much choice, to his way of thinking. Jean had taken the day off and Lawrence needed someone he could trust to manage the lift. The horse had to pull a lot of weight, what with the slate in addition to the lift itself, not to mention the drag on the block and tackle, and Andrew was a lot better than he let on.

The youth had grown, both physically and in his demeanor, and Lawrence wondered if he, himself, had changed, as well. He still felt like the same person he had always been, and wondered how to tell if he was having any success at becoming the man he wanted to be. What did such a change do to you? Was it real or was it merely like putting on another man's clothes while remaining the same naked person underneath?

Maybe it was the season, he thought, trying to understand his dismal mood. With winter full on, so much of the countryside looked dead. In the summer, the heavy green foliage of the pressing wilderness was like a leafy cocoon, wrapping and smothering. Now, however, he could see the trees as individual twists of trunk and limb. The rough fiber of forest seemed to roll on and on endlessly, revealing something wild and desolate. It made him wonder if he, too, weren't stark and twisted in some way that was obvious to others if not to himself.

"Do you ever wonder why your pa decided to live here in the first place?" he said.

The abruptness of the question and the seriousness of tone got Andrew's attention, and he shot Lawrence a sideways glance.

"Why would you want to know something like that?" Andrew asked.

"Just wondering, that's all," Lawrence said, but he could tell the youth wasn't convinced.

"It doesn't really matter, does it?" Andrew said.

"Perhaps not," Lawrence said. "I just think of who he is and where we are, here in the middle of nowhere. I have to think of how different it must be from what he used to know, and I wonder what it was that brought him here. What it is that makes him stay."

"This is our home," Andrew said.

"I know. But what if something happened that made him think he had made a mistake?"

"Is that what *you* think? That you made a mistake?"

"No, not at all," Lawrence hastened to say.

"Then why're you asking such dumb questions?" Andrew said, and Lawrence had no response. It wasn't that he had cold feet. But having found Catharine, the thought of losing her filled him with a loneliness he couldn't fully fathom. The man he would be without her was nothing like the boy who'd crouched in a corner of the brewery and missed his mother. That man was not even like the youth who'd searched for a love he hadn't yet found. Finding something and losing it too soon was much worse than never having had it in the first place, and he didn't know how he could bear such sorrow.

◆　◆　◆

It was dark by the time Lawrence arrived at the inn in Watertown, where he and the architect were staying. A large fireplace occupied one whole wall, a sooty mantle lidding a maw of crackling, crawling flames that slowly consumed a pile of firewood. The room's single occupant was LeBlanc, who sat hunched over a loaf of bread and a large tankard of ale. The man looked up, his dark hair like a clump of matted grass, his penetrating eyes peering from either side of a beaked nose.

"Come in from the cold," LeBlanc said, nodding toward the empty chair opposite him. Lawrence opened his coat, but left it on as he slid onto the seat. The heat of the room radiated against his face, but the cold he had brought in clung to him like an envelope of frigid air.

"I see you are comfortable enough," he commented.

"I work best when warm and well fed," LeBlanc said.

"Does your work include actually visiting the construction site anymore?"

LeBlanc grinned sardonically, as if to remind him that his contributions are essential, on whatever terms he wishes to provide them. LeBlanc had the annoying habit of looking at something with both mild interest and a broader disdain, and he required libations before discussions of any import could be had. But Lawrence decided to ignore these shortcomings, if shortcomings they were. Of more immediate concern was the unaccustomed lassitude Lawrence had felt of late, and which his earlier conversation with Andrew had done little to dispel.

Still wearing his coat, he ordered an ale.

"And the progress, it is good?" LeBlanc asked, solicitously.

"Well enough, I imagine, for as brutally cold as it is," Lawrence had to admit. "The roofers keep the fireplaces burning all day long, making what little warmth they can."

"You wasted too much time on the barn," LeBlanc said, in that dismissive way of his. "We could have had the house closed up by now and the men would not have to suffer so much in the cold. But the barn—it put us behind schedule. We could have waited and built it later."

"I can't board my horses at the Laux farm forever," Lawrence snapped in his own defense.

"All the same, if you had asked me, I would have told you that the house comes first. People come first, not the animals."

"Not here, not in the country," Lawrence said.

"Ah, yes—the country." LeBlanc's lip curled.

Lawrence looked at him thoughtfully. On the one hand, he found the architect to be annoyingly sanctimonious. On the other, however, the man had been around. His familiarity with Old World structures and the culture that surrounded them was the very thing that made him so useful to Lawrence, here in the colony.

"Say, there's a question I've been mulling over that I'd like to ask you—if you don't mind?"

"You pay me to listen," LeBlanc said.

"Aye, well this is a little off the subject of our normal discussions. I've found your advice useful in matters of design and construction and some of the other things, like what you said about adding a vineyard. You know what I mean. But I have a query of a more personal nature that you might not be altogether a stranger to. Something I've pondered and wondered about. To wit . . ." He paused, searching for the right words. "Well, I presume you've built other châteaux . . ."

"Of course. If you're wondering at this late stage about my credentials—"

"No, not at all. Rest easy, my friend. It's a question on an entirely different matter. You see, I've been wondering . . ." He paused again, then soldiered on. "I've been wondering, in your experience, when a man builds an abode like a château, does it change him?"

LeBlanc looked confused. Without moving his shoulders, he pulled his head back, then shifted uncomfortably in his chair. He studied Lawrence carefully.

"That is a complicated question, monsieur," he said. His eyes drifted. "Many châteaux are very old. They go back centuries, in fact, to a time when such homes were not only symbolic but also had to serve as protection—as fortresses, if you will. Nowadays, people who build them might already have similar homes in the family and want another for a son or for some other reason." He shrugged. "Then there are those who have found good fortune, of course, just like here in these colonies of yours." He shrugged again, this time apologetically. "But to answer your question, important people like to have—how shall I say it? Hmm—*notable* accommodations. They seek homes to reflect who they already are."

"So what you're saying is that a man is who he is and nothing can change that?"

"No, no, not at all," LeBlanc said, quickly. "All by itself, a house—however grand—is only an empty space. It is the person who counts. A man is destined to fill his home to whatever fullness it represents. It takes a big man to fill a big house and an even bigger man to fill a château. Oui, monsieur, I think this is the answer that I have for you. Yes, most definitely. Whether a château is the reflection of who a man already is, or the man builds a house like yours and must then grow to fill it, it is all the same. It takes a certain kind of person to live in such a house, yes, most definitely."

LeBlanc paused, as if balancing on a fine point of purchase. He seemed to struggle before finally venturing to address his employer that little bit further. His eyes widened, rolling in Lawrence's direction.

"Do you feel you are changing, monsieur?"

Lawrence had to allow that it served him right to be put so terribly on the spot. He was the one who initiated the conversation, after all. But he'd already revealed far more than he intended, and his question had been answered in overabundance. What he needed now was ale. Quite a bit of it, actually.

TEN

J ean had taken the day off from work on the château to visit Timmy Souder. Rumor had it that Timmy had stolen his father's squirrel gun and run away from home, intending to never return. A young man without a farm or trade or some other way to make a living was in dire straits, and Timmy had undertaken the extraordinary effort of walking to Massachusetts to join the provincial army. That was the last Jean heard of him until the clerk at the dry goods store in Watertown announced Timmy had returned like the prodigal son—much the worse for wear—but that Timmy's father must've missed the part in the Scriptures about a warm welcome with open arms.

Jean tightened his grip on the reins and touched his heels to his mount. His father, Pierre, took pride in his horses. He said that you got what you started with and you had to start with a good horse and make it better. You had to let them know what you needed from them and take care of them along the way, and you found good horses on the Laux farm—not the slack-eyed, shaggy beasts you saw hanging their heads over the fences of neighboring farms. Maybe that was how the horse seemed to know exactly what Jean wanted, responding with a quick change of gait, shoulders tensing, hips flexing, the hooves springing into a longer, quicker stride along the muddy snow of the road. Jean loved the surge, the feeling of power, the sense that his human brain was as connected to the horse as it was to his own body.

The Souders raised dairy, and Jean could smell the cows before he saw them, the sharp, acidic odor of their manure that made a horse person's nose wrinkle. The log house was like the hub of a broken wheel, with brown spokes trailing through the snowy landscape to a leaning barn and other outbuildings, and Jean's horse blew clouds of impatient breath, stamping a foot. Jean helloed and a woman came to the door. She had deep-set, hesitant eyes and blistered skin. Under the hem of her print dress, her feet were bare despite the cold. Jean was well aware that you never knew what to expect on one of these isolated farms, and a sense of caution had kept him in the saddle.

"You be here for Timmy," she said, in a flat, uninterested voice that did not invite response. She shuffled back a step. "You kin come in if'n you want."

"I'm fine—thank you," Jean said, nervously. "Maybe if Timmy's there he can come out and me'n him can take a walk or something."

The woman disappeared, rather like a body sinking in dark water, and the gloomy doorway stood empty. There was an exchange of voices from inside and then Timmy finally appeared, dressed in the gray homespun that men wore in the fields. He had narrow, puffy eyes and a premature bend to his back. His mouth drooped and twisted to the side.

"What you here for?" he said, squinting. "You here to say 'I tol' you so,' like all the rest?"

The stabbing nature of the remark took Jean aback. In the old days, he had run into Timmy from time to time—just chance encounters at the flour mill or dry goods store—and knew him well enough to exchange greetings. But they were hardly friends.

Even then, the boy had been just a little too different. You heard things, such as a father and husband being too quick with a belt and it made you leery, as if the family were diseased and you didn't want to get too close.

"Timmy, it's me. Jean Laux," he said.

"I know who you are, and I know what you all're thinking, too," Timmy muttered.

"What who's thinking?" Jean asked, trying to sound upbeat.

"What all you's thinkin'," Timmy said, in the same dull voice his mother had used. "Thinkin' maybe I don't have what it takes," he continued, defiantly. "Thinkin' I couldn't cut it, but by God there was nothin' to cut and that's the truth of it. No glory in marchin' on old Indian trails to the ends of the earth and then campin' there in the mud until you run out of food and have to walk back on an empty stomach."

He turned sideways and made as if to spit, but nothing came out.

Jean's chest tightened. He had come to the Souder farm hoping to connect with someone who had gone forth and done some of the very things he himself dreamed of doing, and the soiled rag of a human being he saw in front of him now was dispiriting, to say the least.

"Timmy, I just wanted to talk to you, that's all. I've been thinking of a military career myself and hoped you could tell me a little bit of what it was like. Where'd you go and what'd you do? You know, did you have to fight?"

"A career—is that what you call it?" Timmy scoffed, then hardened. "Sure, I did some fightin'," he said. "I fought for my share of piss-poor eatin' food. I fought to keep the rain off of my neck. What I didn't fight was any damned Indians or Frenchers—just the muck of the swamps we tramped through and mosquitoes big enough to eat, by God, and would've been better eatin' than the shite we had when we ate at all."

Jean felt queasy. "They said you went all the way to the St. Lawrence," he said, his voice rising, as if he had been called on to explain himself.

"How to good God do I know where we went?" Timmy said. "We marched through the goddamned woods until we stopped marchin' and then we camped in tents while the rain ran under us and soaked our blankets and our clothes. The only time I shot my gun was at a muskrat and I missed, goddammit. And then the powder got wet and we couldn't've shot at anything if we'd'a wanted to. The colonel said we had shite for brains as backwoodsmen and what the hell? Who said anything about being backwoodsmen? We were farmers is what we were!"

He wiped one of his filthy sleeves against his eye and down the side of his face, and Jean had to look away. It was too much for him to bear—the deep-set eyes, the yellowish pallor of the youth's skin, the way the body twitched and jerked. Jean felt as if he couldn't breathe.

"Bloody army," Timmy said.

Jean backed his horse up a step.

"Yeah, look, I gotta go," he said. "It was good to see you."

"Lyin' arsehole."

By now, Timmy was shivering hard, his body jolting. His face seemed frozen in a contortion of anger and shame, the eyes tunneling and then lapsing into bitterness, and Jean wanted nothing to do with him. He tried to convince himself that he and this unhappy youth had nothing in common and that he, himself, could never sink so low and become so disgusting. He refused to believe that someone like Timmy really mattered that much after all.

◆ ◆ ◆

JEAN COULDN'T GET AWAY FROM the Souder farm quickly enough. His encounter had distressed him and now everything else was insufferable as well, the snow and the cold, the time it took to travel from one place to another, the road itself that had given him so much hope before. Timmy's words stuck with him, like a grime that couldn't be washed away, making him feel dirty and unclean. For a fleeting, unchristian moment, he wished Timmy had faced the enemy and been killed in the fields of battle, unsullied, untarnished, raised up unto Glory.

Reining his horse impatiently, Jean left the road and cut across an open pasture to the trees on the far side. He had hunted the backcountry and knew of an old game trail that contoured the mountains. The trail cut deeply into the ground and was visible even under the covering of snow. It passed above several homesteads, and from it, he could drop down to the main road again and eliminate more than a mile of otherwise painstaking progress.

The woods were quiet as he walked his horse, nursing his wounded spirit. A woodpecker flitted from one cold-barked tree to another and Jean envied the bird its freedom from human concerns. Far below, he saw a farmhouse with smoke rising from the chimney, a good, righteous farmhouse of river stone, and he tried to imagine it held a mother and sister like his very own, who tended a welcoming hearth at which one could forget all about the Timmy Souders of the world.

Then, the pounding of horse's hooves caught his attention. He could see them below, through the bare trunks of winter hardwoods, two dark horses making long strides, a man hunched over each, urging it onward. The one man had something across the saddle in front of him, something thick and heavy, like a rolled carpet or a large duffel. The men kicked their heels and the horses lengthened their strides and Jean's interest flared. It was no way to ride a horse, he thought, not across an open field covered with snow, with rocks and holes and broken tree branches possibly hidden from view. The men drove their horses like desperados. They fled from the direction of the river stone farmhouse, crossed a meadow, and angled up through the trees, and Jean saw that what had appeared to be a duffel was the rump of a human being, the hem of a dress jerking and flapping, a white, shoeless foot bouncing with the horse's strides.

Something seemed wildly irregular. Why would a man be carrying someone across the front of a saddle, someone with bare legs and no shoe in callous disregard of the bitter cold? Something needed to be done, but what? If the men were making a getaway, what were they getting away from? Where were they headed and who was to stop them?

The men headed toward a narrow pass in the ridge above, and Jean knew that beyond this point lay the wildlands, where the farmers hunted and sometimes found Indian sign. Heeling his horse, Jean felt the power of the beast as it surged forward, not recklessly but with purpose. By heading straight up through the trees, he was able to get to the pass before them, and he quickly dismounted, hiding his horse in a clump of hemlocks and positioning himself at a rock outcropping.

The woods seemed to mushroom with silence around him. From below came the sound of a hoof against rock, the crack of a branch, the grunt of a laboring horse. Jean could no longer see the men but knew they would lurch into sight soon, and his thoughts flew and fluttered like trapped birds banging against a windowpane. His musket lay on a rock before him, but he had never so much as pointed it at another person before. When he thought about joining the marines, he had been thinking of adventure and glory, and not the other thing, at the meanest level, the pulling of a trigger against a fellow human being.

Suddenly he was out of options. The men appeared, the head of one and then the shoulders, the head of the other. The man at the rear used his reins to lash his horse and it bent its head and muscled forward, climbing toward the pass. Jean lay down against a rock and sighted along the barrel of his musket. He cocked his flint back and his hand shook so hard he was afraid the gun would discharge before he could aim it. And still he didn't know what to do. Surely, the men were up to no good. He had heard the stories of women and children who had been kidnapped to be traded as slaves or far worse, but what was he to do about it? What would his father do if he were here right now and had to act?

His finger touched the trigger and the gun kicked back into his shoulder. A fog of smoke belched out in front of him and one of the horses reared. It was the second horse, the one carrying the girl, and a man shouted, cursed. The lead horse bolted left and took off back down through the woods, angling away, the rider whipping it with the tail ends of the reins. The other horse bucked again, and the rider clung to the saddle, then flung the girl from her position across his lap. She hit the ground and flopped to her side, where she lay without moving, and the rider threw his weight forward, righting the horse and kicking it in the flanks. The horse bolted toward the pass and the man rode hard and out of sight in a matter of seconds.

The girl lay in the snow and Jean reloaded his musket, shivering with both cold and the violent shakes of adrenaline, the ramrod missing the borehole of the gun again and again before he was able to drive down the new charge. The magnitude of what he had just done rolled in on him and he crouched behind a rock and gasped for breath, paralyzed with fright, waiting for the men to come back. He watched and waited until his fear gradually subsided. The girl had not moved and he thought his bullet may have struck her and that she was dead.

Resolutely, he forced himself to approach her, and he squared his shoulders, preparing for the worst. Her eyes were closed. Her forehead and cheeks were blue, and he placed his hand to her mouth, where he felt a faint breath. Leaning his gun against a tree, he crouched down and picked her up, carrying her to the clump of hemlocks where his horse waited. The girl's eyes opened and she stared up at him, expressionless.

"Are you all right?" he said.

She didn't respond but stared at him vacantly.

"We gotta get out of here," he said. "Those men could come back. If they knew it was only me, then we'd both be in trouble. If I put you on the horse, can you hold on?"

Slowly, she roused. One of her hands tightened against his arm, and he sat her on the horse and held her steady in the saddle.

"Who were they?" he asked, his heart hammering. He wanted desperately to hear that the men were indeed the outlaws he had assumed them to be, and that firing his weapon had been the right course of action.

She didn't say anything but reached out and grasped the horse's mane.

"You're freezing," Jean said, shifting his focus to what mattered most in the moment.

Taking off his coat, he draped it across her shoulders. He wrapped his muffler around her bare foot, tying the ends of the scarf together. The cold bit into him hard and he started to move. Holding the horse by the bridle, he led it down to where his musket leaned against the tree. Briefly, he scanned the woods for any sign of the men before continuing his descent.

"I heard a sound," the girl said, dully.

Jean stopped the horse and waited to make sure she was all right. "Cold . . ." she said.

He steadied her and then led the horse a few more steps, looking back over his shoulder, pausing, leading the horse on and then pausing again. The girl swayed. Hunching in the saddle, she held on to the horse's mane and pressed with her knees, and Jean led the animal on the easiest downhill slope he could find.

They finally emerged from the woods onto the white expanse of meadow. Twilight already purpled the air and, cold as it was, the temperature dropped even more. Jean didn't know if the girl came from the river stone farmhouse, but that was the nearest shelter and they both would die of the cold if trapped outside overnight. As they approached the house, the door flew open and a woman charged out, waving a broom above her head as if it were a weapon. But when she saw their faces, she threw the broom aside and ran toward them, arms outstretched, fingers wide. Grabbing hold of the girl, she pulled and Jean helped the girl get down from the horse. The woman clutched her and sobbed.

"My baby, my baby!"

The girl had trouble standing, and Jean picked her up and carried her into the house. The woman wouldn't let go of the girl, and he had to drag them both along. Inside, the heat from the fireplace enveloped them. There was a wooden table and chairs, a bearskin rug. Cooking pots hung from the mantle.

Jean carried the girl into a second room, where he found two beds. He placed her on the first one. She still wore his coat. The woman yanked at a comforter, pulling it up over the girl, and the girl closed her eyes and started to cry.

"There, there," the woman said, kissing the girl's eyes and forehead.

The girl clutched at the woman's shoulders, her breasts.

"You're all right now. It's all right. You're home. We're safe."

Jean backed out of the bedroom. His knees gave way and he sank down into a kitchen chair. His hands and feet were still numb from the cold, and the heat of the fireplace made them ache. But he was safe, and it began to dawn on him that something extraordinary had happened. He, Jean, had saved the life of another human being, and long forgotten was the unfortunate visit to the Souder farm and any second-guessing he might have had about a military career. At the same time, however, he felt more and more aware that anything could have gone wrong. He could have been too far away to attempt a rescue. The shot fired could have hit a horse, leaving Jean to scuffle with the rider on the ground. Or the shot could have killed the girl, as he had earlier feared. Had the kidnappers realized he was alone, they could have circled back around. In retrospect, he and the girl were both lucky to be alive.

◆ ◆ ◆

THE SMELL OF FRESH BREAD woke him. He was still slumped at the table. The woman wouldn't eat with him. She wanted to wait for her husband, who had gone to Watertown for supplies and was due home any minute. He would want to talk with the young hero, she said, and Jean wondered to whom she was referring. Then he remembered, and a sense of uneasy fulfillment carried him into the night, when he lay on the bearskin rug covered with blankets, while the stoked fire hissed and fizzled and the log timbers of the house made cracking sounds against the outside cold.

True to his wife's word, the farmer dragged from him every detail of the afternoon's rescue. The farmer and his wife had one remaining child, having buried two others, and the farmer had had to go to town. The ruffians came to the door pretending to need help and then kidnapped the girl when they found the women alone. The farmer's face twitched as he listened first to his wife's story and then to Jean's. His fingers bent and flexed. Finally, he cried out and wept, and Jean had never experienced anything like this before, another human being—a grown man—weeping with gratitude at something he, Jean, had done.

The following morning, he rose and left early, the family watching him off at the door. The girl stood between her mother and father. She wore a blanket around her shoulders. Her eyes had come alive again and she leaned her head against her father's shoulder. Jean saw that she was probably no older than his brother, Georgie, and pretty, which only added to his humble gratitude that they had both survived.

Leaving the family behind, he rode his horse with a straight back and squared shoulders, the reins in his right hand. The day was as bitterly cold as the one before, but today the chill didn't touch him. He nudged the horse into a canter and stood in the stirrups, rising above his conflicted emotions, thrilling at the impact of the horse's hooves and at the speed with which he was swept along.

About halfway home, he saw three riders approaching. It didn't take him long to recognize his father, with Andrew and Georgie on either side. Fully aware of the concern that must have driven them to search for him, he raised his musket in salute. They approached warily, suspiciously, looking past him as if searching for clues as to why he'd caused them such worry, and he didn't care about the interrogation that was sure to follow.

"You got some explaining to do!" Georgie cried out, his youthful voice piping.

Pierre Laux pulled his horse to a stop in front of Jean and looked at his son somberly, his eyebrows slowly climbing. Andrew walked his horse past Jean's and reined it around, coming up beside him.

"I had to tell Pa where you were," he said.

"We thought maybe you fell in a hole or something!" Georgie said.

"Maybe you fell in with bad company," Andrew suggested.

"Maybe he met some girl!" Georgie hooted.

"Let's give him some breathing room," Pierre said, and that was it. Jean couldn't wait to tell them of his adventure. But for now, it was enough to have their company, and they rode along, together, heading home, like a small but invincible army.

ELEVEN

B eatrice had never thought raising boys would be easy, but the notion that Jean had purposefully put himself in harm's way took some getting used to. When he said he wanted to be a soldier, she hadn't taken him seriously. After all, her own father had been a tailor, and nothing in her personal life had ever suggested that a person just went off on his own, looking for trouble. She wanted Jean to be happy. But if farming wasn't in his future, she didn't understand why he couldn't become something more sensible—such as a tradesman or merchant like Mr. Kraymer. She cast a sidelong glance at Lawrence, who rode next to the wagon that she and Pierre occupied. Beatrice was sure she couldn't have found a better future son-in-law. But goodness, none of them were easy— boys, that is—and what a trial even Lawrence could be at times, thinking he had to build a château before he was good enough to get married and then putting things off until the last minute. Beatrice was convinced that if Catharine hadn't nearly died from the dog bite, Lawrence still might not have formalized his bid for her hand.

She sighed, dwelling on her many thoughts, and as they neared Watertown, the country sounds gave way to the man-made stir of the settlement. There was always the rumble of the wagon and the clipping of the horse's hooves, but the bugling of the redwing black-birds and the cries of the jays gave way to barking dogs, the ringing of a blacksmith's hammer, the shouts of children at play. After such a long, cold winter of ice and snow, the buildings seemed worn out. But the vernal sun was doing its job of awakening them, readying them for something new. It was remarkable how a little bit of warmth could make the world seem like a better place.

"Greetings!" said the plump, middling man in a lumpy sweater and wool pants, who answered their knock on the church door. Bowing slightly, he held out his hand to the men, pulling them deeper into the building, clucking like an old hen, his voice echoing in the gloom. There were about a dozen pews. The air still smelled like fresh paint and sawdust, and the minister led them to his office, where he beckoned for them to sit in straight-backed wooden chairs arranged in front of a large, uncluttered desk.

"I was wondering when you would call on me," he said, angling around to his side of the desk and taking a seat. His eyes sharpened and his voice lost some of its unctuousness. His lips pursed and he leaned back in his chair.

"The whole town is talking about the wedding . . ." he said, very nearly pouting.

"You know how men are, pastor," Beatrice said. "Always with the best of intentions and sometimes short on the wherewithal. We meant to speak to you earlier—much earlier, in fact—and would have done so had my Catharine had her way. But this is not a matter for the bride to concern herself with. It is up to her parents and, in this case, the groom—an upstanding man, as I'm sure you already know."

"Yes," the minister said, thoughtfully. "A fine young man," he agreed. "So new to our humble community and already such a man of consequence. They say he's building a castle in the woods."

"It's a château," Lawrence corrected him.

"I see," the minister said.

His eyes sharpened as they shifted to Pierre, and Beatrice had a momentary fright. She had never particularly worried about her husband's soul, as she had always thought he was a Calvinist. But the Cathars' visit to the farm had shaken her considerably. She had never heard of a Cathar before and to discover Pierre's mother was one had taken her breath away. What did that say about Pierre, she wondered. Were the Cathars even Christians, and if not, what if the minister found out? The Reformed Church of Watertown took a dim view of what it considered mixed marriages, which was when a member of the congregation wed outside the faith.

But the minister was only looking at Pierre to see if he had anything to say about Lawrence's château. Perhaps the minister supposed the château to have been Pierre's idea in the first place. But if the minister thought he would get any explanation from the reclusive, aristocratic farmer, he was very wrong, Beatrice thought, glad to be off the hook about the mixed marriage issue. The kind of house Lawrence wanted his wife to live in was really none of the minister's business, anyway, as far as she was concerned.

The minister agreed to perform the wedding ceremony, and the conversation descended into small talk. But Beatrice's earlier scare had awakened a sore point that stuck with her. Pierre had received some rough treatment early in life, and she couldn't hold his claim to be an agnostic against him. But she couldn't rest easy with it, either. She was, after all, a God-fearing woman who couldn't help worrying about the choices her loved ones made. As a practical person, she didn't indulge herself very long in matters beyond her control. But there was always that shadow of a doubt—the grubby little fingers of concern—and she was sure that Heaven would be little better than another hell if her husband weren't there with her.

◆ ◆ ◆

As far as Pierre was concerned, the meeting at the church went well. There had never been any doubt in his mind that the minister would give his blessing. Regardless of the positions he took in the pulpit, the minister's financial welfare lay in the hands of his congregation, and the Kraymers would be an important investment in his future endeavors. Pierre saw it in the minister's eyes when Lawrence talked about the château. The minister's interest in the new construction was far more than passing, and Pierre didn't have to guess at his thoughts.

That was the thing with small communities. People were well up on each other's business, and what one person did often mattered to someone else. Sometimes it mattered very much, and Pierre hazarded a guess that the minister was having second thoughts about his newly completed church. People measured themselves by what other people did, and Pierre had a suspicion that, compared to the impressive château, the minister found his own building lacking.

In any case, Pierre and Beatrice had other errands to run in Watertown. While Lawrence headed back to the château, they found their way to Horrocks's Mercantile.

"Well, look who's here," Horrocks said, leaning on the counter of his store. His shoulders were narrow but thick, and his big white hands lay like plucked chickens on the flat surface in front of him. Particles of dust clung to his hair and eyebrows, and he wore a big, dusty apron.

"We're needing some lamp oil," Beatrice explained.

She gave her husband one of those glances that said she might want to look at some other items in addition to the oil, and drifted deeper into the store. Pierre followed her with his eyes, but remained at the counter. He had known Horrocks for almost twenty years, and they had an amicable relationship. On this particular occasion, Horrocks regarded him with an unusual degree of brightness.

"So . . . how's our hero doing?" Horrocks asked.

"Our hero?"

"Oh, come on," Horrocks said, teasing. "Your boy, Jean—that's who. Overbrook was here just the other day and told me all about it, how the outlaws kidnapped his little girl for God knows what purposes and would have gotten away with it, too, but for a certain young man who shot one of them right out of the saddle and saved her life. Put a hole in him as big as daylight!"

Pierre gazed at the other man, solemnly. The incident had happened several weeks ago, but stories develop lives of their own in small towns, where entertainment often comes at someone else's expense. He was proud of his son, but not deliriously so, and the town's chatter disturbed him. Jean was a good boy and turning into a good man, but pride was a funny thing, like a coin with sharp edges. Better it should be spent and forgotten than collected in a pocket where it could turn and cut a hole.

"Nobody got shot," Pierre assured him.

Horrocks gave one of those knowing smiles that indicated he thought he knew better. His head wobbled from side to side, as if he were weighing how to press on without offending.

"It doesn't much matter, does it?" he said. "The way most people see it, the miscreant deserves whatever punishment he got."

"I have to feel sorry for the poor girl's mother," Beatrice said, as she placed a tin of lamp oil on the counter. "Almost losing a loved one like that . . . As a mother, myself, it makes me shudder. No amount of punishment in the world would have healed her broken heart, if that's what it had come to."

"Lucky for everyone that Jean came along when he did," Horrocks agreed, his eyebrows climbing his forehead as he marked the transaction in his account book. He asked about the family in general, and Beatrice let him know that all was well. That was the way errands tended to go, simple transactions followed by chit-chat, or vice versa. People were hungry to know what went on in each other's lives.

For his part, Pierre waited to one side. He found the word "hero" to be particularly troublesome, for he well knew how differently events could have gone. Outlaws were an unpredictable sort, and Jean was plain lucky to have survived the encounter with his skin intact. Additionally, Pierre had to consider what would have happened if Jean's shot had not missed. The result could easily have been the burden of a dead man on the conscience of an impressionable youth, and Pierre found no comfort in an outcome that had been too much like the flip of a copper coin.

CHAPTER

TWELVE

———————●———————

L ong before Martin Luther, Jean Calvin, and the Protestant
Reformation, there were a number of groups, in addition to
Catholics, who called themselves Christians, and while their
beliefs differed in fundamental ways, one of the problems they
all shared was explaining how a just, all-powerful God could
countenance evil in the world. The Cathar solution was simple. According to them, there were two gods—a New Testa-
ment god of goodness and light, and an Evil One, who ruled
the physical world, where unholiness prevailed. Pierre may have
reached the point where he no longer wished to think of himself as a religious man, because he had witnessed firsthand the
malevolence of the followers of a so-called loving god, be they
Catholic, Protestant, or otherwise. But his mother had been a
devoutly religious woman, whether he liked it or not. He could
reject her Catharism. But he couldn't reject her love, no matter
how problematic it seemed, and the seed of her faith followed
him to the New World, where all things were not as new as he
might have hoped.

Little had prepared him for that desperate ocean passage into
what was then still largely an unknown. People left the European
ports and but precious few came back, and at the age of thirteen,
Pierre found himself on a ship crammed with hollow-eyed men,

huddled women, and sickly children. In extremis, a person needs a sustaining thought, something to hold onto, and he thought of horses. The manoir had had a stable and he remembered the smell of them, their sighs and shuddering vocalizations, their settlings and shufflings. As a young child, he would press his cheek against the massive velvet noses and breathe the same air they breathed, imagining he was running with them through lush green fields. He dreamed he was one of them, heart to heart and soul to soul, and on the rolling and tossing ship to the New World, the word for them was the first that he learned in English.

His teacher was a Norman boy who worked as a deckhand and whom he would meet on the bow, where the fresh breezes blew. The Norman had a blistered, brick red face and blue eyes pale as water.

"You talk funny," the Norman said.

"If that's what you think, then you should hear yourself. I can hardly understand a word you say."

The Norman gave a snort.

"You're kind of quiet, aren't you, and now maybe I know why. If people can't figure out what you're saying, then why say anything at all? Right?"

The Norman laughed at his own joke, but both boys knew it was not always easy for one person to understand another. In the land they were from, residents of one village struggled to talk to the residents of another, and a person from as far away as another valley was sometimes impossible to understand. The fact that the boys could speak to each other at all was due to Pierre's education—which was not at all a common thing—and his familiarity with the language of the Far Court, as his father had called it.

"So, tell me," the Norman said, shaking his head. "With all of the English words that I know and could tell you about, why do you want to know about horses? I've never had a horse—have you? Only rich people ride horses, and you don't look any richer than I am. You're not rich, are you?"

This was a challenge that could not go unanswered, as Pierre's friendship with the Norman was based on what they had in common, not what set them apart. What they had in common was youth and proximity, the sense that they were impoverished vagabonds in a world that loomed large. What would set them apart was anything one had that the other lacked.

"I just like them," Pierre said. He felt the weight of the pouch of gold coins under his shirt, against his skin, and knew that he had to guard its secret well.

"If you like them so much, why are you here? Why not just be a stable boy and spend your life cleaning up turds?"

"Let's change the subject."

"I'm just having some fun with you," the Norman chided. His eyes softened and his chin relaxed, as he eased into his role as teacher. "*Eh bien*," he said. "*C'est ce que vous voulez. Pour le cheval, le mot en anglaise, c'est horse*. Ha-oh-are-ess. Ho-arse. Horse."

"Seriously?" Pierre said, in his native Occitan.

"*Quoi?*" the other boy said, in his Norman French.

"It's such an abrupt, ugly word for such a noble animal," Pierre said.

"*Mais oui, vous avez parfaitement raison*," the Norman said, grinning. "You can only know the true spirit of something in your own language, *n'est-ce pas?*"

"Yes," Pierre said, nodding and thinking the statement profound. Indeed, he had already come to the realization that he might never hear his own language again, that the lyricism of his youth was gone forever.

◆ ◆ ◆

By the time his ship arrived in Philadelphia, Pierre knew a smattering of English words but still lacked the confidence to use them. The wharf was a busy place, with immigrants arriving and then branching off to their various indentures and destinations. But not all of the newcomers had a place to go. Children who had lost parents during the crossing were a particularly sad lot and many were reduced to begging.

Word traveled quickly that a certain tailor shop handed out lumps of bread at the back door. The tailor was a man named Mr. Hesse, who was a Protestant—but one of the good ones, the rumor went, unlike so many of the others—Protestant or otherwise—who were just as likely to call the police as to lend a helping hand. It never occurred to Pierre to go to the back door, like the other starving wharf rats. He went in the front, as befitted a person of manners, making the bell ring and standing there among the stacks of linens and Indian cottons with no idea of what to do next. Mr. Hesse could very well have shooed him off. Instead, finding the lad curious, he invited him to take some tea at a small table in the rear of the shop, where the boy held his cup with practiced but trembling hands. But it was how the boy spoke that got the man's attention. After a brief attempt at English, Pierre fell back on the dialect that his people spoke in the Pyrenees, like any other refugee who spoke his or her native tongue. When this didn't work, however, he spoke French—what he called *la Langue du nord*. Mr. Hesse was a gruff man. "Speak

German or hold your peace," he said, and Pierre responded in the language of the *Allemand*.

Amazing, thought the old man. He signaled to one of his clerks. Eyeing the boy, he dictated some measurements and told the clerk to tailor a suit of clothes. Nothing fancy. Something practical. While this was happening, the lad fell asleep, right there in the chair, with a half cup of tea still in front of him, and Mr. Hesse shook his head. Realizing the boy was exhausted, he instructed the clerk to set up a cot in the storage room.

Days later, when the boy had rested and was dressed in his new clothes, Mr. Hesse approved of what he saw and decided to hire him as an odd-jobber, a trial employment to see what the lad was made of. Chewing on the end of his quill, Mr. Hesse studied Pierre, thinking about what to write in his ledger.

"*Du Laux?*" he said, squinting and then and shaking his head. "A name like that sounds too noteworthy. Like you're from some-place important. Like maybe it even matters."

Pierre remained silent and the old man leaned forward in his chair. He lowered his voice, as if even in his own shop it was best to keep a confidence.

"We have all kinds of people in the colonies and they're not all good," he said. "We have the English and the French and the Spanish, not to mention the misfits from New Amsterdam, and one nationality is not as good as another, depending on who you talk to."

The boy stared as if he didn't understand a word the old man said. It was the blank, sunburned stare of someone who had seen hard times and too much ocean and too little food for too long a stretch. Mr. Hesse decided to make allowances.

"Look, lad, let me give you some words of advice," he continued, in a fatherly tone. "Maybe you've heard the colonies are a place to start over, and for some it is, I'll grant you. We're in a natural state here, or as close to it as you might find in the civilized world. But don't think it's natural for people to get along, because it's not. Far from it, lad." The man shook his head. "People don't look for reasons to get along. They look for a reason not to, and that's the sad truth of it. There's something about you that stands out, and that's good, up to a point. But don't give anyone reason to think you're too much different from them."

He dipped the tip of his quill into the inkwell.

"Now, about the name . . ."

He pursed his lips in thought, then wrote in his ledger.

"Laux is what we'll call you. Just plain Laux. A different kind of name but hard to peg. I like it. There. It's done. Now get busy," he said, placing his hands on the ledger and pushing it away from him. "I've got some bales of fabric that have to be sorted, and after that, I might put you on measurements. You know how to use a tape, don't you?"

Pierre just gave him a sunbaked look.

"Go on now," the old man said, affectionately, wondering if the boy knew anything at all when it came to the menial tasks at hand. He didn't know if the boy would even last a fortnight. He certainly had no clue, at this point, that Pierre would go on to marry his daughter, Beatrice.

◆　◆　◆

PIERRE LOOKED DOWN AT HIS hands. His tenure in Mr. Hesse's tailor shop had lasted only five years, and the twenty that followed had transformed them from the big hands of a strapping boy into the browned, cracked, deeply lined paws of a farmer. They were working hands, used to grasping and lifting, gripping and swinging, tightening and twisting—hands like his father had never had. Hands the seigneur could never have imagined for his son. Pierre had lost so much more than a mere childhood home—not that a home is ever a trivial thing. Having watched his father ride away and then fail to return, he lost hope that he would ever see him again. He then lost his mother, putting her to rest while the drunken soldiers slept, placing her so deep she would never be disturbed. With the loss of his parents, he lost his heritage as well, for without proofs to the contrary, he was just another vagabond, cut loose in the world, with whatever flickering flame of life he had. And he lost his religion, because his mother's death stilled the tongue that used to speak God's name.

Here, in a new land a world away from the one he had once known, he enjoyed the loamy richness of the earth, in defiance of his Cathar training that the material world was evil to the core. He loved guiding the ploughshare against the moist, giving earth, breaking open the ground and turning it, his shoulders and back aching, leaning into the plow to keep from stumbling. He loved the snapping of grass roots and the burst of dark, earthy odor in the heavy vernal air that he breathed. Looking up, he saw his son, Jean, striding toward him, and he couldn't help the swelling of his chest that was dangerously close to pride. He simply couldn't believe, as the Cathars did, that the material flesh was evil. His mother's *Cathari* would have said that of the things that made a person, only the spirit came from God, and Pierre shook his head in disbelief. Watching the youth approach, he just could not believe that Jean's lucid brown eyes and springing step came of anything but goodness.

But an early indoctrination is hard to shed, and he couldn't escape it entirely, the tiny but enduring seed his mother had planted.

The seed of fear that there was an Evil One who was rampant in the world. That even in the so-called New World, the Evil One knew who a person was and where he lived, what he loved and what he had yet to lose.

◆　◆　◆

TURNING THE PLOW OVER TO Jean, Pierre headed to the springhouse to wash up before returning to the house. He marveled at how much his son had changed since rescuing the girl. The youth now brimmed with confidence, and Pierre could see the man in him, the calm and competent adult he would become. But everything had its shadow. The youth was more determined than ever to join the Royal Marines. Pierre was no stranger to harm's way, but he had never sought it out. It had come to him, unbidden and unwelcome, and while he recognized Jean's martial spirit as one of the enduring traits of his family heritage, he could not be happy about it.

Fighting a heaviness of heart, he dipped his hands in the cool water of the cistern, swirling them and then cupping them, raising them to his mouth. How good the water tasted. Drinking deeply, he splashed the water over his forehead and cheeks, then used a handkerchief to mop his face and neck.

The springhouse was cool and quiet, and he thought he heard his daughter Magdalena's voice. The pipe on the wall dripped water into the rock basin, making sounds like "Pap" and "Papa," and he spun around, thinking for sure he would find her standing there.

◆　◆　◆

THE PATH FROM THE SPRINGHOUSE led up past the barn to the wire gate in the fence around the yard. The two remaining mastiffs bounded to meet him and he couldn't help but think of Romulus, and the terribly close call his daughter Catharine had had. The two dogs that remained had earned his trust, but there had been a time when he trusted Romulus, as well, and he was reminded how quickly fate can change everything you thought you knew.

Carrying these dark thoughts with him as he went into the house, he heard voices coming from the sitting room, where he had set up a table for Beatrice and Catharine to work on the girl's wedding dress. Beatrice had covered the table with a bed sheet and bolts of cloth. She was smoothing out a pattern that she had made and Catharine stood at her mother's elbow, her hands clutched in front of her, as if she carried a dove she was afraid might get away.

"It's easier to wear linen in the winter than to wear wool in the summer," Beatrice was saying, in a reassuring tone. "Besides, how many times will you put on such a dress? We're not city dwellers, you know, and how many special occasions do we have?"

"I want to wear it as often as I can!" Catharine said.

"Of course you do, dear. You will look perfectly beautiful in it, I promise."

Pierre cleared his throat and Catharine gasped, spinning around to face him.

"Sorry to interrupt," he said.

"Oh, Papa, how you talk!" Catharine said, making him smile.

"I'm looking for Maggy," he said.

"She's upstairs taking her nap, of course," Beatrice said.

"That's odd. I was just out in the springhouse and was sure I heard her voice."

"I already told you where she is," Beatrice said. "In fact, she's been asleep for a while, now. If we don't get her up soon, she won't sleep through the night."

"I'll look in on her," Pierre said.

He crossed the kitchen and went to the doorway in the far corner, where the stairs led up to the second floor. The boards of the stairs creaked under his stockinged feet. At the top, he turned and went into the bedroom where he and Beatrice slept, and there he saw the little girl, her eyes closed and her cheeks flushed, her ringlets of red hair damp against the pillow.

Pierre sat on the edge of the bed. Extending his hand, he held it a short distance from her temple, where he could feel her radiating heat. Little beads of perspiration dotted her forehead. He didn't want to use his handkerchief, but it was the only thing handy, and he touched it to her forehead, dabbing at the drops.

The eyes opened, bright blue and soft with drowsiness.

"Papa, you came back," she said.

"Where else would I be?" he murmured.

"I had a bad dream," she said, her chin starting to quiver. "I dreamed there was a black cloud that came down from the sky. It made everything dark and I couldn't see. The cloud had yellow eyes and lightning came out of its mouth."

"It was just a dream," Pierre reassured her.

"I looked for you but couldn't find you. I couldn't find you anywhere. I called out your name but you didn't answer."

Tears bubbled in the corners of her eyes.

"I will always be here for you," he said.

"Promise?"

"I promise. Now, it's time to get up. Do you want Papa to carry you?"

She stuck her small ivory arms in the air and he scooped her up, pressing her warm body to his shoulder. Her legs dangled down.

"Don't ever go away again," she said, clinging to him, tightly.

CHAPTER

THIRTEEN

———————————●———————————

Throughout the construction of the château, there had always been spectators, villagers who sat on their carts at a distance, watching the hired men lever rock into place, swing hammers, and work the shingles. They would sit and watch and then turn their wagons around, sometimes pausing to look over their shoulders, but usually just heading back the way they had come, as if they had seen enough to talk about until such a time as they might want to see more. There were other visitors, too, who came from the forest, materializing from the woods as if they were one of the many shadows, some wearing little more than breechcloths. They would stand for a while and watch the goings on, then disappear, and Lawrence never worried about such scrutiny. He figured it was just part of what you had to expect when you built something as unusual as he was endeavoring to do.

The church delegation, however, actually expected a tour, which was an unwelcome intrusion for a man who was trying to finish such a massive undertaking before he ran out of money. The minister had set up the tour, making arrangements through Mrs. Laux—whom Lawrence could hardly say no to—and now the man stood looking up at the lofty edifice as if trying to imagine himself in possession of such a thing. Two deacons and their wives accompanied him, picking their way through the mud, craning their necks upward, and Lawrence could see it on their faces, the rigid reserve of people who were astonished by something beyond their imaginings and therefore, at the same time, stubbornly suspicious of it.

"Look out below!" a man shouted from high atop the scaffolding that was being dismantled, board by board, from where it hugged the granite wall. A long, slightly warped piece of wood clattered as it struck the other boards on the ground, like a warning bolt from the clear blue sky—and one of the women jumped, her hand flying to her chest as if to restrain a surging heart.

"Goodness," the minister said, though he didn't appear particularly alarmed. His eyes drifted. His mouth fell open as he breathed.

Lawrence waited as patiently as he could in front of the château.

"Careful there, pastor . . ." he said. The minister's shoe sank in the mud and Lawrence held out a hand. McDonall happened to be hovering nearby, and Lawrence directed him to bring some of the boards for the church people to walk on. But the delegation had already picked their way through the worst of the mud. The porch had not been constructed yet, and to enter the house, they had to climb some log rounds standing on end in front of the open door.

"My word," the minister breathed, pausing in the spacious gloom, his eyes owlishly large. The tip of his tongue darted out to moisten his lips. "Was a time when a church was the grandest building in a town. Supposed to make a man feel humble, it was. But this . . ."

His voice trailed, his head turning, his eyes searching to the sides and upward, as he tried to take everything in. The deacons and their wives crowded around him, as if piling up against an invisible barrier.

"Look yonder," one of the women said, pointing to a room that stood apart from the others. It had its own hearth, a dry sink, and spacious counters. The hearth had an elongated extension. A pit made of stone had metal doors that opened to a firebox.

"It's the kitchen," Lawrence said.

"You're going to burn wood in that?" the woman said, pointing at the box.

"It'll have a metal plate on top and vent through the chimney," Lawrence said, proud of the innovation but hesitant to explain it much further. The disbelief in his guests' eyes already bordered on hostility and he saw no reason to unnecessarily antagonize.

"I'm sure it'll make a lot of smoke," the woman sniffed.

Lawrence led them into the adjoining room, with its high ceiling and tall windows.

"My word," one of the deacons said.

"It won't seem so big once the furnishings are in place," Lawrence said, self-consciously.

In a rear corner of the room, a ladder extended through a hole in the ceiling, through which the sloping interior of the roof could be seen.

"And that?" the deacon wanted to know, pointing.

"That's the upstairs, where we'll have the bedrooms. We haven't built the stairs yet, as you can see."

The man's wife made a clucking sound. Already, the guests had started to squabble, pointing out details they found disagreeable in one way or another, some expressing astonishment and others making a show of dismissiveness, as if such extravagance had no place in a frontier life. Someone went so far as to pronounce the château a good example of the kind of pride that went before a fall.

Lawrence began to feel very tired, wondering why he was wasting his time with these people. He didn't value their opinions very much. However, he was not insensitive to them, either. This was, after all, the community in which he planned to live after he sold the brewery and no longer had to make the trips back and forth to Philadelphia. These were the people who would be his neighbors, though he had a hard time imagining them as friends.

"Mrs. Laux made mention that you planned to have a vineyard," the minister commented, and Lawrence brightened. The vineyard had become a passion, and he thought about it night and day. Arrangements had already been made to ship some root stock from southern France, where Pierre was from.

He led the delegation out the back of the château, where the group paused, squinting in the bright sunlight. Lawrence pointed out the field behind the barn, where stumps of felled trees still studded the ground and piles of limbs and other trimmings waited to be burned. The minister shaded his eyes. He stood like a man in a dream.

"I intend to plant the vines right there," Lawrence said, pointing toward the gently sloping hillside. He told them about the vines and the grapes and the wine he intended to produce.

"We don't drink wine, do we?" said one of the deacons to the other.

While the Reformed Church, in general, was not entirely against drinking alcohol, the minister had railed from the pulpit against the evils of all alcoholic beverages—the intoxicating spirits, certainly, but also beer and wine, as well, which in his view had led many a righteous person astray, and the deacon looked to him for approval. The other deacon hastily reminded the rest of the delegation that whereas some churches used wine for communion, their particular church used common grape juice. But the minister raised a hand, gesturing for them to be still.

"Very impressive," he said, speaking to Lawrence. "You're a man of accomplishment, no doubt about it." The minister shook his head in shrewd admiration. "The Lord could use a man like you. A man like you and we wouldn't have to abide the firetrap of a building that we worship in now."

As a businessman, Lawrence had learned the importance of knowing what another person was thinking, and the minister did not make it difficult for him. A church was no small thing in the minister's eyes. A church was the earthly gateway to Heaven and the minister was in the process of discovering how lucky he was to have a resource like Lawrence on hand. Lawrence reminded the minister that the church he already had was still so new that you could smell the paint on its walls, but the minister dismissed the comment.

"With a man like you, we could have built in stone," the minister said. One of the deacons had taken a piece of paper from his pocket and was frowning at it. The other stood with his arms folded across his chest, as if unhappy to find himself outside the conversation and trying to decide how to get back in the good graces of his shepherd.

"There is so much mud," his wife said, looking around, distastefully.

It was one of those awkward moments that might have lingered. But a man appeared at the far side of the clearing, emerging from the trees as if disengaging from them. He had a shaved head and wore a buckskin hunting shirt and leggings that twisted around his legs like tree bark. Placing the butt of his musket on the ground, he leaned casually on the long barrel.

"Who's that?" one of the women asked.

"Goodness, is it an Indian?"

"An Indian?" said the deacon who had been writing on the piece of paper. He looked up and cast about, observing where the others were looking.

"Here?" the other deacon said, uncrossing his arms with a convulsive gesture.

"Excuse me," Lawrence said, his attention on the newcomer.

◆ ◆ ◆

JOHN WATCHED LAWRENCE APPROACH. HE recalled taking Lawrence on the fateful hunting trip a year and a half before, never imagining, at the time, that such a simple gesture would result in a house built of stone and as big as a mountain. The land was changing. The forests where his people had roamed were turning into woodlots amid a patchwork of cultivated fields. His people, the Lenape, had been on mostly friendly terms with the newcomers. But that did not save them from the fevers and sickness that followed the Europeans wherever they went. Out of his whole village, only John remained.

The two men clasped hands, stiffening their arms and giving each other a good shake.

"It's good to see you," Lawrence said, and John agreed. You never knew, when you said goodbye to someone and went off into the forest, if you would ever see them again. Too many things could go wrong. A bear could avenge a misplaced shot or a body could fall from a rocky ridge. A broken ankle could well prove fatal if it meant a bad fever or a stomach that went too long without food. A man alone in the wilderness walked in the shadow of the Great Spirit, who did not always pay attention to where he was going.

Lawrence asked him where he had been, and John had to consider the question. The Europeans had a curious way of thinking, as if they walked in a straight line and could easily account for where they had been and what they had done. John's paths meandered. The one day that turned into the next seemed very much the same to John. It was the forest that changed, dappled sunlight that moved the shade, rain that turned to sun and fog, wild game that ran away or fell to his musket, enemies that he avoided as much as possible. Why a Lenape would choose to winter in New York would have been difficult to explain. Even more difficult would have been to talk about who he was now that his tribe was gone. Where was a man like John to go, when he was a stranger wherever he went?

He and Lawrence had talked about this, during the campfire huddles on their hunting trip. Lawrence had wanted to know what it was like being an Indian, and John shrugged, gazing into the flames. He didn't know, he said. His father was white. His tribe had accepted him as one of them. But they could see the difference when they looked at him and he could feel it as well, the thing that they saw, the little bit of him that was not quite the same as they were.

In return, John wanted to know what it was like to be a European, this thing that he, himself, was part of but didn't understand. He'd actually hoped to find an answer, but Lawrence appeared stumped by the question and John had to accept that his friend was not going to be much help. He wondered if what made them different wasn't less important than what made them the same. In any case, he had many long nights of lonely campfires ahead of him, and here was something to filter through his head as he sat in front of the glowing coals.

◆　◆　◆

JOHN HAD SOMETHING IMPORTANT TO tell his friend, but didn't know quite how to go about it. Danger was a part of life and certainly something to be aware of, which was why some native villages had palisades and why braves kept a lookout for any sign of trouble. Along with danger came uncertainty, which you lived with every day, like the deer that lived with the panther, but still fed and bedded down and lived the life it had been born to. The problem, as John saw it, was that in his experience, the Europeans had trouble with uncertainty. They had their disagreements and their wars, but unlike the deer, they found uncertainty itself to be an enemy that had to be attacked and defeated. They had little tolerance for threats of any kind.

"Things are very bad up north," he finally said. "The Haudenosaunee are making trouble. Many white men have died and many women, too." His gaze drifted toward the clump of people who stood next to Lawrence's house, as if they didn't know whether to take a stand or turn and flee.

"Seems to me I heard something about it," Lawrence said. "There's a man they call the major who has been going about in the area, trying to put together a militia to spell relief for some settlers in New York. Jean Laux already signed on with him. He's one of my fiancée's brothers."

John did not like this news and had to mull it over.

"This major's war party is a bad idea," he finally said. "I have heard of him. He has taken many Indian scalps and knows the woods. But the men who follow him will be like children. They are farmers, not warriors. They will make mistakes—too many, I think." He brooded on this last thought. "What about you?" he said, reluctantly, fearing one of the answers he might receive.

"Me?"

"Will you join the war party, too?"

"Goodness no," Lawrence said, glancing toward the towering château. "I've got a house to finish." He shook his head slowly back and forth. "This is where I belong—right here. I don't have time to go running off into the woods."

Lawrence flushed as he spoke.

"Good," John said, nodding. There was a lot of rough country on the way to what the settlers from across the big water called their New York Colony, as if anybody could take a whole swath of country-side and call it theirs. There were tall timbers and swamps, not to mention the bands of unhappy Haudenosaunee, who could be very difficult. John thought the major was begging for trouble and was relieved that his friend would not be a part of it.

◆ ◆ ◆

WHEN LAWRENCE RETURNED TO THE church delegation, they looked at him as if they thought him somehow changed, that close proximity to a native had infected Lawrence in some way, or worse, that they had just discovered something in him they hadn't known before. The minister stood in front of the group like a little barn-yard rooster, looking at Lawrence intently through the glass circles of his spectacles, and the deacons hovered over their wives, as if uncertain how to play the protector, should the need arise.

Lawrence had no patience now to continue with the tour. For one thing, he was concerned about Jean Laux, who had joined the major's band. If John thought the expedition ill-advised, what did that portend for Lawrence's future brother-in-law? Secondly, there was something else, and it had to do with the château. After a year and a half of construction, it was nearly completed. There was a common perception in the colonies that if one settlement was threatened then they were all in danger, and it took Lawrence's breath away to think that the home he had birthed after such a long and hard labor could be in danger. The mere possibility that it could come under attack made him sick at heart.

FOURTEEN

⎯⎯⎯⎯⎯⎯⎯⎯⎯ ● ⎯⎯⎯⎯⎯⎯⎯⎯⎯

The major was a man of grim countenance. His eyes were pale blue—the color of ice, when viewed at a certain angle—and a scar ran down from his right temple to the corner of his mouth. He had received the wound while in the company of the famous wilderness ranger Colonel Benjamin Church nearly thirty-five years earlier. The wound had gotten infected and subsequently healed, but it still looked like raw meat, which only served to remind the major of the glory of being young and fighting under a commander of renown, fighting a guerilla war like the Indian himself, and surviving, by God, to tell of it.

The difference between the starry-eyed youth he had been back then and the man of more mature years he had become, was that after campaigning in the woods for many years, he knew of the many dark places and secret hollows where an enemy could hide and how large a role luck played in your ability to draw another breath. You either had to run like a deer to outpace your enemy or hunker down like a cottontail so the fiend couldn't find you, and even then, luck could thwart your plans to stay alive. The woods could be a dark and terrible place, and had someone told him they planned to take a militia to New York, he would have advised sticking to the established roads. But he was better at giving advice than taking it, and in this particular case, he would not have accepted his own counsel. Time was of the essence and he planned to cut through a swath of wild country he had ranged through from time to time, but that few other Europeans had ever traveled. Even the French *voyageurs* to the north usually stuck to the river paths and generally wouldn't risk the dark timber the Indian called home.

The problem with assembling a militia was that you didn't always know what you would get. He had heard of Jean Laux, the lad who had taken on a small army of miscreants and killed the half of them—as the story went—in defense of a woman's virtue, and knew he could hook such an apparently ardent youth to his cause. He had also heard of the castle some fancy man was building in the settlement, and thought he could use such a stage to benefit his recruitment efforts. All that mattered was that he got a half dozen or so good men, and maybe the good didn't even matter, as long as he could somehow get them to New York and join their muskets to the cause. This would be a one-way trip for the major. Once in New York, he had no intention of coming back again, and once the people he called the Iroquois had been repelled, any men still alive would be on their own.

When he first approached Lawrence Kraymer about using the château as part of his enlistment efforts, the man had declined, like one of the damned Quakers that couldn't seem to get off their pious haunches, saying he didn't want to get involved. Old Ben Church never had to deal with such poltroons up in the Plymouth Colony, that was for sure. But the major hadn't lived so long by not being crafty, and he'd heard that Kraymer was building the château for some beauty who just happened to be Jean Laux's sister. The next time he visited Kraymer about using the château, he took the Laux boy with him and proceeded to get a lot of pleasure out of getting what he wanted. He pressed his luck and tried to recruit

Kraymer, in addition to getting the use of his house, but had no success on that front. That's how luck was. It could turn bad just as easily as not.

"Welcome to the new militia!" he shouted, standing on the hastily constructed porch of the château and cutting the air with a sword. He glared at one man and then another, scaring them with his visage. "The Mohawk have been hitting the New York settlements and I have it on good faith that this settlement could be next. So what do we do about that—men like you and me? Do we sit around and quiver with fear? No, that's not what a man does," he said, singling out Lawrence, who stood with his arms crossed at the back of the group. "We take the fight to the enemy, that's what we do. Our New York brethren need us and we're here to help. We're here to give the Indians some hell. We'll show them the stuff that Penn's marksmen are made of!"

The scattering of about twenty men, who stood in front of the platform, shifted under the weight of his words. Some leaned on rusty muskets, their linen shirts sticking to their bodies in the summer heat. A couple carried pitchforks, as if some sort of weapon were required for such an occasion and pitchforks were the best they could do. They watched the major with glum expressions, and a few gave each other sidelong glances, gauging the mood of their peers.

"We're all here because of the burden we feel," the major went on. "The burden to protect our brethren in their time of need. The burden to serve them as they would us, if the situation was different and we were the ones under attack." Again, he directed his gaze at Lawrence, taking satisfaction from the red blooms on the man's cheeks. "We're here to do for them what they can't do for themselves and to push the Iroquois back to the lodge where he belongs."

A muttering ran through the assembled group. The major took this as a good sign. Some of the faces looking at him were shadowed and dismissive, but others were bright with strengthening resolve.

"Thems of you that's got the balls for it, meet here at dawn. Put your affairs in order and say goodbye to your families. Give your wives a kiss and your babies a good pinch. Tell 'em you'll set things right in the eyes of God and come home a hero." This time, his gaze shifted to Jean, who stood at Lawrence's side. "Bring all the ball and powder you can carry," he said, directing his words at Jean Laux, as if the youth were the only one present. "We'll be moving fast and living off the land as we go, so if you got some jerky or Indian pemmican to bring along, good for you. Bring a blanket to sleep in and anything else as long as you can carry it yourself and not be a bother to anyone else's progress."

He gave Jean a nod and could see the youth's chest swell.

"Will we be seeing action?" a man wanted to know, shouting out his question.

"Damned right you'll see action," the major growled. "Unless the savages take one look at you and run for their lives."

Some of the men hooted.

"Is it true that women and wee ones are being dragged off as slaves?" another man called out.

The major glared, then turned and spit.

"Aye, but not no more. Not with the likes of you standing in the way."

More hoots and the major gave his sword a flourish.

There were more questions, which he answered with grim and compelling determination, and the group broke up and drifted apart. Even would-be heroes had homes to go to and words to be had with the families waiting there. Even the most enthusiastic had to admit that the future was uncertain. But no one thought they had anything to worry about, personally, especially with a man as fearsome as the major in charge. Even the smallest glimmer of hope was enough to light the darkness of the most dubious cause, and these men had an abundance of optimism. They had strong feelings for their compatriots. They saw their own reflection in each other's eyes and saw the plight of their fellows as a plight of their own.

Lawrence approached the porch, where the major still stood.

"Well, that was damned inspirational," he said.

The major heard sarcasm in the remark and chose to ignore it. He had what he wanted. He had Jean and was sure he could count on several more. As a colonial ranger, he had accomplished plenty with a lot less.

He had no intention of telling anyone his real reason for calling out a militia and taking this extraordinarily risky trip. It was his own goddamned business, the way he saw it, and whether or not anyone chose to join the expedition was theirs. The idealism of the Laux boy could have pricked his conscience if he dwelled on it for very long. No one wants to be the hammer that drives the nail. But there were other considerations, far more important to the major than what happened to a lad in the woods. Youth was a fine currency, no doubt about it, but how you spent it was on your head and no one else's.

FIFTEEN

I t was the last night before Jean's departure and the family was all together. Beatrice had taken three hens from the coop and young Georgie had plucked them and cleaned them, saving the hearts, livers, gizzards, and unlaid eggs. After oiling and seasoning the birds, Beatrice roasted them hearthside, while Catharine baked the bread, snapped the string beans, and set the potatoes to boil. Pierre fetched a slab of bacon from the smokehouse, and Catharine used it to flavor the beans. Everyone pitched in, even Andrew, who had been such a stranger to the house of late, performing their tasks with quiet deliberation, unified in their efforts while at the same time wrapped in an envelope of their own separate thoughts. Smelling the food and perhaps unnerved by the unusual somberness of the occasion, the dogs were agitated and whined throatily from the porch.

The chairs scraped as they pulled to the table.

"Did you feed the dogs?" Pierre asked, looking at his youngest son.

"I've been busy!" Georgie said, in case his father hadn't noticed.

"You know the rule," Pierre said. "Whosever turn it is to feed the animals doesn't eat until they do."

"Fine!" Georgie slapped his hands down against the table and pushed to his feet. He slammed the door on his way to the out-kitchen, where his mother kept the scraps that they fed to the dogs. The whining intensified and padded feet scuffled on the floorboards of the porch.

"Goodness," Catharine said, arching her eyebrows and glancing at Lawrence, who sat next to her. He shrugged, as if to say that everyone was tense and could easily be pushed out of sorts, even one normally so blithe as her youngest brother.

Georgie stomped back into the house and flopped back down in his chair. Hunching forward, he took his fork to the buttered potatoes on his plate.

"Did you give the dogs fresh water?" Pierre asked.

Georgie held his fork suspended.

"Can't they drink at the creek the way they do all day long?" he said.

"Is that what you want to do when you're thirsty?"

Georgie's chair shot back as he lurched to his feet again and spun on his heel, returning to the porch.

"Mr. Laux, dearest, must you be so hard on him?" Beatrice said, coming to her son's defense. "Everyone is a little on edge with Jean leaving us so soon, and Georgie's doing the best he can, just like the rest of us."

"That's no reason to make the animals suffer," Pierre said.

Georgie came back and stood stock still, his hands raised. "Anything else?" he said. "Should I feed and water the horses all over again? How about the cow and the chickens?"

"Stop being foolish and sit down before your supper gets cold," Beatrice said.

"I just wanted to be sure," Georgie muttered.

By this time, most of the others had finished, and Catharine stood up and reached for Lawrence's empty plate. Unusually helpful,

Andrew carried his own plate to the counter. Magdalena fidgeted, as if unsure whether or not her father's lap was as available as it usually was. Old enough to know that the occasion was momentous but still too young to understand its full portent, she looked around from one face to another, searching for clues.

"I was thinking of having a smoke," Pierre said, looking at Jean.

"Do you mind if I join you?" Jean said.

"What? He can smoke now?" Georgie said, pausing in his rush to finish his meal. Pierre had never allowed his sons to smoke. What you put in your body becomes part of it and you need to be strong, was a thing he liked to say.

"I guess if he's old enough to bear arms in hostile country, he's old enough to smoke," Pierre said.

"It won't be the first time, I'll wager," Andrew said, dryly.

Jean felt the bulge of his pipe in his pocket. He had, in fact, already smoked in private, because taking tobacco was one of the things men did and he'd been impatient to try it for himself. In retrospect, carrying the pipe around with him was not a very effective way of hiding a bad habit. But none of that seemed to matter now, as he followed his father out onto the porch, where the warm, muggy night enveloped him. Crickets made a dense chorus that billowed in waves of sound and lightning bugs spotted the darkness with their flaring and waning glows. Father and son walked for a ways, not saying anything, and Jean was reminded of being a young child, when his father would lead him off somewhere, not to punish him, but to question him in private about something he had done wrong.

Pierre stopped at the edge of the apple orchard and stood for a long time, a shadow in the surrounding darkness. Apparently coming to some decision, he took a pipe from his pocket and put a pinch of tobacco in it, tamping down with his little finger, then held out his pouch. Jean accepted the tobacco pouch with one hand, as he fished his pipe from his shirt pocket with the other, and Pierre took out a tinderbox and removed a piece of charcloth. He paused to glance at Jean, then placed the charcloth on his flint and struck his steel until he got an ember. Holding the ember to his pipe, he drew the spark into the tobacco and then held the glowing charcloth out for Jean.

They smoked in silence for a while.

"Are you all right?" Pierre asked.

It was such a simple question and yet so difficult to answer.

"Sure," Jean lied. "Of course I am. Why wouldn't I be?"

"You're not the first, you know, to leave home and head into unknown territory. Our family has a history of moving from one place to another, and it's usually someone particularly daring who leads the way. Our earliest known ancestor was a man named Iñigo. He was probably no older than you when he left his home in Navarre over seven hundred years ago."

"You never told us that story!" Jean said.

Pierre shrugged, or at least so Jean imagined. The nighttime was so thick and dark around them that it was hard to see anything at all. Now and then his father's pipe glowed and the tobacco smoke made a fragrant cloud. He heard his father sigh.

"Family origin stories are sometimes difficult because things change so much over time. It was easier just to say we were from France and let it go at that. But the fact is that France was once a lot smaller than it is now. It grew by enveloping other lands and kingdoms and absorbing the people who lived in them. But taking a people's land and gaining their hearts are two separate things."

He paused and his pipe glowed. Jean waited with bated breath. If Jean could have frozen this moment for all time, he would have gladly done so. This was his father at his best, digging deep into the reservoir of what it was he knew. And he knew a lot. Apparently more than he had told in the past and probably more than he ever would. Jean wanted the voice to go on forever and never stop.

"Ancestries aren't always very exciting, but we have to remember that each name was a real person, just like me and just like you. They were born and had childhoods, maybe even liked some of the same things you do—a cool draught of water on a hot day, the smell of baking bread. Maybe they heard the bells that hang from the necks of bellwethers and thought of distant lands. They had moments of happiness and fear, got married and had wedding nights of trepidation. They had children and maybe, if they were lucky, they even found love.

"Some believe Iñigo was a Basque who married a Spanish princess from Logroño. As the story goes, he crossed the mountains during the Great Expansion, when Navarre spread up into what is now France. Some think he lived for a while in a place that became known as the Aquitaine. What is known for sure is that he built a great house in what was then part of the Languedoc and that his family thrived for hundreds of years. We were seigneurs of the land. Our men became courtiers and chevaliers, men of letters and accomplishment. Our women were famous for their learning and their wisdom. You have to understand how the Languedoc was back then . . . It was much bigger than it is today. It was the land of poets and troubadours. Some called it a land of milk and honey.

"This is your family, son. This is who you carry with you and who, in part, you are."

"I love you, Pa," Jean said, in a sudden rush of emotion.

"Aye . . . And I love you—remember that, always. You have chosen a difficult road and I don't know what lies ahead—none of us do. But never forget who you are. No matter the circumstance, remember that you are not an island of fear and despair. You are a man of substance."

Pierre fell silent and the night rebounded. The harsh rasping of cicadas joined the crickets. A medley of frogs from down along the creek thrummed like a swollen river of sound. Father and son were hardly more than shadows in the darkness, but an arm snaked out. A shoulder was embraced. The two bodies drew together as one.

CHAPTER

SIXTEEN

———————●———————

The following morning twelve men showed up at the château, and the major lost no time setting the expedition in motion. They hiked cross-country, but the woods were fairly open this close to the settlement, and the men were in good spirits. The major had warned them that a man in farmer's boots would walk through the forest with the stealth of a pregnant cow, and some wore moccasins, which met with the major's approval. He warned them that the troop would not slow down for any ninnies that couldn't keep up, and to a man, they couldn't imagine that he was talking about any one of them, in particular, as it took a tough and self-confident lot to start on such a mission in the first place.

As the youngest, Jean brought up the rear. He had a lot to think about after the conversation with his father the night before, and he hardly noticed the passage of time. He imagined he was in the Pyrenees with a Spanish princess. During the cold nights, he gave her his blanket and she kissed him in gratitude. What a lucky man the Basque must've been, he thought, to have such a beauty as he imagined the princess to be.

When the men finally stopped for lunch, they ate venison and beef jerky, along with chunks of bread they pulled from their packs. "Don't eat everything you've got," the major warned. "We've a long way to go and hunger's closer than you think!"

And the men paid attention, up to a point, like children listening to the overly cautious lectures of a parent. They may have put back a piece of bread they had intended to eat, but they were still too excited with the adventure of just starting out. A dour outlook may be second nature when it is born of experience, but when it comes of mere admonition, it fades in the bright sunlight of an otherwise beautiful day. The outing was still too much like a vacation and lunching in the woods a picnic for farmers used to the hard work of pushing and sweating and swearing at livestock.

Toward late afternoon, they stopped again, this time to make camp. They collected firewood and made a circle of rocks. Flint was struck and a flame started, a red, darting soul that leaped up through the kindling. The fire hissed as more wood was piled on.

Jean sat on the ground and leaned back against a fallen log. As accustomed as he was to hard work, he was not used to marching many miles over broken terrain. His head started to nod and he drifted off to sleep, where he dreamed of a dark-eyed girl. In the dream, she could fly and when he opened his arms, he could fly too. All he had to do was think about it and they soared above the treetops. They flew to the top of a mountain, where they stood on a bald rock and looked at the moon, together, side by side.

The smell of food woke him. A couple of the men had wandered with their muskets. They brought back a brace of squirrels, which the man called Dutch prepared for the iron pot and slipped in with the beans. Dutch was a square man with a drooping mustache, who wore a felt hat pulled down to his ears. The major had said there would be no extra meat, but Dutch managed to produce a slab of bacon. He cut off a piece and slipped it into the pot with the squirrel pieces and the beans, giving the men a sly wink.

"These squirrels'll be tough as a horse harness and the beans haven't had much time to soak, but the chewin'll be good for ya," he said, laconically. He grinned, looking up from the cook pot as if to share a wonderful and unexpected idea. "If anybody don't want his portion, he can give it to me."

Still in a fog from his dream, Jean watched. He had only ever seen his mother or his older sister at the cooking hearth, and it amazed him that a man like Dutch was so adept with the wooden spoon, scraping at the contents of the large iron pot, adding liquid from a nearby spring, and pulling the aromas toward his nose with an open hand. Up until that point, Jean had always thought of soldiers in the context of guns, but he realized the fine weapon a cooking pot could be in the hands of someone who knew how to use it. The men went to bed with full bellies, trading jokes back and forth as they lapsed into sleep, the ribald humor of men without women.

One by one, the voices dropped off until the camp was quiet, except for the popping of coals in the firepit, and Jean lay on his back, staring up through the trees, picking out the bright points of starlight. The stars were distant and cold. It was a comfort to think they were the same stars he had viewed from home, where he was safe and secure. But he couldn't help but think they were different, now, because *he* was different—further away from home than he had ever been before and so very much on his own. If the same star could be viewed by two different people, or by the same person in two different places, under entirely different circumstances, was it indeed the same star after all? He looked for signs, any signs at all, that he was on the right path and found only the cold indifference of a wild and unforgiving landscape that had no regard for him whatsoever.

◆ ◆ ◆

THE NIGHT ON THE HARD ground had dissipated the frivolity of the previous day. Except for the major, none of the men had ever been in a militia before, and they stuck one foot in front of the other with a growing awareness that this adventure was different from any they had ever had. They trudged forward with a growing wariness.

When the sun was high overhead, obscured by the trees but still leaking through with its buttery warmth, they found a path etched into the forest floor. The trail was four feet wide and over a foot deep, packed firm with cloven animal hooves and the smooth footprints of humans. The unseen presence of other people spooked and sobered the men, who thought of this wilderness as theirs for the taking even as the heart and soul of it eluded them.

"You think that just because you've never been here before that no one else has, either?" said the major, his mouth twisting and his eyes crinkling. "Just because we call 'em savages doesn't mean they're just plain old wild, like the wolf and the weasel. They got what you might call cities, just like us. They got roads. They've been here a long time before we ever knew they existed."

"They're murderous!" one of the men exclaimed.

"Some are, same as us."

"But they're unchristian!"

The major paused and turned to the side to spit, as if that were all the comment he cared to make. He had done his recruitment and started off the expedition with an apparent generosity of spirit, but Jean realized the major was not a nice man. The scar on his face was enough to give anyone pause. His cold blue eyes made Jean shiver.

"If we follow their roads, won't they know we're coming?" said the man they called Abe.

The group had bunched up on the trail like so many cattle and the major just shook his head. "They knew we were coming soon after we left," he said, wryly. The men looked around, peering back over their shoulders. "We be where they hunt and live," the major added. "You think you wouldn't know if someone tramped through your farm, your home? You think you wouldn't know if a stranger was in your house?"

"If they know we're here, why haven't they attacked?"

The major shrugged.

"Maybe they got other things to worry about." The major shrugged again, his mouth dragging open with callous amusement. "Maybe they know how important lunchtime is to us, and want to give us a chance to rest. That's pretty damn near Christian of them, by my way of thinking!"

"That's very funny, there, major. Go ahead and joke if you want. We're out in the middle of nowhere and a long way from any kind of help, should we need it."

"Are you saying you don't trust me?" the major said.

The men stirred, hunching their shoulders and shuffling their feet. Some looked back the way they had come, their faces registering the predicament they were in. Maybe they could backtrack and eventually return to the settlement. But they weren't really skilled woodsmen, after all, in spite of what they would have liked to believe, and it occurred to each and every one of them that, on their own, without the major, they were already lost.

"Anyone wants to head back, just go on ahead and be gone with you," the major said.

"I'm staying the course," Jean said, stepping forward.

"Aye, that stands for me, too," Abe said, giving Jean an unhappy nod.

"Do we need any more discussion on the matter?" the major asked, looking from one grim face to the next. He waited long enough to give anyone who wanted it an opportunity to speak. "Then let's not waste any more time jawin', because like I said, we be on an Indian trail and they know full well we're here. The more ground we cover the better from now on."

The major resumed his forward march, and the men fell into place behind him, sullen but resolved, and not another word was spoken for some time as they trudged along. One of the men waited until Jean was next to him and then walked by his side.

"That was right brave of you, stepping up the way you did back there," the man said.

Jean nodded without looking at him. He wasn't at all sure what bravery was in the context of their particular situation. Was it bravery to admit to yourself and the world that you really didn't have much of a choice?

"I've been watching you," the man said. "You're the one who saved the Overbrook girl, aren't you?"

"Nothing like that much matters anymore," Jean said.

"You're him," the man pressed, making Jean feel uncomfortable.

But the man's eyes had drifted and he stiffened. A young boy sat alongside the trail—up on the bank and a little ways back, but plainly visible. He sat on his haunches, his knees drawn up, hands wrapped around his ankles. His black hair was long and ragged at the ends, his eyes dark shadows in the gloom of the forest. He just sat there, watching, watching.

The men walked past hesitantly, looking straight ahead and then glancing sideways and back at the boy, then looking front again, then back, then at each other, from side to side.

"Who was that?" one of the men whispered, hoarsely.

"It was an Indian, I think," a second man responded.

"Should we 'ave, you know . . . shot 'im?"

"Christ's love, man, he's just a boy!"

"Just walk on and hold your tongues," Dutch grumbled through his mustache, and the men filed along in uneasy silence.

CHAPTER
SEVENTEEN

A round midafternoon of the following day, a turkey flushed hard from underfoot and the men recoiled, crouching down and gripping their muskets. They had left the trail and headed into the deeper woods, following the major, forcing their way through tangles of laurel and dank, rotting masses of deadfalls. The turkey exploded from the ground and went up through the trees, breaking off dead branches and showering them with debris, and the men straightened back up, unbending sullenly, giving each other furtive, guilty looks of relief.

"Ol' Abe here just about shite his pants," one said.

"Kinda like the way you dumped in yours," Abe muttered.

"Let's keep sharp," the major said, pushing on.

But later in the afternoon, the major raised his hand for the troop to stop. They had left the dark woods and worked their way through a dense fringe of sumac, arriving at a grassy apron of land that dropped down to a small river valley. Below them, a river of slow-moving water wound through a meadow of tall sunflowers.

A warm, moist breeze had shifted their way, pushing gently against the men's faces, and the major turned his head to the side, as if listening. There were no sounds, not even a bird call, and the men grew anxious. The major tilted his head back and sniffed, standing very still and then sniffing again.

"Do you smell that?" he said.

"Smell what?" one of the men said.

"The smell that's not you," the major growled. "I know the stink of you all too well by now and this-un's different."

Water, mud, smoky clothing, the acrid smell of human bodies. The major put his hand out and stepped forward a little bit, distancing himself from the group so as not to confuse their body odors with the other spoor that tugged ever so slightly at his senses. He knew the smell of a bedded deer and the reek of a black bear, and this was not either of those. It was very nearly subliminal but still there, almost a tease, a faint odor that he might have overlooked had he not been in a cautious state of mind.

"I don't like it," he said, eyeing the meadow suspiciously. "I don't like it one bit." He glanced at the man named Abe. "You—go on down there and take a look around. Give us a wave if everything looks okay."

"Me?" Abe said, his voice rising from a whisper with concern.

"Just do as I say. We'll be right behind you."

"What am I supposed to look for?" Abe asked.

"Just go on, now," the major said, angrily.

"Shite," Abe said, stepping past the major and looking back at him, then moving his head forward and following hesitantly with his body. The men watched him stumble in the thick mat of grass.

"The rest of you be watching those rock outcroppings," the major hissed. "You see anything move, don't bother asking yourself what it is. Just shoot it, you hear me? Anything moves gets shot."

"What about Abe?"

"Abe is fine."

They watched Abe struggle through the tall grass, stepping sideways like a crab. He held his musket with the barrel up at an angle, at the ready, first crab-stepping and then stopping to peer back over his shoulder at the rock shelf behind him, then moving forward again. When he got to the edge of the sunflowers, he stood for a long time without moving, the sunflowers nearly up to his shoulders. He looked back at the men, his eyes wide, silently imploring them as to what to do next.

"All right, Jackson, you head on down there, too," the major said.

Jackson's head turned, his eyes wide.

"I will," Jean said, stepping forward, and the major gave him a hard look. The major liked the boy. He hesitated, then shrugged. Best get whatever was going to happen over with, and the boy was as good as anyone else. He could see Jean's face stiffening with resolve, and he liked that, too. The boy might well need all the grit he could muster.

Holding his musket aloft, Jean waded down through the grass. The major watched as he reached Abe's side and then went on past, heading off through the sunflowers. Now and then, he dipped out of sight among the profusion of bright yellow blooms, only to pop up again a little farther along. When he reached the riverbank, he paused, then turned to give a cautious wave.

The major looked at the men gathered around him. He gave a sharp nod and they filed down, one after the next, until they stood with Abe at the edge of the sunflowers. By then, Jean had crossed the river and stood next to the woods on the far side. The major waited. When nothing happened, he motioned for the men to cross the river.

A sharp whoop cut the air and a man wearing warpaint stood up in the sunflowers, pulled back a bowstring and loosed an arrow, which leaped from the bow and arced through the air, sticking into the body a man in the middle of the river. The wounded man shrieked and stumbled to the side, then turned and fled back to the riverbank. "Fall back, fall back!" the major shouted, jerking his musket to his shoulder and bracing himself as he aimed and fired. There were more whoops and the boom of a gunshot, and then another. Another painted man rose from the sunflowers and aimed an old musket, which flashed, puffed, and issued a dense cloud of smoke. The ball cut through the sunflowers, snipping off stems and causing the flower heads to fall. Another man rose, this one with a bow, yanking on the string and sending off the arrow. Muskets discharged amid shouts and curses, the fog of gunsmoke bursting one way and then another, hanging above the water and settling into the sunflowers until it was hard for a person to tell friend from foe.

The major didn't have time to reload. Holding the musket by the barrel, he swung it like a club, a savage thrill ripping through him as he sent one man to the ground and turned to engage another. But then something happened. His leg went out from under him. There was no pain at first, just a numbing jolt that left him in the mud, down among the sunflower stalks, the fog of burnt gunpowder pressing down around him. He tried to move but couldn't. The damned leg wouldn't work, and then the pain started, an awful, crushing torment the likes of which he had never felt before, even when an Indian knife had split his face in half those many years ago.

◆　◆　◆

JEAN SAW THE MAJOR GO down and charged into the river, splashing through the water in a desperate attempt to reach him. A body floated face down in the river with two arrows sticking from it, and Jean surged past, splashing up through the rocks and mud. Although he had seen the major fall, he had a hard time finding him. The sunflowers were nearly as tall as Jean's head, and the burnt gunpowder made a dense cloud. He kicked around, looking for the major, when a man with a tomahawk charged him. Jean raised his musket and tried to fire, but nothing happened. He pulled on the trigger as hard as he could, but the gun wouldn't shoot, when suddenly a loud discharge came from close at hand. The man with the tomahawk went down and Jean saw the major, lying in the mud at the base of the sunflower stalks, a smoking pistol in his hand. Grateful to the major for saving him, but concerned that his own gun hadn't fired, Jean looked down and saw that he had failed to cock it.

"Major!" he shouted, standing over the fallen man.

But now another man rose from the sunflowers. Jean got his musket up first, making sure that it was cocked this time. Smoke belched from the muzzle of the gun, and the man disappeared, the sunflowers jerking and twitching where he had stood a moment before. Shots were fired from every quarter. Jean whirled around and raced to the major's side.

"We gotta get out of here," he shouted, grabbing hold of the fallen man's collar and starting to pull.

"Reload!" the major gasped.

"We gotta get back to the trees," Jean said, yanking on the collar.

"Load your damned gun!"

Jean stopped and reloaded as hurriedly as he could, then grabbed the major's collar again and yanked him upwards, throwing an arm around his waist. The major screamed as his mutilated leg was dragged through the sunflowers, but they reached the grass, where Jean paused and then threw his musket aside. He might have been a boy by some men's reckoning, but he was nearly as big as his father, and he bent down, threaded an arm between the major's legs and hefted him up onto his shoulders. Striding heavily, he stomped through the grass until he reached the sumacs, where he placed the major on the ground, then dashed back to retrieve his gun.

Muskets continued to discharge, though not as often now, and the men that were left began to stagger out of the sunflowers, emerging like specters from the fog of burnt gunpowder, crouching and lurching toward where the major lay. "We need to find cover— up there!" Jean shouted, gesturing toward one of the rocky shelves above. The men looked at him dully, as if unable to comprehend his words. Their faces were blackened with smoke and mud, smears of blood.

"The major's been shot!" Abe said, stating the obvious with dull horror. The man called Jackson sat down on the ground and started to shake. He drew his legs up and wrapped his arms around them.

"You heard what the man said! Let's get out of here!" Dutch cried. He grabbed one of the major's arms and Jean hauled up on the other. Between them, they dragged the wounded man. The others staggered after them. One stopped and swore under his breath as he ran back for Jackson, who still sat on the ground and who by now had his head between his knees. The man grabbed Jackson by his shoulders and tried to pull him up, but Jackson wouldn't budge and the one standing finally abandoned him and ran after the others.

Scrambling to the top of the ridge, they huddled behind a piece of broken outcropping. Dutch and Jean placed the major on his back. "We need to be ready for the next attack!" Jean said, crouching to peer down over the rocks, toward the strip of sunflowers below.

"What do we got?" the major grunted through clenched teeth. His face was ghastly white. "What d'we got left?"

"I count seven men and five guns," Jean said. "The mule's gone with all our supplies."

"Shite, I lost me pouch!" one of the men cried, slapping his hands against his sides. He spun around, searching the ground at his feet.

"See to your ball and powder, men, your ball and powder!" the major gasped, his eyes squeezed shut. He lay panting, his chest rising and falling mightily.

A silence fell over the group, and the stillness of the forest welled up around them. There were no more whoops, shouts, or gunshots, only the rasping breaths of the men—and then even these sounds subsided. A thin copse of birch grew along the ridge, and through the twisted trunks of the whitened trees, the men could see that nothing moved.

"Where's Jackson?" one asked.

"He's still sitting down there where we left him," another replied.

"What's he doing?" Jean said.

"Just sitting there. Wait, he's standing up and looking around. He looks like he doesn't know where he is."

Jean stood up and waved back and forth. A couple of the other men rose to a crouch.

"He sees us," one said.

"Here he comes."

They heard feet sliding against the rock scree, labored breathing, and then a man's head came into view. He didn't have his musket. When he looked up at the others, his face was calm, nearly childlike. His eyes looked vacant. He stood among them and then took notice of the major, staring down at the wounded man as if from a vast distance. He seemed to channel the awareness of the others, and they all shot hard looks at the major, then lowered their eyes to the ground and off to the side, looking away.

The major was nearly unconscious from pain and loss of blood. A musket ball had shattered the lower part of his leg, and Jean tended him the best he could, wrapping a strip of torn bedding just above the knee and tightening it with a short stick to slow the bleeding. He gave the other men a look that begged for help, criticism, anything, but the other men remained expressionless, the desperateness of their plight taking hold, hope draining like the blood that still leaked from the major's wound.

"We're buggered," one of the men said, his voice thick and low, hardly more than a whisper but clearly heard by all.

Several of the eyes shifted to Jean. For not one among them considered him to be a boy anymore. In the difficult situation they found themselves in, they shared a common plight and Jean had proved himself. He had rescued the major, carrying the man on his very shoulders, and now he was the one they turned to, weighing the odds that those shoulders were big enough to carry whatever else lay in front of them.

◆　◆　◆

JEAN HAD NEVER FELT SO alone. His father was too far away to lend a hand, the major lay nearby in a dismal state, and the men who had survived the skirmish were too traumatized to be of much assistance. Remembering one of his father's sayings, that an idle mind was the first step toward trouble, he set about giving the men jobs to keep them busy. Of the six left, not including himself, he sent two to collect firewood. Three he posted as guards. That left Dutch to help with the major, who shook with fever, and Jean built a fire to keep him warm. The major's leg had swollen, and Jean spread his own bedroll over the injured man, trying both to warm him and to keep the blowflies and the meat-eating wasps away from the wound. The cook squatted down and lifted the bedroll a little bit, peering underneath.

"Oh my . . ." he said, shaking his head, unable to finish the thought. Even such a gruff man as Dutch was shaken, and he looked to Jean for any kind of reason or comfort the youth could provide. Jean felt both the need to act and, at the same time, the desperation of not knowing what to do. If the major had been one of Pierre's horses, he would have been put down by now. Pierre had often opined that some horses were better than most men, but you still put them down because that was the merciful thing to do. With a man such mercy was unthinkable. You did what you could but mostly you waited.

"I'm sorry I killed you, son," the major said, startling him.

Jean had thought him unconscious. But the major's eyes were open, gazing at him with fatalistic regret. The sun had set. The whitened trunks of the birches had turned purple and black. The firelight pulsed against the major's face.

"I'm not dead yet," Jean said.

"It's all my fault," the major said. "If we'd stuck to the roads, we'd've got there in one piece instead of shot to hell and useless like we are now. We might've been able to make a difference . . ."

His voice trailed. He swallowed and struggled on.

"I took us the way we did to speed us along," he said. "It was a shortcut, supposed to get us to New York faster, you know, cut across the land straightaway. One of the settlers being attacked is my brother," he continued, his eyes reddening. "He's every bit the son of a bitch I am, but he has a wife and children, two baby girls. As good a woman as I've ever known and two young'uns of such a tender age . . . I've killed us all for the love of angels."

"You haven't killed anybody, and I don't want to hear you talking like that. Those of us who followed you did so of our own accord. It was a choice we made, and who is to say it was the wrong one? What does it matter that the people we tried to save are your kinfolk? Now you just rest. You're going to need every bit of strength you've got left."

The major hissed.

"I knew a man like you once, all full of his own piss. You can't make a man like that. He has to be born that way. But by God you can see the giant in him and I would've followed Old Ben anywhere." The major's eyes brimmed and teared to the sides, but then opened wide. What he saw was anyone's guess. "Ho!" he said, with a hoarse mustering of breath. "Ho, I say!"

Dutch was sitting nearby. He caught Jean's eye and shook his head, sadly.

Later, while the major slept, the men stood off to the side, where the edge of the fire's warmth lost its battle with the chill of the night. Dutch explained the situation. "I've done a little doctoring from time to time—broken bones, a bit of sewing—but this isn't anything quite like that. The bone's a mess and the leg mangled. The major'd be dead already if Jean here hadn't applied the tourniquet as well as he did, but even that isn't enough. The leg is already getting sour."

"What are you saying?" Abe asked.

"You know what I'm saying," Dutch said.

"What do we do, draw straws?"

"To what end?" Dutch said. "To have someone not suited to the task end up having to do it?"

"Aren't none of us suited to something like that," the man said.

"I'll do it," Jean said.

"Of course you would," Dutch said, with appreciation. "But much as I'd like to pass the wretched cup, I'm the one with the most experience, paltry as it is in the present light. I guess a man is not so different from his beastly brethren, not in the ways of the bone and sinew. The way I see it, the burden's mine, God help me."

"I'll assist the best I can," Jean said.

"We'll do it together," Dutch said, quietly.

◆　◆　◆

JEAN STOOD WATCH FOR MOST of the night, propped between two rocks with his musket across his knees. The major had passed out during the surgery and had not yet regained consciousness, and Jean couldn't shake the images from his mind, a man being held down while a part of him was cut away, the major screaming in spite of the stick in his mouth, bucking and straining. When he finished the job, Dutch walked away and threw up, and Jean cauterized the wound with a hunting knife heated in the fire. Dutch came back and apologized. They packed the wound with pieces of blanket and pulled a wool sock over it to keep it in place, and then, when it was over, it was Jean's turn to be sick.

Nothing had prepared him for this and everything was changed, everything was different. He thought of Lawrence Kraymer and how both lucky and irrelevant he seemed now. Lucky to at last have found what he was looking for in a château that would have made a European prince proud. And irrelevant because, here, in this moment, atop a stone outcropping in the middle of nowhere, what mattered was life itself, the ability to keep breathing, to tend to your wounded and get your men back home. The ability to survive the next attack they all thought was sure to come. Here, in the middle of Indian country, the château was a puff of smoke, like the dream of a Spanish princess and flying to a mountaintop. A hot ache rose up in him, sheer amazement and contempt that he could ever have been so naïve.

A sudden movement next to him made his heart lurch. It was Abe, the man who had performed heroically, despite fearing his own shadow. Abe, who had gone down into the sunflowers alone and done as the major ordered.

"I woke up and couldn't go back to sleep," Abe said.

"Give it another try. You'll need it."

"I might as well do something useful," Abe said, holding out his blanket. "Here, I won't be needin' this."

Jean didn't want the charity of a man who had so little to give, but the dawn was still some time off, and the air was cold. The warmth of Abe's body still clung to the blanket, and Jean accepted it with gratitude, thinking about what the major had said, that the major had somehow killed them all because of the decisions he had made. Some of us are still alive, Jean thought, with a numb tenacity. If the major has killed us, he hasn't killed us all. Not yet.

He didn't remember pulling the blanket around him. It seemed to have moved of its own accord and he wondered if Abe had done it. The place where he sat was a fine lookout post, and he thought maybe Abe should have the spot instead of having to search out another location to keep watch. But while thoughts trickled through his head, his body stayed right where it was, sitting on the cold ground, leaning against a rock. He remembered his father's voice, saying he would not be an island of fear and despair, and indeed he felt free of fear, though certainly aware that death might be little more than a halted breath away. And he didn't feel despair, just a stubborn will to survive. But there was something else his father had said, something important. What was it, he asked himself, struggling to stay awake. It was there, he could feel it. He could almost reach out and touch it. But his chin had lowered to his chest. His eyes closed and he found himself in the open arms of sleep.

◆　◆　◆

UNABATED THIRST IS A TERRIBLE thing, and the men suffered greatly. They clung to the protection of the rocks, waiting for the attack they felt sure was to come, licking dew off the stones in the cool damp of the mornings and suffering through the heat of the day.

"We can't make it," one of the men muttered on the morning of the third day. His eyes were bloodshot, his breath rank with thirst. His lips were blistered and his mouth hung open. His tongue had started to crack.

"We'll make it," Jean said.

"What're we going to do?" another man muttered.

Jean raised himself up on his knees and peered over the rocks.

"The river's right there," he said.

"But so's the Indians just waitin' to kill us. They're down there with all that water to themselves, thinking we don't have a choice. Here we are drying up, while they have all the time in the world."

"Indians aren't like that," Jean said, with no idea of what he was talking about. He was trying to calm the men, that was all. "If they want to attack, they attack. They don't just sit around doing nothing."

"They got us right where they want us."

"They've got nothing," Jean said, coming to a decision. He leaned on his shoulder to cast a look at the other men, who lay sprawled among the rocks. His eyes fell on the major, who gave back a glassy stare. "Abe, give me your empty water bag," he said. "Anybody else got anything that will hold water?"

The men just stared, as if trying to comprehend. Abe handed over his collapsed water bag and Jean looked at the men, sure he was seeing them for the last time, then slid around one of the rocks. He crawled on his belly, using his elbows and knees, slowly making his way down the escarpment. When he hit the scree, he paused, and turned so that he went feet first. His foot slid, sending a small cascade of rubble clattering down the hill. Nearby, a thrush sang in a treetop, and Jean put his head back and listened, wondering if he had ever heard a bird sing so beautifully. The thrush stopped and silence pillowed around him. Finally, he slid a little farther down the hill. Once again, the clatter of stones gave him away and he stiffened and waited and then slid some more. The noise couldn't be helped, and he slid the rest of the way quickly, finally arriving at the patch of sumac that bordered the meadow.

Gripping the empty water bag tightly, he rose slowly to a crouch. The ground was thick and soft with sumac leaves, and he scuffed down through the dense stand. A sound like the roar of wind through trees filled his head and his neck throbbed. He tried to moisten his lips, but they were as dry as tree bark and he struggled to get his tongue back in his mouth. It felt like a pinecone had gotten caught in his throat. Dashing through the matted grass of the meadow, he made it as far as the edge of the sunflowers before stopping again, kneeling down until the cool moisture of the mud chilled his knee. He looked up toward the escarpment, but saw no evidence the men were there.

A buzzing came from near at hand, and he saw a black cloud like a smudge of smoke, and crawled forward on his hands and knees.

Heavy-bodied flies zipped and looped among the sunflowers. Then the stench hit him and he saw the naked foot, the calf. A man lay face down, his body stripped of clothing, the top of his head a red patch of bone, his face mercifully turned away. He lay on his belly with his arms back and his palms turned up. Animals had already started to feed on him, and a rib bone glinted, already dry. Death seemed so overwhelmingly complete that it was hard to imagine life had ever been there in the first place and Jean's eyes burned. His stomach heaved but there was nothing inside of him to move up into his throat, and he turned away and stumbled sideways, plunging past the body and beyond the stench to where the air was sweeter. His eyes felt like aching craters in his head, and he cursed his weakness. He cursed the major for leading them astray, and he cursed himself for following. He cursed the river for being so close and yet so interminably far away.

And then it was there, right in front of him—the riverbank, the water's edge, the smooth, languid roll of the current. A small riffle held some rocks and a small brown bird hopped from rock to rock, head bobbing as it busily searched for food. Past the riffle, in a deeper pool, mayflies danced above the water, dropping to the surface and then rising again. The water dimpled at the rising of a fish, and there was a sound, the deep note of a bullfrog, and then another sound, the piping of a red-winged blackbird, stirrings and sounds seemingly incongruent with the nearness of death. Sliding on his belly to the water's edge and drinking deeply, he didn't see the buckskin-clad figure until it was too late.

CHAPTER
EIGHTEEN

—————————●—————————

J ohn watched as the youth flopped down on his belly and buried his chin in the water. It was a careless act, but not surprising. The settlers were not always known to pay nature its due, wandering where they didn't belong, taking what wasn't theirs, and failing to recognize there was a price to be paid for the simple blessing of being alive. The price was death and all living things paid it, sooner or later, be they young or old, lucky or not. The youth was oblivious and John could have killed him easily.

But that was not his purpose. Lawrence Kraymer had sent him. Lawrence had feared for this young man's life, and with good reason, John mused. The major was crazy to have tried to lead a troop of farmers across the wildlands, where a life always hung in the balance, and fate could tip it one way or another with little warning and no regret at all. Lawrence had asked his friend to look after this pup, and John had complied, following the abundance of spoor the pitiful militia left behind them.

Looking up and seeing him, the youth scrambled frantically, trying to find the gun he had left laying behind him on the river-bank, and John watched with the same dispassionate interest with which he might have watched a deer take sudden fright. At any point John could have finished him, extinguishing the boy's light with a musket ball or tomahawk. Lenape boys were warriors by the age of this youth, and John would not have hesitated to take his scalp under different circumstances.

But he was there as a favor to a friend, and leaving his side of the river, he strode into the water, which surged to his knees and thighs, before lowering back to his calves as he neared the other bank.

"What do you want?" the youth demanded. Perhaps realizing John could have shot him if he'd wanted to, the young warrior pointed his gun but didn't pull the trigger, and John was grateful. He wasn't usually so careless with his life, but friendship complicated matters. It made him take risks he'd just as soon have avoided.

"Are you Jean Laux?" he said.

Jean's face grew slack and his eyes widened with astonishment. John said he was there at the behest of Lawrence Kraymer, who had no love for the major and who was concerned for Jean's welfare. John looked around. The ones who had attacked the militia were no longer there, he said, but they might return. They could return at any time and Jean had to make his escape now, while he was able.

But Jean struggled to understand what the native was saying.

"Lawrence sent you?" he said.

Having already explained himself, John ignored the question. He scrutinized the ridge above the meadow, where he knew full well the other men waited. After what the troop had been through, he knew they would shoot him on sight, and he wasn't very happy about it.

◆　◆　◆

IT WAS JOHN'S IDEA TO give his musket to Jean and make it appear as if he was the boy's prisoner. He thrust out his gun and the boy took it, though he didn't seem to know what to do with the weapon once it was in his hands. John had to explain that if the men above thought he was Jean's prisoner, then maybe they wouldn't be so quick to shoot, and Jean looked at him with dazed comprehension. John took the lead and the youth followed, stumbling along behind him.

Walking with his hands in the air, John found footing to be difficult, especially when they reached the scree. Balance had a lot to do with how the body was positioned, and with his hands in the air, John's uphill foot slid out, driving him down on his thigh. He angled to the side to regain his balance and then continued the steep climb. They were within a stone's throw of the outcropping, now, and still none of the men showed themselves.

When they had climbed the last several feet, they saw the major on a grimy bedroll. His hand was lying across his belly and he held a pistol that he raised and aimed at John's chest. John thought it was a shame he was about to die and called on the Great Spirit to receive him. But the young warrior intervened. He stepped past John and shielded the native with his own body.

"Hold on, there, major," the youth said, hurriedly, and John began to realize there was more to the boy than met the eye. He might have been confused, down along the river, and he might have been slow to comply with John's plan to approach the rest of the militia. But he now spoke with a command that belied his age, coming from behind and taking charge when it mattered most. "This is a friend of mine. He's not one of the ones that ambushed us. He's a friend that's here to help us out."

"Here to help us, is he?" the major forced out the words. His face was pale and his eyes bloodshot. His mouth looked like a blackened hole.

"He's not one of the ones that fired on us," Jean said.

"Is that what he says to you?" the major said.

"Just listen to me, will you?"

"I dearly want to pull this trigger," the major said, ruefully.

As he spoke, the other men appeared, some standing up, others stepping around rocks, their muskets pointed at John. They were a grizzled bunch, with hard, gaunt faces. Their eyes were empty except for a meanness John recognized all too well.

"Shooting him would not be a good idea," Jean said to the major. "In the condition you're in, this man is our only hope of getting back to the settlement." He turned to look at the rest of the men, who had him and John surrounded. "This is John, and his only sin is wanting to help us. Anybody here think we don't need a helping hand?"

The major closed his eyes, letting his hand with its pistol drop back against his belly. John was relieved, but still keenly aware of the other men with their muskets. He had no doubt that but for Jean, the guns would have had their say.

"Maybe he's just here to scout us out so that he can go back to the others and tell them what he saw," a man snarled.

"There aren't any others. They're gone," Jean said, with the strength and composure of a chieftain.

"Says who? Him?"

"His name is John. John Three Sixteen, to be exact."

"John Three what?" the man asked.

Some of the eyes blinked.

"Do you vouch for him?" someone asked.

"That I do," Jean said, evenly.

"Damned if I could be friends with an Indian," another man said.

Glaring at John with unbridled suspicion, the men lowered their weapons. The river now beckoned to them irresistibly, and one of the men started the descent to the meadow. Two more quickly followed. In a moment, only Jean and John remained behind with the major.

"Who is John Three Sixteen?" John asked.

Jean's eyes danced.

"That's you for now."

"My name is John. Not any Three Sixteen."

"It never hurts to get Biblical with God-fearing men," Jean said, with a triumphant look.

John didn't know what to make of the comment.

"Will you old ladies quit the jabbering so a man can get some shut-eye?" the major said.

◆　◆　◆

LONG INTO THE NIGHT, JOHN stood at the edge of camp, with his musket in the crook of his arm, ostensibly standing guard against the outside world but guarding against the colonials, as well. He had shared his pemican with them, thinking that whatever strength it gave them would help on the long journey back to the settlement. But Jean said they had to bury their dead before going anywhere. By the time they were done, it was too late to travel, and the men had huddled by a fire as twilight fell.

Now, a shadow among the deepening shadows, John stood alone while the others slept, his face blank, but his mind active, tactile, pushing, sifting. As a young child, he had lain on his sleeping skins and watched his father in the flickering light of the wigwam fire, watching the way his father comforted his mother and wondering what it meant that the man had come from another land on the far side of the big water. John tried to hear the words his parents shared, wondering if his father spoke a secret language that only he and John's mother could understand. But the murmurs were too low to hear. They were like the wind in the pines, which could whisper incessantly about nothing at all.

◆ ◆ ◆

IF IT WASN'T ONE THING it was another. First the settlers had to bury their dead and then they had to figure how to transport a grievously wounded man. The major's leg had been amputated below the knee and John didn't understand why they insisted on trying to sit him astride the mule, which he had recovered for them and brought back to the camp. They ended up building a travois, using strips of beaver hide to tie the major's bedroll to two birch saplings. But this was not much help, either, as the mule balked at pulling it. John could well imagine the beast bolting, with the travois and the major attached, ruining the sled and causing further harm to the injured man.

After much coaxing, the men gave up on the mule and took turns pulling the travois themselves, as they left the rock outcropping and climbed into the dark woods. When one man was not strong enough to pull the sled, they tried two, but neither could go very far before falling to their knees with exhaustion. Confronted with a deadfall, they put a man on each pole, so that four could carry the major between them. But they had trouble synchronizing their footsteps. When a man stumbled, they all went down, spilling the major to the ground.

That night, they camped without a fire, and the following morning the major could not be awakened. His face was the color of dirty snow and the scar on his cheek stood out in ugly relief. The stump of his leg had bled during the night.

"The major can't travel," the man with the mustache said, shaking his head.

"We can't stay here," one of the men said, with a stricken look.

John agreed. "Must move on," he said.

"I thought the Indians decided to let us alone?" another of the men said, plaintively.

John shrugged.

"Indians are men and men change their minds, maybe. We should go."

The men looked as one to Jean, who studied the major with misgivings. He told the others to go on ahead and send back a rescue party when they got to the settlement. He and the major would be fine, the young chieftain said.

"Maybe it don't matter none," the man with the mustache said.

"Of course, it matters," Jean said. "We can't just abandon the major and I can't in good conscience ask anybody else to stay with him."

The man with the mustache shook his head, resolutely. He pointed. The major's lower jaw had slackened open and to the side, and his chest no longer moved. The mustached man placed an ear to the major's chest and then placed the back of his hand to the major's mouth. Looking back at the men, he shook his head.

◆　◆　◆

JOHN CONTINUED TO LEAD THE way, and unburdened by the major, they now made good progress. Skilled as he was in the wild, the woods were different than what he remembered as a child. The

Europeans changed everything they touched, with their hunters tramping into the backcountry, shooting game the natives relied upon to survive, and the settlers' feral swine rooting up native gardens. The newcomers couldn't live with the forest. They had to alter it, turning ancestral lands into something John no longer recognized, and for him, entering the fringe of the settlement was like taking a plunge from a high rock into a pool of murky water.

The one that the men now called captain wanted to show John his appreciation for the militia's safe return, but John found that he couldn't accept this gratitude. The settlers were still too unknown to him. The youth wanted him to come to his family's habitation and enjoy their hospitality, eat their food and rest. He assured John he would be received well. But John didn't want to be received at all. Much as he had grown to respect the young chieftain, he declined, for he knew he could find no rest in such a place. The woods were his solace. As infected with the European presence as they had become, they were still the only home he had ever known.

CHAPTER

NINETEEN

———————⬤———————

J ean was relieved to be back with his family, but something wasn't right. His family was overjoyed at his safe return and the farm looked the same, but something was different. As a child, he had never worried about his security, just as he never doubted the intrinsic rightness of anything his parents thought or said. The idea that the house and its cluster of outbuildings were vulnerable to destruction would never have crossed his mind. Neither would the notion that his parents were as human as anyone else in their community, and perhaps just as prone to errors in their judgments or pronouncements. But now there was an edge. Now he saw the thread upon which a person's welfare hung.

For some families, this thread had already snapped. Wives would never see their husbands again and children had bid a farewell that would last forever, and immediately upon returning home, Jean set out on the rest of his mission, the final phase of an ordeal that didn't end with men who now took their permanent rest in Indian country. Five men had died, not counting the major, and the next four calls were as difficult as Jean had imagined they must be. For a man's life was bigger than just the breath he took and the labor he put his back to. If he was a good man and a productive farmer, then his life meant the life of his family, too. His death could mean untimely ruin if crops wasted in the fields and animals couldn't be fed. Fortunately, the first four families had teenaged sons who could handle the plow and sweep with the scythe, doing what needed to be done to put bread on the table, and the wives took the news of their husbands' deaths with the stoic reserve of hardworking frontier women. Their sorrow was palpable, and with the news delivered, they wanted nothing more than that the bearer be gone and maybe even gone to hell, he and his more fortunate lot, he and his stumbling, clumsy words of consolation that meant little to them now that their worst fears had been realized and the men who had been so quick to leave their farms and families would never, ever return again.

But the last was by far the worst. The rough wood of the door bit into Jean's knuckles as he knocked, the sound dull and hard, bone striking wood and wood resisting with the fortitude of its rough-hewn nature.

"Who is it?" asked a voice that sounded small and distant.

"It's Jean Laux, ma'am."

"The one what was involved in the expedition? The one who saved the Overbrook girl?"

"The same," Jean said, his voice catching in his throat, as if the words were too big to come out.

The door opened a crack and he saw a vertical slice of forehead and hair, an eye that peered at him, a piece of cheek, and the linen cloth of a dress, where the neck went into the collar. The door opened further and he saw an unkempt head of hair that looked as if it had been combed with fingers, eyes that regarded him suspiciously, a small mouth with the lips pressed together, an arm that was crooked to hold a bundle, the bundle a blanket-wrapped baby with a big head and open eyes and arms that waved jerkily. The woman held the baby tightly to her chest, staring at the man whom she knew only slightly and who was not her husband.

"My husband's not here. I mean, he's with you and the others what left here for to help those others up in New York."

"I know," Jean said, dropping his chin and raising it slowly, his eyes moving past the woman and on to the dim interior of the cabin, where a toddler stood looking at him. The cabin had the musty smell of soiled diapers. The fire in the hearth was down to a glowing coal and the tinge of smoke burned Jean's eyes. Maybe it was the smoke that made him blink. Maybe it was more of a wince, something else entirely. He found it hard to breathe.

"May I come in?" he said.

"What do you want?" she demanded.

"I need to come in and sit down," he said, gesturing toward the wooden table with the three wooden chairs. "We need to have a word," he added, giving her an imploring look.

She backed away, giving him room to step past. He pulled a chair away from the table for her to sit on and then pulled out the chair opposite, sitting down on the edge of it and resting his elbows on the table, holding his face in his hands, before looking up at her and taking the deep breath he needed to go on.

"What do you want?" she repeated, softer this time, as if she knew and feared what he had come to say. The baby she held started to fuss. It had sagged in her arms and, closer to the breast, started to grope with its mouth. She hoisted it back up, higher, moving her shoulders back and forth, her eyes never leaving Jean's.

"It's the worst," Jean said. "I'm sorry. I'm so sorry."

He explained that the militia had run into trouble, that they had a skirmish and that some men didn't survive. The men had fought heroically and five of them had died. Six, if you included the major, himself, who passed away somewhat later, from the grievous wound he had received.

"Where's my husband?"

"He was one that didn't make it," Jean said, quietly.

The woman stared at him as if he had spoken in a language she couldn't comprehend.

"My husband?" she said, finally. "Are you saying he's dead?"

"I am, ma'am, and I'm sorry."

"But how can that be?" she said, her eyes starting to jerk. "We have a farm to run and a family. He has a baby and a boy still in diapers and a girl too little to help out. He can't be dead. What am I to do? What am I to do with the farm?"

She looked past Jean, searching the room, as if reaching and grasping and failing to grip hard enough, slipping from one fixture of her life to the next, her voice rising but quietly so, the words floating and hanging in the air. The toddler in diapers waddled to where the woman sat and stood in front of her chair, holding onto his mother's leg for support.

"What am I going to do?" she said, again, tears snaking down her face. "He was supposed to cut the rye grass when he got back! He was supposed to sell one of the pigs so we could get a new butter churn and some sugar. He promised me the new churn, so that we could have butter again. He promised me as soon as he got back . . ."

Her chest rose and fell rapidly. Her cheeks were growing shiny and wet.

"It's not fair, and I'm sorry," Jean said.

With eyes averted, he rose from his chair, grieving. The young mother still sat at the table. The baby reached up and tugged at the collar of her dress. A small girl ran out of the house's single bedroom with a cornhusk doll in her hand, stopping short when she saw the stranger and looking up at him.

"You will have nothing to worry about," Jean blurted. "I will send a couple of men to help out and do whatever you want them to do. They'll bring a new butter churn and a sack of sugar and you can keep the pig. They will bring in the crops for you. They'll cut the hay and put it in the barn when the time comes. I'll open an account for you at the dry goods store in town—whatever you need for as long as you need it to get back on your feet."

Backing away, he stumbled, then turned around and ducked out of the cabin, right foot crossing the threshold and then the left, the fresh outside air bathing his face but failing to beat back the heat that he felt. The door of the house gaped behind him and he couldn't get away from it fast enough. In another sense, however, he couldn't seem to get away at all. Something tethered him to the place, with its sadness and misfortune. It pulled with a weight that restrained and bound.

◆　◆　◆

JEAN'S LAST STOP OF THE day was at the château, where he wanted to pay Lawrence his due and thank him for sending John. But Lawrence took the opportunity to disparage the major and Jean took umbrage. Jean didn't disagree that organizing the doomed militia had been a mistake. But he didn't want to hear about it from a man who hadn't marched with the major, who hadn't fought with him or held him down while part of his leg was cut away. The major certainly had his flaws, but Jean thought a man like Lawrence was hardly in a position to criticize.

"Look, I didn't come here to talk about the major," he said, impatiently, interrupting Lawrence's diatribe, and maybe it was the youth's tone of voice that gave Lawrence pause. For Jean was a different person from the one who had left the settlement a scant two weeks ago. Jean wasn't done talking about John, and made inquiries about the native, asking how Lawrence had met him in the first place.

Lawrence regarded him, cautiously. "Well, it's a long story," he finally offered. His gaze drifted upward and around the room. He seemed to sort through several possible responses, before settling on the simple truth. "It gives me no pleasure to say it, but my grandfather used to sell his ale to the Indians, along with spirits from the West Indies. That's where much of the money came from to pay for all of this." He looked Jean in the eye. "When I inherited the brewery, I stopped the practice, and John was part of a delegation that came to thank me."

"Ah . . ." Jean said. He had already awakened to the realization that there were people in the world who made coin from taking advantage of others, as if a person's wellbeing were a jewel to be plundered and stolen at will. He was not surprised to discover Lawrence's grandfather had made his fortune in such a manner. He should have known as much, he thought.

They stood in the empty great room of the château, and his gaze drifted to one of the windows. In addition to thanking Lawrence for sending John, he had intended to see if his sister's fiancé could spare some men to look after the widow whom Jean had offered to help. But through the window, he saw a man torching a pile of tree stumps, and maybe it was the trauma he had so recently undergone. Maybe it was the stress of having to tell married women they now were widows. Quite possibly it was sheer exhaustion, but a fury took hold of him.

"What's he still doing here?" he demanded.

Lawrence peered out the window.

"McDonall?" he said. "He's harmless. Mostly, he just cleans up and burns things."

It was just too much for Jean.

"No—I don't want that man anywhere near my sister," he said, hotly.

Lawrence blinked in the face of Jean's high color.

"Fine, I'll let him go."

"Do I have your word?"

"I said I would, didn't I?" Lawrence snapped, getting his back up.

Jean nodded, assuming they had an agreement. He realized he had crossed the line, but was nevertheless resolute. He would take care of the widow, himself, and give her the butter churn and somehow arrange for the men she needed to harvest her crops. But for now, he was up on the bluff overlooking the sunflowers, holding night watch after the slaughter. The perfidious calm of the night, the dank smell of pine boughs and leaf rot, the mineral odor of rock, and the faint whiff of the mud down along the water. In his mind, he still waited for an attack he was sure would come, if not now, then soon, if not today then tomorrow, an assault that could come from any quarter and occur when he least expected it.

CHAPTER

TWENTY

L awrence considered Jean's concerns about McDonall to be over-
blown. The man was not a hard worker, by any means. But he
was steady, in his plodding way, and did whatever he was told. For
more than a year and a half, he had worked the limekilns, which
was about as unpleasant a task as a man could do. The masons and
carpenters got most of the respect, leaving someone like McDonall to clean up afterward. Tearing down scaffolding, burning trash,
digging out the stumps that still dotted the field where Lawrence's
vineyard would go. Nothing was too menial or demeaning, and
when one job was finished, he hung around until a new one was
assigned—unlike the other men, who packed up their tools and
left. Men like McDonall were hard to find, and Lawrence couldn't
understand what Jean had against him.

Now that the exterior of the château was complete, Lawrence
felt like the landed gentleman he had so desperately wanted to
be, and he would need a man like McDonall to help caretake the
grounds. Not that he, himself, would be idle. There was still the
finishing work inside the château, not to mention the furnishings
and the procurement of floor coverings. After the cost of building
the château, he had no money left to spend and had to buy the sofas
and beds on credit. The carpets came from India, and he had to see
a banker in Philadelphia about coming up with the money to pay for

them. But his chest swelled with pride when he entered the house and smelled its newness, and realized over and over again that this was who he now was. No longer the mistreated orphan who had inherited a brewery, but a man of substance in his own right, and he thought of Catharine day and night, dwelling on the bouquet of her hair and the lightness of her smile. Giving up his room at the inn, he started sleeping in the house, and at night, he would sometimes awaken and light a small fire in the hearth to take off the early autumn chill. He would sit in one of the chairs made in Philadelphia, and imagine that he shared the hearth with Catharine, her face flickering in the firelight, a blanket warming her legs as the sight of her warmed him.

That was when he knew he had a soul, when he thought of this woman he was finally ready to marry. That was when he thought that love was too big for a man to hold all by himself and that there must be a God to help with the carrying. Lawrence didn't care much for the particulars of religion and it mattered little to him whether a Reformed or a Roman Catholic said the words that he wanted to hear. The nuptials had been planned for January, but the minister was happy to move the date up to October, in view of the discounted rock Lawrence had agreed to supply for the new building project the minister had in mind. Lawrence was a happy man. With several successful businesses, a château, and Catharine's promise to become his wife, he was ready to take the next step in what had all the appearances of a worthy life.

◆　◆　◆

BEATRICE WAS NOT ENTIRELY THRILLED at the change in the wedding date. She didn't expect Lawrence or even Catharine, for that matter, to understand the amount of work that would go into the celebration. The château would take care of the venue, but there were the accommodations for the guests to think about. Then, there was the wedding feast to follow, which in and of itself was no small thing. There was the food to think of, the courses to plan, not to mention the various preparations. She intended to have the celebration outside, weather permitting, where the autumn foliage would add to the overall grandeur. If Beatrice had her way, the guests would have an experience they would long remember.

She scrambled the best she could, enlisting the help of a couple of church ladies, and the day arrived as fair and lovely as she could have hoped. The bride wore the pale blue dress Beatrice had sewn for her, with a white veil that draped to the shoulders and matching white lace on the sleeves. Her silk gloves and fitted leather wedding boots were of the same color as her dress, and she walked with her hand lightly on the arm of Lawrence Kraymer, who wore a coat of a darker blue, over a brocaded red waistcoat and fawn-colored breeches. Pierre followed with Beatrice on his arm. One of the sacrifices Beatrice had had to make for the earlier wedding date was that she didn't have time to finish her own dress. She and Pierre both wore their Sunday best, which would just have to do. Little Magdalena skipped ahead of them and the three brothers brought up the rear, wearing new frock coats and stepping with pompous care.

In such a small community, the event would indeed be remembered and discussed for many years, the beauty of the bride, the good fortune of the groom, the amazing attributes of such a regal family, and Beatrice was not immune to pride. It was not easy raising a child to adulthood. So many things could go wrong. So many little things, like cuts and scrapes and toothaches, not to mention the grippe and any number of other ailments, and she couldn't help feeling that the occasion was a rite of passage for her, too, as a mother, to have successfully birthed and nurtured a soul into meaningful existence. The minister caught her eye and she thought he understood. She fancied he even went so far as to give her a nod of appreciation.

◆　◆　◆

AFTER THE CEREMONY, THE GUESTS turned to the out-of-doors, where tables with linen tablecloths stood beneath the few remaining grand old oaks. The oaks stood like towers in their red fall robes. A couple of Lawrence's men turned a whole hog on a spit. There were creamed potatoes, all manner of casseroles and breads. Trays of nuts and sliced root vegetables such as carrots and radishes. There were hard ciders from the ongoing harvests and the usual ales, but also bottles of wines from Pierre's cellar.

The mood was festive, and Pierre was particularly at ease with himself. As a father, he had worried whether or not his daughter was making the right choice—not because of any specific concerns about Lawrence, but because part of giving someone away was the letting go, and this was something he had never done. Pierre had often teased his daughter that had they lived in the Old Country, he could have chosen her spouse for her and thus saved her the trouble. She retorted that if this had been the case, she would most likely have ended up as her Aunt Esclarmonde, not because she was already perfect, but because of the imperfection, in her father's eyes, of any likely suitors.

Pierre could well see his daughter's point and even chuckle at the thought of it, now that the vows had been solemnized. In the spirit of the happy occasion, he even felt charitable toward the French architect, LeBlanc, whom he spied seated among the guests. As a holy woman known for her wisdom, Pierre's mother had had many sayings apropos to different situations. One of these was that a lightened load is easier to carry, and Pierre was prepared to let go of some of the resentment he had borne so long toward the *Langue oui*.

LeBlanc looked up at Pierre's approach. He sat over a heaping plate of food and his mouth, which had been chewing, sagged open.

"I would have thought you'd be long gone by now," Pierre observed, with an ironic twist of the mouth intended to be friendly. But perhaps LeBlanc didn't take the comment in the spirit in which it was intended. The skin of his face seemed to crawl back a little from around his eyes.

"Speak for yourself," he said, starting to chew again, the jaw sagging and angling to the side, clenching and unclenching. There was something defiant about him. Something mean and truculent.

The spot at the table opposite LeBlanc was empty, and Pierre swung his leg over the bench. Even seated, he loomed over the smaller man, and LeBlanc eased back a little, to create more distance between them.

"This is my home," Pierre said, with a shrug.

"Oui," the architect said. "So it would seem. And it appears that congratulations are in order." He gave his head a wobble that encompassed the château and its grounds. "You have done well, my friend. We root you out of the Languedoc only to find you here, flourishing like a weed."

It was a statement that alluded to the conflicts between the north and south that had raged in France for several hundred years. The northerners had gone so far as to refer to the provincials as farm animals, and Pierre felt a bitter coldness gather in his body. The goodwill he had felt evaporated. He studied the smaller man, who was sitting back on the bench and chewing furiously now, as if mastication were a form of self-defense. Pierre looked to the left and right, to see if their conversation was overheard. Indeed, one of the neighboring farmers eyed them warily.

"You speak boldly for a guest," Pierre said, giving LeBlanc a hard look. The farmer who sat nearby stood up. He begged Pierre's pardon and went to sit elsewhere. This seemed to amuse the architect, who followed the man with his eyes. His mouth twisted with a dark thought that he apparently chose to keep to himself.

"Why are you here?" Pierre said.

"Me? Here? Why, the same reason as everyone else, monsieur," LeBlanc said. "It is a happy occasion, yes? The nuptials of a wealthy man and his 'Cendrillon'. I am led to believe there will be music and dancing."

Pierre spoke the northern French to Leblanc to make himself completely understood.

"What I mean is, why are you still in the colonies? You have made your unhappiness plain. Why did you come here in the first place, and now that your employment has ended, why do you linger?"

"I believe the answer to that is obvious. I am a man who must follow the winds of opportunity in order to ply his trade. With better winds, I might have ended up in a better place."

"Perhaps this is where you belong, after all," Pierre observed.

LeBlanc stopped chewing. His eyes narrowed.

"Maybe you are just another colonial now, like the rest of us," Pierre added.

LeBlanc brought his fist down, the butt of his knife striking the table.

"You should be wary of the words you speak, monsieur," he warned.

"Maybe you have become just another of the *racaille*—what is called the riffraff, here, eh?"

"Jamais!"

Pierre shifted onto his left hip and took a coin from his pocket. It was a piece of gold he had carried as a token these many years—one of the coins from the leather pouch his mother had given him shortly before her death. Reaching forward, he placed the edge of the coin on the table and then snapped it down flat.

"Out of a kindness you ill deserve, I will not send you away empty-handed," he said.

"What makes you think I'm going anywhere?" LeBlanc said.

Pierre stood up and LeBlanc's face paled. His gaze dropped to the coin and he looked ill.

"I don't expect ever to see you again," Pierre said.

"Maybe you think we are back in France, where families such as yours think they have the privilege to tell others what to do," LeBlanc sneered.

Pierre looked down at him with cold disdain.

"Don't ever speak of my family again," he said.

The architect flinched, and Pierre stalked off. Another of his mother's sayings was that a temper that ran too hot burned everyone, and she certainly would not have approved of his state of mind. But his past was always there, like the shadows that lurked beneath an otherwise placid pond. Even a pebble made ripples, and then there were rocks. He considered it bad luck to have an altercation on his daughter's wedding day. But some things can never be forgotten, no matter how hard you tried. Pricked too hard and they can't be forgiven, either, he thought, clenching his fists.

CHAPTER
TWENTY-ONE

The sudden departure of the architect troubled Lawrence. They had spent a lot of time together, and while LeBlanc could be unpleasant on occasion, Lawrence had thought of him as a friend. It had not been easy, introducing an Old World relic into the colonies. The settlers bridled at anything to do with social class. On the one hand, they were fascinated by what Lawrence was doing. On the other, they were appalled, and Lawrence had come to consider the architect as a comrade in the fight to bring a bit of European antiquity to the colonial wilderness.

But the disappearance of an erstwhile companion soon became a matter of small concern. Winter was always a difficult season, when the world turned cold and time seemed to slow to a crawl. It was the perfect time to be newly married, however, because other than feed whatever animals you happened to have, there was little to do outdoors, and Lawrence reveled in the joy to be had in the close company of another person. Those early days in the château were about discovery, both of the home he and Catharine now had and of each other, and the first several weeks they spent their days in bed. On their brief sorties from the pile of blankets, they built roaring fires and sat in front of them feeding each other. They told stories, baring their souls, and laughed together over the things that had once vexed them. The weeks turned to months and time passed in the blink of an eye.

The first indication Lawrence had that everything was not perfect came in the spring, when he ventured forth from the house to spend time in his new vineyard. The first batch of grape cuttings he planted did not flourish. Their growth was stunted and the leaves unballed grotesquely, as if the green shoots were reluctant to leave the soil, clinging to the root and recoiling from the sunlight. He crushed the new leaves with his fingers and sniffed at them warily. He scraped the stems with his pocketknife, looking for parasites or anything that might explain what was happening. He pulled up some of the plants and inspected the roots, dabbed a fingertip to the moist earth and tasted the gritty substance. With such nurturing sun and ample water, he didn't understand why the vines didn't thrive.

There was plenty to keep him busy on an estate that had never before seen European cultivation. There were grasses to plant and fences to build, beef calves to be purchased at auction. There were the garden crops of the corn, beans, and squashes that the Lenape had grown long before the first settlers arrived. But the vineyard called out to him in its plaintive, sickly voice, and as June and July came and went, and the hot days of August crowded in, he spent as much time as possible among his struggling vines.

A small, horse-drawn cart came up the lane to the château, and Lawrence stopped what he was doing and walked around the corner of the house, wiping his hands on his pants. From down by the barn, the sound of an axe smacked sharply in the air, where McDonall split kindling for the hearth.

"Hello, pastor," Lawrence said to the man, who climbed down stiffly from the cart.

"Greetings, friend," the minister said, forcing a smile.

"Don't happen to know anything about grapes, do you, maybe a little sermon or something to give them a nudge in the right direction? Trying to get them to grow is like trying to get a mule to act against its wishes. Talked to different people and some say maybe it's too much sun. Others think maybe I'm watering the plants too much. Then there are those who say it must be the soil, maybe it's too good for growing grapes. Have you ever heard such a thing? Can there really be such a thing as too much of something good?"

The minister glanced at the house that loomed beyond them. His lower lip pushed out a little, as if whatever he held inside of him was too much to keep entirely contained. He cleared his throat.

"I'm sure you'll figure out what the problem is and solve it," he offered, graciously.

Lawrence liked to think he was right, but wasn't so sure. In any case, the minister hadn't come to talk about grapes. The road from Watertown was dusty, and the fine powder had stuck to the minister's thinning hair and eyebrows. It coated his shoulders and forearms.

"Pastor!" a cheerful voice sang out.

Catharine Kraymer had opened the door of the château and stood on the front porch, her hand in the air. Her hair was tied back and she wore an apron that showed the small bump in her belly. She beckoned to him.

"Come into the house, please. Lawrence, don't let the man just stand there. Please come on in, the both of you!"

Casting a lingering look at his vineyard, Lawrence ushered the minister inside. Catharine led the men on into the dining room, where a long table stood in front of a China cabinet filled with the dishes Catharine's mother had given her—dishes that Beatrice's own mother had brought from Germany. A large vase of daisies sat on the table.

"I must say, I was wondering how you were going to get on in such a grand abode, but I see you have done well," the minister said, with admiration. "You have a very well-appointed and comfortable home, with some very nice touches. The fresh flowers are especially nice. I would like to think they were for my benefit, but I'm afraid my visit has caught you by surprise."

"Thank you, pastor, please have a seat," Catharine said, her cheeks and neck reddening.

Lawrence took a chair opposite the minister and seated himself, placing his elbows on the table and folding his fingers together. Gazing at the minister, he was the model of rapt attention, the good host grateful for the unexpected visit. But the problem of the grape vines continued to vex him, and he wondered if the issue he faced might not be the particular region of the land overseas where the cuttings had come from. Maybe the cuttings were at fault. Maybe they were diseased. Maybe he should look elsewhere for the next batch.

"I hope I'm not abusing you with my presence," the minister began.

"On the contrary," Catharine said. "We so love visitors, don't we, Lawrence?"

"Yes, of course," he said.

"I hear you plainly," the minister said, nodding. "For my part, a little solitude now and then is a good thing. It clears the mind and helps with the contemplation. But I imagine too much of it can be a burden."

"I don't think we'll be enjoying the solitude much longer," Lawrence said, with a flush of warmth and pride. He glanced at his wife. "Another few months and there will be none at all."

"Why, Mr. Kraymer, hush now," Catharine said, modestly, her hand stealing to her belly, where a new life lay in wait.

"Aye . . ." the minister said. He gave one of those inane smiles of a man used to reveling in blessed events that had little to do with him, personally, and went on to praise the bounty of the Lord's grace. While he spoke, his face reddened, a face much like a peach in so many respects. He drank a glass of cool tea and then had another, the perspiration running down his temples and past his ample jowls.

Lawrence was sure the minister's visit had something to do with the church—not the wooden one, but the brand new one that was to be made of stone, like the château. The minister had been insistent that the Lord, himself, had spoken to him about the matter, and Lawrence had long since relented, offering the granite at cost. He would have donated the rock for free had he not been suffering from strained financial circumstances.

It didn't take the minister long to confirm Lawrence's suspicion. He brought the subject up hesitantly, begging his hosts' forgiveness, protesting that he did not want to burden them in any way. More than anything, he assured them how grateful he was for their generosity and how the whole congregation owed them a debt of gratitude. Once completed, the new church would be a remarkable standout in a community where some worship groups were of such humble finances that they still met in people's homes for lack of more suitable gathering places.

But there was a problem, he went on, and Lawrence felt his spirits fall. One of the challenges of owning a business was that there were always problems, and Lawrence didn't welcome the news. The minister said the rock deliveries had slowed, and Lawrence didn't want to hear about it. He had already dealt with a similar issue when he, himself, needed the rock for the château, and the minister's complaint rang too much like of a repeat of the same old thing.

A great weariness came over him and Catharine gave him an inquiring look.

"If there's a problem, I'll take care of it," Lawrence said.

Perhaps sensing that he had presented an unwelcome development, the minister made a tactful retreat. He lapsed into small talk, and when even that had run its course, he excused himself, saying he had other calls to make, a ministry unto the sick and home-bound, he called it, and Lawrence walked him to his waiting cart. Lawrence turned to find Catharine by his side.

"That was nice," she said, watching the minister's conveyance trundle away.

"What was?"

"The visit. It's nice to have a visit now and then, even if it's about a problem someone is having." Lawrence placed his hand on the small of his wife's back, and she gave him a glance. "You know, I love our home and it's been wonderful having you around. But the pastor's dilemma brings to mind a matter that has been troubling me. I haven't mentioned it because you've been so busy and I know you must know what you're doing."

"Yes?" he said, sensing her concern.

"Well, it's your businesses, isn't it?" she said. "I mean, you have Andrew looking after the sawmill and I know he's doing a good job. But then there's the quarry, which has been nothing but trouble, and you haven't been to Philadelphia in almost a year. I'm not sure how you manage to keep things going."

Lawrence did not want to talk about his businesses. Even thinking about them made him feel heavy and tired. All he wanted to do was work in his vineyard and not think about anything else.

"Please don't worry yourself on the matter," he suggested, hoping she might change the subject.

"But I do. How can I not?"

"I've got everything under control," Lawrence said.

"You'd tell me if there were problems, wouldn't you?" she said.

"Of course I would," he said, reassuringly.

But Catharine had raised a sore point. The sawmill was indeed in good hands. But if Lawrence had everything under control, they wouldn't be having issues with the rock deliveries for the new church. And in all fairness, the revenues from the brewery had declined, as well. His wife had the annoying habit of speaking truth, and his businesses did indeed need his attention.

TWENTY-TWO

An unwelcome burden often makes other tasks more difficult, and Lawrence had to catch a horse. Several of them were in the pasture below his barn, and the one he wanted for the ride to the sawmill didn't seem to appreciate the distinction. It raised its head from the lush green grass and stared at him in defiance, then tossed its head and moved off, lowering its muzzle to the green pasturage while keeping an eye on the approaching man.

"Come on, you. Don't be so damned stubborn," Lawrence said, reassuringly, as he held out his hand, and the horse waited until the man was close enough to touch, before it moved forward and away, its nose still down as it ripped up a mouthful of grass. "Come on, you stupid beast," he said, trying to keep his voice low and calm.

The horse continued to evade him and he tried misdirection, approaching the other horses and scratching their forelocks, rubbing their necks. His fingers became powdered with their dander and the smell of them filled his nose. The one he wanted turned away and Lawrence pretended to walk past it, then stepped quickly to its side, grabbed a fistful of mane and started to scratch the long, sleek muscle of the neck. Slipping the halter over its head, he led the horse to the barn and tied it to a rail outside the open door.

The next challenge was the saddle, which seemed so much heavier than usual. The weight of it stretched his arms and neck muscles and the bulk of it banged against his thighs. The horse pushed him off balance, and he caught himself. But the saddle slipped from the horse's back and fell to the ground. Lawrence swore an oath, jamming his shoulder against the animal to push it out of the way.

"Are you all right?" Catharine said, coming up behind him. She carried the egg pail over her arm.

"Aye," Lawrence said. He picked the saddle up again and hefted it resolutely to the horse's back.

"You don't have to go see Andrew today, do you? Why not wait until tomorrow?"

Lawrence had told her of his plan to turn the problem with the quarry over to her brother, who had a head for business and a way of working with men.

"The sooner I can get it all behind us, the better," he said, wearily. "The pastor brought the delivery issue up again last Sunday at the back of the church, when we were shaking hands after the service. He just doesn't give up, and I have to wonder what he's going to want next. I'm surprised he hasn't asked for free lumber. Probably just hasn't thought of it, yet."

"You've a kind and generous spirit, Mr. Kraymer. People will want to take advantage, from time to time, if you let them. And speaking of taking advantage, if you're bound and determined to visit Andrew today, do be careful. He's turned into quite a different person than the one I once knew. He's very canny when it comes to other people expecting things of him."

"Is that what you think—that I'm trying to take advantage of him?"

"I'd be careful, that's all. If you want him to do something for you, he'll want to know what's in it for him. Just something to keep in mind. That's all I'm saying."

"Well, you've said enough," he said, grudgingly.

He gave her a kiss, and the sweet taste of her mouth went into him, as it always did. He could hardly remember what it was like to be without her. His life seemed to have started the day they met, and now that he had the château, even the ghost of his grandfather kept a tactful distance.

◆　◆　◆

ANDREW LAUX SAT BEHIND THE large desk in the office of the sawmill. He wore the fresh face of a youth on the rawboned body of a man, lean of frame and all elbows and knees. The desk was an old, wooden behemoth Andrew had scavenged from somewhere, and was flat and empty but for a tin of quills and an open ledger book. Andrew studied the book, his elbows on the desktop and his knees wide, sitting on an empty keg.

"You know, you don't have to sit on a barrel," Lawrence said, looming large in the office doorway.

"I'm fine with it," Andrew said, without looking up from the ledger. "The chairs are for the men, when they come in and have something to say. That's what you do, you know, for the sake of good morale. You make the men feel like their opinions are important. You put them at ease."

"You're pretty sure of yourself for one so young," Lawrence said, shaking his head, as he took a seat in one of the chairs in front of Andrew's desk. He tensed, preparing to speak of the matter that was on his mind, but Andrew stole the moment.

"What do you think about credit?" the youth asked.

"Uh . . . What?"

"What do you think about credit?" Andrew repeated. "Seriously, with the settlement growing the way it is, business is great. People're buying lumber at the rate they can afford, but we're not anywhere near capacity. With the waterwheel doing the work of six men, we could saw a lot more logs than we are."

Lawrence let the words sink in. While he had worked day and night to finish the château, Andrew had performed the monumental task of dismantling the old mill and moving it to a new location. The young man had built a road through the limestone ridges to the Delaware River, where a feeder torrent provided the power to turn a waterwheel and where the river itself served the purpose of floating logs. Lawrence was impressed with the ambitiousness of the project. He had to admit that he, himself, might never have thought of such a thing.

"I'm not sure what that has to do with credit," Lawrence said, defensively. "Credit is for people who have access to money to begin with. Most of the people around here barely make ends meet. They raise crops to feed their families and livestock rather than to sell. Build them a house on credit, and it seems to me, you run the risk of building it for free."

Andrew looked at Lawrence with searing, intelligent eyes.

"The flour mill runs on credit. The dry goods, too."

"That's because people need to eat, and they need supplies to live."

"Like they don't need lumber?" Andrew said. He plucked a quill from the tin and started waggling it, flipping it back and forth between his first and second fingers. "Building a house or a barn is a slow process when money is in short supply. What if we could speed things up? If people could build faster, they might want to build more and, in turn, have to buy more lumber. We could put in a second waterwheel."

"I'm just not so sure about credit . . ." Lawrence said, skeptically.

"You know what your problem is?"

The sudden shift in the conversation caught Lawrence by surprise, and he did not have a response. Catharine had been right. This new Andrew was different from the one of old, more confident and challenging. Far more difficult.

"The problem with you is that you've lost your daring," Andrew said, tapping his quill against the desktop.

The effrontery of the statement stunned Lawrence. Anger flashed through him and then just as suddenly ebbed. He didn't know what to say.

"A little success and the boy thinks he's an authority," he said.

"I'm serious."

"So am I," Lawrence said, rising abruptly. He still thought of the sawmill as his—as it ostensibly was. But Andrew was the one who'd had the idea to start it in the first place. He'd run the operation back when men used handsaws to cut the logs. He was the one who moved it to its present location and who made it profitable. Lawrence saw very little of himself in the business and felt more and more like a stranger on the premises.

◆　◆　◆

IN THE AFTERMATH OF HIS experience at the sawmill, the decision to sell the quarry came easily, and Lawrence felt greatly relieved. The way he looked at it, the sale solved several problems. He had the minister off his back, because now that Lawrence no longer owned the quarry, he could not be held accountable for the cost of the rock and the timeliness of its delivery. He'd avoided indebting himself to the ambitious and increasingly arrogant Andrew, which was no small consideration, and the sale gave him a lump sum of cash that didn't hurt, either. In retrospect, he should have sold the thing a long time ago and saved himself a considerable amount of trouble.

"You're very quiet," Catharine said, stirring him from his reverie. They had been married for almost a year, now, and another autumn was creeping in. The fall chill had come early and they sat in front of a pinewood fire. Catharine, holding knitting needles and a ball of yarn, studied her work.

"I was just thinking, that's all," he said.

"It's the brewery, isn't it?"

"Why do you say that?"

"It stands to reason," she said, watching her fingers as they worked the needles. "The sawmill is doing well and you no longer have the quarry to worry about. That leaves the brewery, doesn't it? Honestly, you haven't been there in so long that I don't know what to think."

Lawrence gazed into the fire, collecting his thoughts.

"No doubt you're right," he said, sighing. "I really should pay a visit."

"Of course, you should," she agreed. "You can't just let a business run itself."

"What if I just got rid of it—like the quarry? I always intended to, you know. I mean, the sawmill's doing okay, like you said, and we get a little bit of money from it—enough to limp along. If I could get a good price for the brewery, we'd have plenty of time to secure another source of income."

Catharine stopped knitting and rested the ball of yarn in her lap. She looked at him.

"If you've lost interest in the brewery, then what's the point of holding on?" she said.

Lawrence felt himself blanche at his wife's words, and stealing a look at her, was relieved to see she had returned to her knitting. During the construction of the château, the trips back and forth to Philadelphia had not been difficult. He had taken them in stride, along with his other challenges and responsibilities. But now even thinking about a day in the saddle made him tired. The thought of leaving the château seemed insufferable. Being separated from his beautiful wife and his amazing home was something he simply didn't want to think about.

◆　◆　◆

THERE WAS NO MOON AND the bedroom was black. In such total darkness, he felt like nothing more than a pinprick of thought, a whim. Catharine lay next to him but he couldn't see her and for a frightful moment he wondered if she was really there, after all. Reaching out, he touched the loose pile of her hair. The warmth of her skin.

"Are you awake?" he whispered.

"Mmm," she said.

He hesitated.

"Do you think . . . You know . . . We could . . ."

"That would be nice," she said.

"But what about the baby?"

He slid his hand under the covers and felt the bump of life through her nightgown.

"Mother says it's fine."

"You talk to your mother about . . . you know . . . us?" he said, aghast.

"Who else would I talk to," she said. She waited. "You can kiss me," she finally said.

But now it wasn't just the baby that concerned him. He imagined Beatrice sitting in one of the bedroom chairs, watching them, and told his wife he wasn't in the mood, after all. He tried to sleep, but lay awake, lost in the blackness of the moonless night, feeling afraid for no reason he could think of.

TWENTY-THREE

Catharine got out of bed earlier than usual. Pushing some tinder under the iron plate next to the kitchen hearth, she made a fire, adding more fuel as she built up the flames. She put a kettle of water on the iron plate, and then went to the pantry where she gathered up several eggs and a loaf of bread that she had baked the previous day. Taking a small kerosene lamp with her, she shuffled out of the kitchen and out of the back door of the house, following the glow that spilled onto the path to the smokehouse. The chilly morning air tugged at her mouth, stealing some of her breath. A side of beef hung in the smokehouse, smelling like molasses, and she cut off a piece of backstrap.

Steak and eggs were not a typical breakfast for the Kraymer household, but this was not a typical day, she thought, as she sliced the meat and put the pieces on a plate. An effervescence of being filled her, a sense of rootedness in the moment. Remembering the potatoes, she made a return trip to the pantry. They were from her garden and thinking of them made her feel good, as if first the growing and then the harvesting of them had accomplished something important. They would last the winter in the root cellar and represented a meal that was always in the offing, an ongoing source of life and sustenance.

Leaving the skins of the potatoes on, she cubed them and set them in the iron skillet with a chunk of bubbling lard. Quickly, she sliced an onion and tossed the slivers into the pan. Using a potholder to take the skillet by its handle, she gave it a vigorous shake.

"What time is it?" Lawrence asked, appearing in the lamplight.

He wore a robe, with his nightshirt sticking from the bottom. His feet were bare. His hair was tussled, and he rubbed his eyes, yawning.

"You have a big day ahead of you."

He looked at her and nodded, raising his eyebrows in a way that acknowledged the difficulties of travel and the challenges ahead. She pushed the potatoes and onions aside and set the steaks to sizzling in the pan. Lawrence went up behind her and circled her with his arms. He pressed his lips to her hair. She leaned back into him and closed her eyes, missing him already.

"If you're going to get dressed, you should hurry up with it," she said. "The meat'll be done shortly and the eggs won't take half that long. Breakfast'll be ready before you know it."

"You trying to get rid of me?"

"I'd quit dawdling if I were you."

"Okay, I can take a hint," he said, letting her go.

Not hardly, she thought, pretending to herself to be cranky with him, as he turned back upstairs to the bedroom. You and a hint wouldn't know each other if you were in the same room together. You and a hint would need an introduction, and even then, you'd likely forget what it was. The thought made her smile.

He shuffled back into the kitchen, dressed but still barefooted, a pair of socks dangling from one hand and a pair of boots from the other, and she put a plate in front of him with the backstrap, three eggs, and a mound of fried potatoes. Sitting down in his chair, he pulled the socks on and slid his feet into the boots, then scooted forward and placed his elbows on the table. Sitting opposite him, she ignored her own plate, watching him eat, watching him cut a piece of meat and spear it with his fork.

He paused, fork suspended.

"Aren't you hungry?" he said.

"I just wanted to watch you."

"Well, it makes me nervous."

"Why would it make you nervous?"

"It just does, that's all. Now come on. Don't make me eat alone."

She acted miffed, but of course she wasn't. She felt the dull pain of his imminent departure and the emptiness that would soon follow. It would happen all too quickly and indeed it did. Barely a heartbeat seemed to pass, and she watched him riding off, a silhouette against the paling sky of dawn.

◆　◆　◆

SHE WORKED IN THE GARDEN, harvesting pumpkins, piling them in small mounds to be picked up by the wagon. The thin, brassy heat of the sun beat down, and she wore a bonnet. Her blouse was open at the neck, and she wore a long dark skirt. Bending and unbending, she took the pumpkins and placed them in piles, now and then stopping to wipe her hand against her forehead and to gaze down the lane Lawrence had taken and the one he would appear on when he returned. He had thought he would be gone a week, maybe two, and it was more than that now. She had visits almost daily from one or another of her brothers, sometimes even her mother, but it wasn't the same as having her husband by her side, and she gazed at the road, waiting for his return and willing it to happen, looking and waiting.

As one day slid into the next, they all became part of the same long solitude that seemed to never end. She cleaned and dusted, prepared her meals, and found more to do in the garden, trying to stay busy. Never in her life had she felt so alone, used as she was to a big family. Her brother, Jean, didn't know why she didn't just come and stay at the farm until Lawrence's return. Jean could be insistent. But she, in turn, could be stubborn, and she stayed at the château and did her chores with an enduring attention to detail. This was her home, she told her brother. This was where she belonged.

She was just coming out of the barn, where she had gone to collect eggs, when she almost bumped into McDonall. Lawrence had kept him on as a caretaker, but she largely steered clear of him. With Lawrence gone, however, she was alone, and McDonall's presence took on new meaning.

"Oh," she said, her free hand flattening against her chest.

McDonall stood in front of her, blocking her path. He smelled strongly of human body odor. His brooding eyes looked like bruises.

"Well, you gave me a scare," she said, with a nervous laugh, expecting him to say something polite and reassuring.

He did not. Instead, he looked at her with a frightening mean-ness. It was as if a darkness had collected in him, and Catharine found it suddenly hard to breathe. She stepped aside, trying to get around him, and he didn't budge. His eyes followed her and she felt them on her. She felt them probing, as if the meanness in him was looking for an excuse to come out.

"Where's your husband at?" he said, and it wasn't the words, themselves, as much as the way he said them that alarmed her. He made it sound more like an accusation than a question, and Catharine paused for a moment, confused. She had been raised to be cautious when outside of the protection of home, as any sensible woman ought to be, so close to the frontier. But the justifiable fear some women have of certain men was alien to her. Her father and brothers had always treated her with respect. Lawrence had done the same, and she didn't recognize the feeling that rippled through her, the weakness in her stomach and knees, the sense that something was terribly wrong.

He stood there glowering and Catharine was astounded to find herself afraid for the first time in her life, and on her own estate, no less—her sanctuary, the place that was supposed to be her safe haven. She could feel the man's eyes on her back. Her skin crawled, and she hastened on to the house. Once inside, she threw the bolt on the door.

Crossing to a window, she saw McDonall still standing next to the barn, looking at the house, and she stepped back, so that he couldn't see her. She took a deep breath and let it out, assuring herself that she was secure inside the château. Shaking her head, she tried to laugh, chiding herself for overreacting. She was her father's daughter and her husband's wife, after all. How silly to think, for even a minute, that a man like McDonall didn't know his place.

◆　◆　◆

AND THEN CAME THE DAY she was waiting for. She heard the hoofbeats nearing the house and looked out from her window to see Lawrence dismounting. Long, greasy strands of hair dangled from under his hat, and the shoulders of his riding jacket were caked with dust. His boots were scuffed and when he stamped his feet, brown clouds puffed up around his ankles.

She rushed from the house and threw her arms around him.

"I'm so glad to see you!" she said.

The embrace was awkward, and he pushed back from her, clearing his throat, uncomfortably.

"We need to talk," he said.

"Let's get you cleaned up and feeling better, first."

Tugging on him, she led him into the house, into the kitchen. They had a boiler next to the cooking hearth that was filled with the spring water they used for bathing, and she dragged a metal tub from its closet and ran water into a bucket that she then dumped into the tub. He seemed to have forgotten how to undress, and she had to help him.

He lowered himself into the tub and she used a pot to scoop water and pour it over his head. Then she took a bar of soap and worked up a lather, pressing her fingers through his hair, against his scalp.

She tried to lift one of his arms but he stiffened.

"I'm sorry," he said.

Catharine paused, resting her wrists on the edge of the tub.

"I thought I could sell the brewery. I really did," he explained.

"I never said you had to sell it," she said. "That was your idea."

"I know, and I really thought I could do it," he said, miserably. "But it's mostly all I've ever known. I've worked in it ever since I can remember, and then, when my grandfather died, it was all I had. I didn't realize how much a part of me it was until I tried to let it go."

"Let's talk about it later," Catharine said, numbly.

Dipping the scrub brush in the hot, soapy water, she rubbed it against his back. This wasn't the homecoming she had expected.

After a solid month of absence, she needed his strength and his confidence, not this self-indulgent display of indecision. McDonall hove into her mind's eye and she started to panic all over again. She scrubbed Lawrence's back harder and harder.

"Stop—you're taking my skin off," he protested, and she flung the brush into the tub and stood up. Her anxiety seized her by the throat, and she fled the kitchen.

TWENTY-FOUR

In the days that followed, Catharine and Lawrence had their first serious disagreement. She stated in no uncertain terms that McDonall had to go, and Lawrence bristled. Running the estate was his responsibility, he said, and he couldn't do it without a caretaker. Catharine responded that having a caretaker was not the issue. The issue very specifically related to the man who currently held that title, and whose name she did not even care to mention. Lawrence demanded to know what McDonall had done to deserve such dismissal. This was a hard question to answer, because in truth, McDonall's transgression seemed trivial when she tried to put it into words.

"He looked at me," she said.

"He looked at you?" Lawrence said, with astonishment. "Men look at beautiful women all the time. It's what they do. It's called being a man."

Throwing his hands in the air, he walked in a circle, as if not knowing which direction to go, and Catharine decided she really didn't like her husband in that particular moment. She felt humiliated and demeaned. The way she looked at it, she and her husband were supposed to be of one mind, and a man like McDonall was beyond consideration. In the end, Lawrence capitulated and let McDonall go. But the damage had already been done, and the way Lawrence reacted to her left a permanent scar.

◆　◆　◆

THE DAYS GOT SHORTER WITH the coming of winter and the house was impossible to warm. Catharine shut the rooms that she and Lawrence did not need and kept the fires burning in the kitchen and sitting room, feeding cordwood to the crackling orange flames. Even then, one had to sit close to the fire to get any penetrating comfort from its warmth. In the evenings, they banked the coals in the bedroom fireplace and huddled under a mound of blankets. By morning, the water in the drinking jugs by the bedside was frozen.

In spite of the seasonal discomfort, however, Catharine found peace. Her belly grew large and she walked with care, rocking from side to side. She still tended the chickens, over Lawrence's objections, saying she needed chores to keep her busy, and when the snows came, she walked the shoveled path to the barn twice a day. Eventually, the snow was banked waist-high on either side of the path—an unusual snow, everyone said. But as her belly grew, the world seemed increasingly special, and even the snow had a magical quality, as if the ferocity of nature had bestowed a blessing of cold, crystalline magic, the frigid air entering her lungs and resting there briefly before she pushed it back out again, slightly warmed, watching how the air took her breath and turned it into clouds.

Sometimes Lawrence worked in the barn, but often he was elsewhere and she had the barn to herself, the horses with their quiet eyes and velvet noses, the stalls with their carpets of straw, the chickens that crooned at her. Catharine liked the barn this way, without McDonall and without even Lawrence, the quiet structure in which everything seemed muffled—the hayloft above where pigeons clapped their wings and the stalls below where the horses nosed their oats and fresh hay. Catharine lingered, in no hurry to return to the house, claiming the quietude as her own, if only for a stolen moment or two.

When she left the barn, she didn't mind the cold air that struck her face as she shuffled slowly between the banks of snow. As difficult as the house was to warm, it was her home and she took delight in an afternoon cup of hot tea. There was little to do during the brief winter days, and Lawrence would often join her, piecing together jigsaw puzzles or trying to read in the dim lamplight. Often, they sat by the fire and dozed, their legs wrapped in blankets.

By the middle of February, she was so big that that the baby's birthing seemed an impossibility. But it was not so impossible after all, and one day it just happened, as inevitably as the melting snow. One moment the house seemed cavernous and empty, and the next her mother was there along with another woman, an older woman with a thin, straight nose and a severe stare, the kind of eyes that seemed to see things that others could not. The woman had long, wrinkled hands that were as soft and smooth as tanned leather. There was a lot of pain and some blood, but Catharine quickly forgot these things as she basked in the glow of her baby's face, eyes still closed but a mouth that opened, a mouth that sought her breast. Lawrence was by her side but she was hardly aware of him, enthralled as she was by the new little man that seemed no less than a perfect miracle to her, that was part of her and needed her and clung to her.

They named the baby Pierre after his grandfather, Pierre Laux Kraymer, with the nickname of Peter—"A chip off the old block,"

Catharine said, smiling at her father, as the older Pierre swayed on his feet at the christening. For a moment, Catharine thought his knees would give out and he would fall, and how she loved her father in that moment, watching the way her mother reached out so effortlessly with an arm that went around his waist, and how he nodded ever so slightly as if forcing himself to accept a profound truth. Having barely survived his own childhood, he now had a grandchild and one that was named after him, no less. Pierre's throat worked up and down and he had to widen his stance.

With the snows finally melted, Lawrence had to make another trip to Philadelphia and Catharine didn't care. The lesson she had learned from his previous trip was that lower expectations resulted in less disappointment. Besides, she had someone else, now. She had baby Peter, who filled her up so much that she hardly thought of her husband. He was gone for a while and then he returned, and it was all the same to Catharine. She hardly listened when he spoke of those things he had done while away.

Then, as the summer approached and the first haying drew near, Lawrence rehired McDonall. The disagreeable man trudged about the estate in his heavy boots, dragging his dark cloud with him. But it was a cloud that existed outside of the house, out in the fields where the man worked, away from the hearth and the heartbeat that now engaged the mother and her child. The house was Catharine's refuge. The baby was all that mattered to her, and she trusted the stone walls to protect her from McDonall and the rest of the world. Her father had often told her similar stories, how the manoir he had grown up in had seemed like such a cocoon, how life as he knew it revolved around him and his mother, and how nothing else seemed to matter, and Catharine thought she understood. It was the same with her, here and now.

The château was an island of happiness to her, and when she had to leave it, she did so reluctantly, tending the chickens, carrying the baby in a sling as she walked barefoot in the turned earth of the garden, bending down sideways to press seeds into the soil. Back in the house, she washed the baby in a large basin, using a sponge to squeeze warm water onto the tiny forehead and brushing back the strands of dark hair. Wrapping baby Peter in a soft blanket, she fed him and changed his diapers, exclaiming at his every function as if each were a laureled achievement.

The baby was three months old when Lawrence said he had to return to Philadelphia.

"I hate to leave you," he said.

"I'll be fine, just hurry back," she said, curious that the pangs of separation no longer seemed to tug so fiercely.

"You're not upset with me because I have to take another trip, so soon after the last one?" he asked, dubiously.

"You have to go take care of your business. Just go on—we'll be fine."

The baby held out his arms, waving them in the air. Dropping her chin, Catharine smiled down at the cherubic face. Little Peter pointed a finger at her and she gave him a kiss.

◆　◆　◆

CATHARINE TRIED TO REMEMBER WHICH day Lawrence had left but could not. The chickens needed tending, the garden needed hoeing, and the housework was endless. But nothing seemed to matter as much as the baby, which mattered more to her than everything else combined, and the chickens sometimes went hungry and weeds sprouted in the garden. The baby was sleeping in a cradle near the hearth and Catharine stole glances at him. Already, she was thinking of Peter's education and the slates she would need. Beatrice had taught her children to spell from the words in the Bible, standing over them while they chewed their lips and squeaked their chalks across their slates. She taught them numbers, how to add and subtract, how to multiply and divide. Pierre insisted they know languages, and Beatrice taught them Latin, in addition to French and German, which were the languages she knew. Pierre himself taught them words in his native Occitan, and Catharine couldn't wait for him to instruct his grandson.

She was pushing an oiled cloth along the dining room table within sight of her son, when she heard a sound from outside. Her brother, Jean, dismounted from his horse. She hadn't seen Jean in over a fortnight, and she caught her breath. It seemed impossible that someone could grow so much in so short a time. His shoulders had broadened and his waist had slimmed. He approached the house with a sense of purpose.

"Hey, sis," he said, standing on the porch, pushing his cocked hat back and giving a stiff smile.

"Oh, Jean—do come in!" she said, and Jean did as she asked. But ever the cautious one of late, he paused first to look around, as if assessing any possible threats the environment might present, and while Catharine appreciated the sentiment, she found it tiresome, as well. He didn't have to act like he was still in Indian country, she thought, and smiled the way she did when her congeniality conflicted with how she truly felt.

Inside the house, he took off his hat. Once again, his eyes searched about, scouting out the foyer and on into the great room beyond. He scratched at the stubble of a beard. Catharine led the way into the great room, where they sat on the sofa. The baby slept in the cradle nearby.

Catharine marveled at how handsome her brother was. His sternness, however, concerned her. Ever since the ill-fated militia returned from the wild, Jean had seemed like a different person. Quiet and withdrawn, but not in the dreamy way he had been as a child. He had grown aloof and untrusting, the way her father was at times. They went through their small talk about the family back at the farm, but Catharine knew that such chatter was not why he had come to the château. She knew him far better than that.

"So, Lawrence's gone again," he said, a statement of obvious fact and not at all a question. Catharine had not told anyone that Lawrence was leaving. She hadn't even given it a thought, frankly. Her family was prone to worrying about things and it was sometimes easier to keep them in the dark.

She admitted to Jean that Lawrence had taken another trip to Philadelphia, and no, she didn't know when he intended to return. It didn't really matter, she said. She had all she needed and the baby kept her plenty busy.

"Lawrence promised me he would get rid of McDonall," Jean said, his expression darkening.

Again, his eyes searched the room, as if looking for hidden dangers in the shadows.

"He did let McDonall go. We had a whole winter to ourselves," Catharine said.

"But now he's back."

"I used to be afraid of the man," Catharine allowed. "But Lawrence is right. We do need help with the outdoor chores. Besides, little Peter keeps me so busy now, I don't have time for other concerns."

"You don't have time to worry about your safety?" Jean's eyebrows arched with astonishment that anyone could say such a thing.

"Honestly, I'm not like you. I don't see an enemy behind every bush!"

The look he gave her almost broke her heart, for she could clearly see the gulf that now separated them.

"I was going to offer my services," Jean said, stiffly. "I'll stay here and work on the estate until Lawrence gets back. We can make boot of McDonall."

"Honestly, what is it about the man that offends you so much?" Catharine said, treating her brother much the same way Lawrence had treated her, when she had first complained about McDonall. She hardly remembered what her concerns had been. To accuse the man of staring at her now seemed patently ridiculous.

Jean searched her face as he composed his words.

"A man doesn't have to do bad things to be a bad man. It is just my opinion, but I have come to believe that evil is something that lies dormant in certain individuals, like a sickness—a disease. You don't run into a man like McDonall very often, but when you do, you have to keep your distance from him, so that what festers in him doesn't infect you as well. You have to be prudent. You have to avoid putting yourself in dangerous situations."

"Says the man who wanted to be a soldier," Catharine said.

But Jean didn't rise to the bait. He remained earnest.

"I could stay," Jean said. "I can remain as long as you want and do whatever you need me to do."

Catharine sighed. She loved her brother. He could be a little frightening at times, the way he had become lately. But she never once doubted his good will and she loved him with all of her heart.

"This is my home," she said. She raised her eyes and let her gaze drift around the room. "I appreciate your concern and your offer. But you have to believe me when I say that I am fine. This is my world. If I can't be safe here, then where? Where would I go and what would I do there? How would I even exist?"

Jean studied her, soberly. Then, with a nod, he tightened his grip on his hat, which he held in his lap. Gathering his strength, he rose from the sofa.

"I will always be available for you," he said. "All you ever have to do is ask. You are my sister and there's nothing I wouldn't do for you."

They embraced and it was one of those tender moments that lingered long after he was gone. Her brothers were changing, heading off in their different directions, as indeed she herself had done. But they had a bond that persisted and a love that endured. When Jean said she could count on him, she knew in her bones that he spoke the truth.

◆ ◆ ◆

THOUGH SHE'D TOLD JEAN SHE was just fine being alone, Catharine still felt heavy and sad in the wake of his departure. The baby started to fuss again, and she was grateful for the urgent little call. A rush of warmth filled her chest and arms as she reached for the small, helpless figure, picking the baby up and pressing him to her shoulder, jiggling and rocking, smelling the damp skin and silky hair, pressing the small head to her nose and breathing deeply.

"Oh, my little man. How is my little man!" she said, rocking from side to side as she held the small bundle of warmth in the crook of her arm.

Sitting down in the chair by the window, she unhooked the shoulder flap of her blouse and exposed a breast, bringing the small mouth to her nipple, feeling a rush as the tiny mouth gripped and began to suck. The little mouth was rimmed with milk and a little hand waved in the air, reaching up to pat her face. Her mind emptied of thought. She cooed, dropping her chin so that she could continue to breathe the hot, sweet smell of the baby's head. Thoughts of her family drained out of her and she thought only of her little one, cradling the small body and holding it just so, breathing its smell, happier than she had ever been in her life.

The baby pulled away and a small jet of milk came from her nipple.

"Oh, you little scamp," she murmured, angling the small head in a way that brought the reaching mouth back to the spot. "You mustn't play with your food. There you are, there!"

The baby sucked and she once again relaxed. Then the baby pulled away again and appeared to smile, the eyes arcing upwards and the mouth opening into a small rosy heart.

"You little scoundrel, you!" she said, delightedly.

But then she heard a sound and looked up, her bones turned to ice water. McDonall had entered her home. He stood inside the open door with a load of kindling in his arm, standing there with his face sagging, staring at her. He had never been in the house before. His instructions were to leave the kindling and cordwood on the porch, and Catharine had no way of knowing that he had tried the door, as a matter of course, every time he brought the wood. She had no way of knowing the surprise he felt, this time, when the door yielded, and how he couldn't help himself. He had to push the door open and see for himself what it was like inside. His mouth hung open and his foul stench permeated the room.

"What are you doing here?" Catharine demanded. She placed Peter in his cradle and then turned away, struggling to button the flap of her blouse.

The baby let out a piercing wail.

"The door was open," McDonall said.

"Get out," she said, straightening up and thrusting a finger toward the door.

The man focused his full attention on her. His mean, bloodshot eyes dwelled on her, then on the baby, then on her again, and Catharine could see the black cloud forming. His face darkened. Moving mechanically, he opened his arm and dropped the kindling into the wood basket. Pieces of the splintered wood hit the basket and bounced onto the hearth, and he turned to look at her resentfully.

"You got teats," he said, as if it were an accusation.

It was an absurd statement and Catharine didn't know what to make of it. She began to panic. Having McDonall outside the house, where he belonged, was one thing, something she could rationalize and cope with. Having him inside with her was an entirely different matter.

McDonall's eyes lifted to grope the room in a grudging, relentless fashion. The walls had exotic wood paneling. There were tapestries and vases. One of the windows looked out on the vineyard, and Catharine could see the effect all of this was having on the man, who in his own opinion had built the place. It was more than he could bear.

Fire began to creep out onto the hearth where the kindling lay scattered. McDonall swayed. Little Peter continued to wail and McDonall raised a heavy hand and pushed it at the air in the direction of the baby.

"Make 'im stop," he said.

Catharine bent down sideways, reaching out until she found the handle of the iron poker that stood in the tool rack next to the fireplace.

"I said get out," she said, icily.

McDonall raised his hands, pressing them against his ears.

"Just make 'im stop!" he said, and when Catharine made no effort to do so, he lurched forward and kicked out with one of his feet. His heavy boot sent the cradle flying and the baby's cries were cut short. In an instant, Catharine was upon him, swinging the poker reflexively. Her hand jarred as the poker hit his face and the man gave a grunting yelp. He fell backward, into the fireplace, scattering half-burnt cordwood and embers. His hair singed and he swore, batting his hands against his head.

At that point, Catharine's only thought was for her baby. With McDonall momentarily subdued, she turned, the poker still in her hand, and saw that little Peter had been flung from the crib. His head had struck the base of the lamp stand and a large quantity of dark blood spread rapidly into the carpet. His eyes were open, staring at nothing, and Catharine shrieked, dropping the poker and rushing to him, reaching for his now silenced, unmoving form. Behind her, McDonall bawled like a calf, but Catharine was of a single mind. She knelt in front of little Peter, afraid to touch him but unable not to, and as she reached for him, a hand clamped around her arm and jerked her back. McDonall was in a rage. Yanking her backward with one hand, he grasped the collar of her blouse with the other and pulled with all his might. The buttons popped and the fabric tore. He grabbed her throat and pulled her to her feet, then pushed her backward, sending both of them crashing into the sofa and toppling the table with the lamp.

Catharine fought with the heart of a lion. McDonall weighed twice as much as she did, and she had little hope of repelling him. But she knew in her mother's heart that her baby was dead. The sounds that came out of her were inhuman and she fought until the last breath left her body.

As for McDonall, he had crossed the line when he first entered the house and by now was too far gone to recover. One thing led to another, and he couldn't stop himself. He didn't even try. With one hand around Catharine's throat, he loosened his trousers with the other, and a sadistic thrill went through him. Only when she stopped breathing and no longer moved did he finally pause, and a stab of horror went through him, not at what he had done but at the fear that others would find out and he might get caught. The scattered embers from the fireplace had already ignited the oil from the broken lamp, which gave McDonall the idea, and he hastened to pile cordwood on the bodies and douse them with oil from the other lamps in the room. The nearby curtains had burst into flames and McDonall fled the room. Angry orange tongues of fire hissed and spat as they climbed the wall, and the room filled with smoke.

TWENTY-FIVE

S tanding in his smithy with a pair of tongs in his hand, Pierre felt the hairs on the back of his neck stand up. The air had an acrid taste, a bitterness that he recognized from his childhood in France when the northerners came down with their dragoons and ragged infantry. He shook his head, trying to dispel the memory but it came back at him, harder this time. For different fires have different odors, and what he tasted in the air was not the pungency of burning leaves or tree trimmings. Rather, it was the kind of smell that the soldiers had left in their wake, after they had looted what they wanted from a home and decided to burn what was left.

The wind gusted, shifting slightly, and the bitter odor intensified. Thunder rumbled. Then a smattering of rain began to fall, large drops that struck with a sudden and popping force. The sky grew even darker, and glancing toward the house, Pierre could see that Beatrice had lit the oil lamps, making the windows glow yellow. More drops clattered against the smithy's roof, then a pale silvery curtain of rain swept in, striking with a dull roar that grew and grew until it became a profound and inescapable torrent of sound. The smithy offered little protection from the spray and icy chill, and Pierre plunged the horseshoe into its cooling bucket and set the tongs aside.

Later, as he lay in bed next to his wife, he had a hard time getting warm. The storm continued through the night, and he drifted in and out of troubled sleep. He was not an overly superstitious man, but something seemed amiss. Something was wrong, and the memories came back. He dreamed he was a child again, when rumors of the soldiers had first started to circulate, and he didn't believe the rumors, at first, because he was just a boy and the life he lived was the only life he had ever known. They said the soldiers had guns and bayonets, that they lived off the land, and in his childish reasoning, he assumed that meant they trapped rabbits and partridges. He had no idea that "living off the land" meant that they preyed on people and livestock, billeting in homes, demanding to be fed, and slaughtering cows and chickens as it suited them. He had no idea that it meant they had their way with the women in the homes and sometimes went so far as to hang the men from trees.

The advance of the soldiers was like a slow-moving wave, and Pierre's eyes were rudely opened. After his father's disappearance and his mother's death, he fled from the manoir on his father's horse, the powerful war machine of a beast that the elder chevalier had loved so much. At the auberge where he sought refuge, he lost the horse and continued his flight on foot. Eventually, he ended up on his hands and knees, finally collapsing in a meadow high in the Alps, where the spongy creekside moss made a damp pillow against his cheek and the towering clouds seemed like the billowing skirts of angels. That was where the shepherd boy found him. The face of the shepherd loomed, the clear brown eyes, the downy, curly beard, the smell of the sheep he tended. A brace of rabbits hung from his belt, and he carried a staff. His simple vest looked like a rough sheepskin turned inside out, with holes for the arms and a piece of rope tying it together at the waist. Before he saw the shepherd,

Pierre heard the youthful piping of his voice singing a love song that would have been ribald but for the exuberant sweetness of the tone. Then there was silence as the shepherd gazed down at him, squatting to look at him closer, reaching out a finger to poke him, as if doubting he were real.

"You must've thought I was a ghost," Pierre said, later, over a bowl of rabbit stew, and the shepherd boy nodded enthusiastically. "I have seen many things in the mountains," the shepherd said, in that triumphant way of his. "I have seen many things and my sheep have taught me much." He raised a finger and tilted his head to the side. "They have taught me that not everything you see is real. Some things you have to poke and other things poke at *you*. Maybe you were a ghost and maybe not—who knew?" the boy said, laughing happily.

That was the way it was with the shepherd, and to this day, Pierre was still not certain the boy wasn't a mountain spirit sent to both save and torment him. They spent many a night with the flickering light of a campfire on their faces, a heavy blanket of stars overhead, points of light so dense and bright it seemed he could reach up and gather a handful as if they were shining grains of wheat. He tried to forget the stench of a house burning down, a bitter smell like ants in the nostrils.

In due time, he was up high on a mountainside, looking down on the rooftops and hearth smokes of Lausanne, where his mother had once told him to go. The shepherd boy, who usually had something to sing about and always had something to say, stood next to him in silence. Amid the many smokes, the roofs of the town looked like a shoal of boulders showing through a sea of haze.

"Why don't you just stay here with me?" the shepherd said. "We could make the mountains our home. The sheep would be our children. We could be happy."

"I don't belong here," Pierre said.

The shepherd shook his head.

"Haven't you learned anything?" he said, sadly. "Up here, we have to worry about wolves and the occasional bear, but down there—" he paused to raise his chin, "—it is your own kind who betray you. The same man who offers you a cup of nourishment holds a knife behind his back. The gods they worship condone murder and genocide. Down there, you will find nothing but meanness and death."

"I don't believe that."

"After all you've been through?"

"I'm going down now," Pierre said, stubbornly.

The shepherd boy gave Pierre his bag of culinary spices, assuming Pierre would have need of them and that a good meal was all he could hope for in the civilized wilds ahead, and Pierre clambered down, through precipitous, boulder-strewn drop-offs. For a time, the shepherd stood in plain view, watching him descend the slope, and then the boy was gone, a bit of cloud hanging where he had been. There was the blue sky, the bit of cloud, the leaning fringes of trees, a little apron of meadow and the rocks, the downslope that soon towered above him, the wood smoke and sewer smells of the city, cows with bells and barking dogs, sniffing, trailing dogs with bristling backs, staring people who watched as he approached and then turned their backs, watching him from the corners of their eyes until he was safely past and beyond the reach of harm to them.

Though no one made a friendly gesture, no one challenged him, either, and he found himself in the town square. In the center of the square was a fountain, with water gurgling up and spilling over a mass of stones. An old woman sat on a bench beside the fountain. She wore a black headscarf and a long black shawl. Gray hair wired out around the scarf and she had a dark, leathery face with a beaked nose. She seemed to doze, hands with prominent knuckles folded in her lap, and ankles wrapped in cotton stockings, heavy black shoes resting with the heels apart.

"Do you mind if I sit next to you?" Pierre asked, and she looked at him with a fierce, stabbing eye.

"If you think you dare," she said.

"Why would I not dare?" he said, cautiously.

"Some say I have the evil eye."

"Do you?"

She gave a contemptuous laugh and shrugged.

"Some say it and that's enough for most," she said, turning her head to the side to spit.

"I'll sit then, if you don't mind," he said, lowering himself to the bench. He paused for a moment, then gave her a sideways look. "But if you do have the evil eye and think you might want to give it to me, I would like to suggest I have had enough troubles without adding to them. I wouldn't mind a reprieve, if you don't mind my saying so."

She opened her mouth and started to silently laugh, drawing in breaths and pushing them back out again.

"I was thinking of taking a nap, sitting here in the sun, but now I think that I won't. You've caught my interest. I don't get a chance for many conversations and precious few laughs. You're not from around here, I can plainly see. As can anyone, for that matter. I bet you got a warm reception."

"Not hardly!" he exclaimed. "No one will even look at me!"

Her shoulders rocked with silent laughter.

"Is it any wonder? You could be the devil himself, come down out of the mountains. Eaten any children, have you? Fancied any of the maidens you might have seen peering at you past partially closed shutters?"

"What makes you think I came down from the mountains?"

"You look like a shepherd and smell like sheep."

"I do?" he said, astonished at the impression he'd made on the old woman and presumably the townsfolk as well. He was a noble-man's son, after all, and still thought of himself as such, in spite of the ordeals he had suffered.

"Shepherds are a scary lot, a little bit wild and unpredictable, all that starry sky on the mountaintops. Living with the winds in the trees and making your own medicines out of nature's herbs. People around here need the likes of you to watch their sheep over the grazing months, but it's best you stay in the mountains where you belong in the in-between times. Stop in a town too long and some might take a mind to burn you at the stake," she said, only partly in jest.

"I'm not a shepherd."

"Could've fooled me," she retorted.

"I'm looking for some people who live here," he said.

"I figured you wanted something. Nobody sits down next to an old woman with the evil eye unless they've got good cause."

He explained who he was looking for and she gave him a sharp look.

"They were big house people and been gone a long time now," she said, choosing her words with care. "Is that what you are—a big house person?"

Pierre's mind reeled at the thought that he had come all this way for naught.

"What happened that they left?" he said.

"To hear it told, it was the house they lived in. It burned to the ground. Some say it was the soldiers on account of they were here-tics. Others say it was people from the town who did it. You know how people can be when they get ideas in their heads. I couldn't rightly tell you what happened, one way or the other."

Pierre stood up to leave and the old woman softened.

"Goodbye, shepherd boy," she said.

"How many times do I have to tell you—"

"I know," she interjected, giving him a rare smile. "But better, perhaps, if you were," she offered.

◆　◆　◆

PIERRE AWAKENED WITH A START, covered in perspiration. He had overslept and the bed next to him was empty. Beatrice was gone. The foul odor of soot from the night before was still strong in the air, and he thought for a moment he was still asleep, dreaming of the big house people to which the old woman in Lausanne had referred. By the time he got to the kitchen, the smell of fried bacon had already gone stale. Georgie still sat at the table, finishing off a bread crust, but everyone else was gone. Except for Georgie's plate, the dirty dishes had already been washed and dried and put away.

"Where's your mother?" Pierre said.

"Aw, she and Jean got to talking, and Ma thought she'd better pay Catharine a visit."

"Is something wrong?"

"How should I know? You know how Jean is lately—always worrying about things. Ma said she had planned to go on over anyway and help take care of the baby."

"And where's Jean?"

Georgie gave his father a look of exasperation.

"You can't expect me to know everything," he said.

Pierre gave his son a grudging nod. There'd been a time when Pierre knew where every member of his family was and exactly what they were doing. That had all changed. Andrew was his own man, now, running the sawmill, and Pierre had no doubt that Jean would leave the farm at the first good opportunity. Catharine was married and living somewhere else, and even Beatrice had gone off without telling him where she was headed. His world seemed to be unraveling. Still vexed by the persistent smell of smoke, he didn't know whether to sit down and have a cup of coffee, follow after his wife, or work at one of the many chores that always needed to be done. It was very perplexing to a man who was used to putting one foot in front of the other in a confident manner.

CHAPTER

TWENTY-SIX

————————●————————

The château was not very far away, and if she were a bird, Beatrice could have been there in no time. But a horse-drawn wagon is a slow conveyance. The horse had to take its time and the wagon had to creak along. A body had to sit there until she got tired of the wooden bench, not to mention that the road was anything but a straight line. Magdalena seemed agitated, and Beatrice had to tell her to settle down. But the girl wouldn't listen, of course. She rocked her body back and forth on the bench as if something inside of her was busting to get out. The look she gave her mother was a cry for help. Her face was flushed, her eyes glassy.

"Whatever's the matter with you?" Beatrice said.

"I'm hot!" the girl complained.

"Are you getting sick?" Beatrice paused the wagon to feel her daughter's forehead. "My goodness, you're burning up, child!" she exclaimed.

The suddenness of Magdalena's condition alarmed Beatrice, who took fevers seriously, and she decided to hasten on to the château, where she could get a cold compress on the girl's forehead and maybe even get her down for a nap. But something was not right, and it had nothing to do with Magdalena. The air had a foul, sooty smell, and when she crested a small rise, she could suddenly see why.

The château was in ruins. A night's steady rain had put out most of the fire, but part of the roof had caved in and tendrils of black smoke still rose from the ashes. Nothing could have survived a fire like that. Magdalena covered her eyes with her hands, letting out a howl, and Beatrice clutched at her, instinctively, pulling the girl hard against her bigger, sheltering body.

◆ ◆ ◆

WHEN BEATRICE PULLED INTO THE farm, Pierre knew that something had to be wrong. She got down from the wagon and hoisted Magdalena into her arms, which she rarely did. Pierre was down at the feed shed, and his legs started to move. He ran. Beatrice hustled Magdalena into the house, with Pierre close on her heels.

"What is it?" he said.

Beatrice shifted Magdalena's weight onto one arm. With her opposite hand, she covered the girl's ear. The face she turned to her husband was bone-white.

"It's the château," she said.

"What's wrong?" Pierre demanded.

"It's the worst," she said, and Pierre spun on his heel. He didn't need to hear more. Suddenly, it all made sense—the smell of smoke over the past day and night, the memories it had evoked of burned homes and lives in ruin. He knew without being told that it had happened all over again, that the past had not been content to rest in peace and was as alive and malicious as ever.

The enormity of what he saw when he got to the château overwhelmed him. The outer walls of the structure still held, but the fire had blackened them and some of the beams that had held up the second story had fallen crosswise and still smoldered. The ashes radiated heat, and he raised a hand to shield his face. He had a desperate hope that Catharine had fled the house with the baby and taken refuge in the barn. But the barn proved empty, as he knew, truly, it would be. Catharine was nowhere in sight. Returning to the smoldering ruins, he stood in the blackened hole in the wall that had once been the front door, shielding his face. He pressed against the heat and it pressed back, and all he could do was wait.

◆ ◆ ◆

THE NEXT SEVERAL DAYS SEEMED to fall into the void the tragedy had opened up. As soon as the ashes cooled, Pierre searched for his daughter and grandson, wearing a handkerchief over his mouth as he worked his way through the blackened mounds, poking with the handle of a pitchfork, probing to find what he knew he must. The house had burned unevenly, with some of the interior reduced to a powder, while other parts were charred but not completely burned. In a corner of what had been the great room, he found the bodies, and the grim story unfolded. Firewood had been piled on top of them and some of the wood had not fully burned. Catharine's clothes lay in a blackened mound a short distance from her body, and when Pierre moved on to the baby, he found that the little skull had been . . . He had to turn away. When he regained control of himself, he turned back and continued the task at hand, carefully removing the charred pieces of firewood and any ash that did not belong to his daughter and her baby. It was clear in his mind that these deaths had not been caused by the fire, which was a small but bitter consolation.

The sheriff was down with the grippe and unavailable for the time. But the doctor went with Pierre to the château and witnessed the circumstances surrounding the deaths. He examined the bodies. The cold-blooded assault upon a mother and her baby, followed by the willful desecration of their bodies, was nigh unto unthinkable, even by frontier standards, and even a man as hardened as the doctor was shaken. The proclamation of a reward of fifty pounds was issued, which was more than enough money for a man to buy a farm. Meanwhile, Georgie rode to Philadelphia to notify Lawrence. He was sixteen by this time and determined to do his part. Pierre gave him the roan.

Three days later, the youth returned to the farm, nearly falling out of the saddle with fatigue. Pierre and his two oldest sons were in the smithy, which had been turned into a morgue. A single coffin lay across two wooden trusses.

"It was no good," Georgie said. "I went to the brewery, but Lawrence wasn't there anymore. No one could find him. They said he sold the brewery and no one knew where he was. I told them what had happened so that they could let him know, and got back here as quick as I could. I didn't know what else to do." He gave his father an abject look, as if fearing he had done wrong. "I could've gotten home quicker, but was afraid I'd kill the horse," he added, his voice cracking. His eyes looked wild, his weary face melting around them.

Normally, Pierre would have comforted his son, telling him he had done his best and thanking him for the extraordinary effort. But Pierre was not himself. The void that had opened yawned bigger. A hand seemed to come out of it and grasp Pierre's heart. The savagery of the murders bred a savage response, and he ached to visit his pain on the person who had so unspeakably wronged his daughter and grandbaby, his namesake, part of the living soul of his life.

"We've waited long enough," Jean said.

"Waited for what?" said another voice. It was the minister of the Reformed Church in Watertown, who had just come from the house, where he had been comforting Beatrice. There was no room for him in the smithy and he stood out in the sun, holding his straw hat by the brim. The man's face was red and damp, his wispy hair sticking to his temples. "All we know is that a crime has taken place. As for who might have done it, only God knows the answer to that."

"*Crimes*," Jean said.

"What?" the minister said, blinking.

"You said crime, as if there was only one. And we do know who committed them. There is no doubt whatsoever."

"We don't know anything for sure. I mean, are we so positive about what happened and who did it that we would take the law into our own hands?" the minister said. He turned to Pierre, as if appealing to a higher and more benevolent authority. "Mr. Laux, sir, if you're thinking what I fear you are, let's talk about it. Let us pray on it, please. Vengeance is mine, sayeth the Lord. The Bible is very firm and unequivocal on this. If Catharine and the baby were indeed intentionally harmed—God forbid—you cannot take it upon yourself to avenge them. That won't make it right and it won't bring them back. Let's talk about it and pray on it, please—I beg of you."

But if he expected understanding from Pierre, he was very wrong.

"This is a family matter," Pierre said, coldly.

"What about Mr. Kraymer, the poor woman's husband? He will want a voice. Catharine was his wife. Peter was his child. We must wait for him to return."

"To hell with him," Jean said, in a heat. "I warned him about McDonall. If he'd've done as he promised and fired the man like he said he would, none of this would have happened. This is all his fault!"

"No, no," the minister said, shaking his head. "I can't believe you really think that."

"I agree with Jean," Andrew said. "We've waited long enough and we're running out of time. Stupid as he is, McDonall is probably hiding out where he lives, like a groundhog in its hole. But he won't stay there forever. Sooner or later, he'll realize that we're on to him. If he takes off, we might never be able to find him."

"This is a job for the sheriff," the minister pleaded. "As a man of God, I have to counsel you to think this through. Put your family first and think of what God can do for us. Do you know why he is willing to pursue vengeance on our behalf? It's because the burden is just too terrible, and he is willing to lift that burden from our shoulders. Vengeance is a poison that kills the soul. In his infinite wisdom, God knows this. Let him do the lifting for you!"

But the minister's words came to nothing. Pierre could not even hear them. They were like the rustling of leaves, caught in a wind that carried them away.

"We will leave in the morning," Pierre said.

He stood with his hands on the coffin, and one by one, his sons joined him, placing their palms on the smooth surface of the wood. The minister still gripped his hat in front of the smithy. His face had reddened and he wobbled, as if not knowing whether to join the Lauxes or keep a discreet distance. Finally, he lowered his head and moved his lips in prayer.

TWENTY-SEVEN

The following morning, the horsemen left at dawn. Concerned that McDonall might make an escape, they had put off the burial, and the coffin still sat in the smithy, awaiting their return. Beatrice was in her bedroom and refused to come out. She said the men could cook their own breakfasts for once and should just leave her alone. Little Magdalena went into her mother's room and lay down next to her, and at first, Beatrice ignored the child, as if afraid that acknowledging her would become a road to even more hurt. But then she opened the blanket and the girl crawled in, and they huddled together in each other's warmth.

Pierre respected his wife's seclusion, though he struggled to tiptoe around her suffering when he, himself, was in so much pain. But he had what she lacked, just then, which was a sense of purpose. She had pointed this out, saying that men had it easy. They had the brute force to flatter themselves with reprisal, she said, whereas she, on the other hand, had nothing, and he was willing to allow that maybe she was correct in this. But he was not in his right mind, in any case, and couldn't think very clearly about much of anything. The fact that his daughter and grandson were dead and that the monster who had killed them still lived was more than he could bear. The fact that the beast still breathed struck him as an abomination.

McDonall was known to live near a town called Kinderville, and this was where Pierre and his sons headed. The road wound through thin, rocky soil, filled with thistle and briar. They passed houses with the mortar leaking from the stones and barns with buckling roofs. Fence rails were bowed like the spines of swaybacked horses and some had collapsed. Pastures were spotty, and fields of corn looked yellow and spindly, with scattered growth separated by bald patches of bleached soil.

On a day when a cloud would have been welcomed—any cloud, even one of the dark anvils that sometimes do more mischief than good—the sky was the palest blue, with a hard sun beating down. The riders rode at a steady pace, reins held stiffly in their hands. Pierre's roan had not yet recovered from the ride to Philadelphia, and he rode one of his draft horses, the tan with the white mane like a badly frayed carpet. The cavernous nostrils sucked in air, and the horse's powerful muscles bunched and slackened as the massive hooves drove against the ground. Jean rode on Pierre's right, his musket crooked in his arm. Andrew and Georgie followed off to Pierre's left, Andrew with his musket and Georgie with a pistol tucked in his belt.

The town of Kinderville had a dry goods store and a livery stable, an old inn with an overgrown, weedy lawn, and a scattering of houses. Pierre swung down from his mount and tied off the reins at the rail in front of the store. His sons climbed down, too, and followed him into the gloom, which smelled of lamp oil and grease. A couple of shovels leaned against one of the walls. A folded pair of work pants, covered with dust, lay on an otherwise vacant shelf and a pair of cowhide work boots sat on the floor. The counter had an empty jar that might have held candy at one time.

"What can I do for you?" the man behind the counter said, suspiciously. He had a round face with gray, wiry hair, and an old linen shirt open at the collar.

Pierre motioned for Andrew to do the talking.

"We're looking for somebody," the youth said.

The shopkeeper's eyes narrowed, moving from Andrew's grim demeanor to Pierre, who stood back and watched. The shopkeeper's tongue crept out of his mouth and he moistened his lips. He made a pass at a cloud of flies hovering in the air above the counter, but they avoided his hand with ease and resumed their hovering pattern.

"I don't believe I know you," the shopkeeper said. His glance slid to the boys and the weapons they carried. "Most folks hereabouts leave their guns out on the porch, on those rare occasions they carry them at all. Otherwise, a body might think you're here on unpleasant business."

"We're looking for a man named McDonall on account of a woman that he killed," Jean said, from where he stood at the end of the counter, closest to the door.

The shopkeeper's eyes widened.

"Oh, I wouldn't know anything about that," he said, shaking his head. "Seems to me I did hear of some trouble over by Watertown. Something about an accident. A fire caused by lightning that burned some rich man's castle. But that's all, I swear. I didn't hear about anybody being killed."

"He's lying," Jean said, turning to his father in disgust.

"Just point us to where he lives and we'll be on our way," Andrew said.

The shopkeeper blew out a breath of air, puffing his cheeks.

"I don't know . . ." he said, shaking his head. "We kind of look after each other around here. I don't know exactly who you are and what proof you have that McDonall did anything. I can't just be pointing out where he lives. I'm sure you understand. If there was a fire, well, who knows what caused it? Could've been lightning, like I said. A man living here lost a barn that way."

"He's wasting our time," Jean said.

Andrew glared at the shopkeeper.

"If we get to his house and he's gone, we'll have you to blame, and we'll be back to hold you to account."

"Look, if you're so convinced it was McDonall who did the wrong, then you should let the sheriff know," the shopkeeper said, his voice getting scratchy. "That's his business, not yours or mine. I don't know about Watertown or wherever you're from, but we have laws around here. When there's a problem, we don't just take matters into our own hands."

"He killed my sister and her little baby," Georgie said, his hand rising to the butt of his pistol.

"A baby?" the shopkeeper said.

He looked from one hardened face to the next and then finally addressed Georgie.

"I'm sorry, son, I truly am. I don't know what else to say."

"He's not your son," Pierre said.

It was the first time Pierre had spoken and it had an effect.

"What?"

"You called this boy 'son,' and he's not your son. He's no part of you whatsoever."

"Well, yeah, I know. I didn't mean to imply . . . All I meant was—"

"We only want one thing from you, and then you can go back to whatever it is you do around here," Pierre said. "Now, we're going to ask you once again where McDonall lives, and you would be wise to tell us."

The shopkeeper moved his tongue around and around his lips, his eyes darting. Pierre's regard of him was cold and steady, and the shopkeeper wobbled. Finally, he stiffened and walked out onto the porch, where he turned to cast a reproachful look at his tormenters, before raising a hand to point.

"I still think you should talk to the sheriff," he said, as the others climbed into their saddles. "Keeping the peace is his job. If we had to fight our own battles, we would be at each other's throats every day. If you had to carry a gun to keep the peace, there would be no peace. Somebody who wanted what you had would just shoot you in the back and take what's yours."

"You mean someone like McDonall?" Andrew said.

"That's for a jury to decide," the shopkeeper said, shaking his head doggedly.

But Andrew had already wheeled his horse around and heeled it to a trot. Pierre and his other two sons followed. The shopkeeper retreated to the shelter of his store and closed the door, where he then stood looking out through the filmed glass.

"I could've shot him easy," Georgie said. He sat in his saddle, shivering as if cold.

Pierre gave him a sharp look but said nothing.

◆　◆　◆

THE ROAD WENT OUT OF town and up through a stand of birch, and that's where they found the house. It was a cabin made of notched logs, with birch poles laid down as a roof. A rock chimney jutted from the roof's far end and the air smelled of creosote. A window at the front of the cabin was shuttered and the door was closed.

"Looks like maybe he was expecting us," Jean commented.

"He'd be pretty stupid to think we wouldn't come after him," Andrew said.

Georgie just sat holding onto the saddle horn, leaning forward as if ill.

"You boys wait here," Pierre said. He urged his horse forward. Stopping some distance from the house, he dismounted. After several seconds with nothing happening, he slowly approached, scouting the side of the cabin for gaps in the mortar through which a person on the inside could fire a weapon. Then, he rapped his knuckles against the wooden door. When no one responded, he used the hammer end of his fist.

"What do you want?" the thin, muffled voice of a woman said from the inside.

"I'm looking for a man named McDonall."

"Go away."

"Is he there with you?"

"He's not here. Now go away or I'll turn you in to the sheriff."

"Open the door," Pierre demanded.

"I have a gun and I'll shoot if I have to."

Pierre stepped back, eyeing the door and the frame.

"I've got children in here!" The woman's voice rose to a wail.

Jean had come up behind his father and lashed out with his foot in a fit of disgust. The door shuddered in its frame and the woman inside screamed. Jean kicked again, and the end of one of the door's boards jarred loose, leaving a gap big enough to stick a hand through. Pierre exchanged a look with his son, then gave a shout, and Andrew fetched a rope from one of the horses. Setting about the task with grim determination, Pierre fed one end in through the gap and out through a space between the doorjamb and the abutting log wall. Knotting the rope, he tied the other end to the saddle of his horse and then, after making sure his sons were out of the way, he urged the horse to take a step backward. The rope tightened. The horse took another step and the doorframe cracked loudly as it was wrenched from the wall in a cloud of dust and caulking.

Pierre stood aside, waiting for the dust to settle. Spots and slanting lines of mote-filled sunlight showed among the birch poles of the ceiling, but the inside of the cabin was so dark he struggled to make anything out. There was a table and a fireplace with a slab of stone for a hearth, and as his eyes adjusted to the gloom, he saw some iron traps hanging on one of the walls. Then he saw the woman, huddled on an animal skin draped over a pile of hay. A small child clung to each of her thighs and a third hunkered between her legs. She sat with her head down and her arms clutching as many of her children as she could hold, clutching and sobbing.

Pierre did not see any gun and he ignored her, striding through the gloomy cabin and kicking open a closed door that led to another room. The room was hardly bigger than the four-post pine bed it held. Yanking up on one of these posts, Pierre heaved the bed against the wall, revealing a heavyset man lying sprawled on his back, pointing a pistol at Pierre's belly. The man had a hideous visage, with a deep gash on his forehead, where the skin had been mashed and grown inflamed. The wound extended to his eye, which had swollen shut, and the opposite cheek bore four scratches. He pulled the trigger, and the pistol's flint clacked as it struck the steel. The flint did not spark and the pistol did not fire. Pierre grabbed the pistol by the barrel and threw it against the far wall. Reaching down, he grabbed the man by the boot and dragged him toward the bedroom door. The man kicked wildly with his other foot, and Pierre ignored the blows. Then the man braced his foot against the door jamb and Pierre wrenched with all of his strength, yanking him through.

The man shrieked. "You broke my leg!"

Memory can be a fluid thing and Pierre could never be quite sure what happened next. He remembered dragging McDonall through the house and out through the hole that had been the front door. Once outside, he saw the yearning look in Jean's eyes as he gazed upon the man who had killed his sister. The look didn't quite register with Pierre at the time, but came back to haunt him later, the look of a man on the verge of becoming someone neither father nor son would have recognized. He remembered Andrew looping the rope around McDonall's boot and using the horse to drag the man across the clearing, where Andrew then tied him to a tree. And he remembered Georgie, sitting off to the side on one of the fallen birch logs, his elbows on his knees, forehead pressed into his palms, with his fingers spread up through his hair.

"I didn't do nothin'," McDonall pleaded in terror. "The fire started all by itself, I swear. I swear it on my wife and children!"

Pierre stood in front of the captive, his head bowed, rubbing his forefinger against his brow. He was not aware of breathing. Every bit of his awareness wanted to crush every bit of life from the man in front of him. But something was wrong. His certainty had begun to wane. Now that McDonall was completely at his mercy, he wasn't entirely sure what he wanted to do. His rage was a living thing. It had driven him to the brink of committing an act that would have defined him and his family for the rest of their lives, and it was only then that his truer nature finally emerged.

"Stop," he said, his forehead resting in one hand while he raised the other in the air. "Wait," he said to his children.

But the kind of rage he'd had does not just wither and die. It left him and went into Georgie, who lurched up from the birch log and staggered like a man possessed. Yanking his pistol from his belt, he cocked it, pressed the barrel against McDonall's chest, and pulled the trigger. Pierre knocked the barrel aside just as the gun discharged, and while the powder burned the side of McDonall's face, the ball passed harmlessly by his head. McDonall let out a shrill wail.

"I'm shot!" he cried.

Pierre stood there with his youngest son in his arms. He crushed Georgie to his chest. The youth's body sagged in his arms, and Pierre gripped him tighter. A victim of violence himself, he had almost bequeathed it to his sons. In his haste to seek revenge for his daughter's death, he had almost turned Georgie into a murderer, and the horror of this fact now overwhelmed him.

"I'm sorry," he said, pressing his son's head against his own and whispering hoarsely in his ear. "I'm sorry," he repeated, over and over.

Jean and Andrew exchanged looks. Shocked at their brother's abrupt loss of innocence, their truer natures had the opportunity to emerge as well, and they moved their muskets aside, pointing them in a safe direction, as if suddenly and for the first time aware of their lethal potential. McDonall leaned against his tree, moaning piteously.

Meanwhile, a cart with two men on the bench had appeared on the road from Kinderville, and Pierre turned slowly, heavily, a man now filled with doubts and remorse. As the cart neared, he heard the thudding of the horse's hooves, the snapping and crunching of stones as the iron-rimmed wheels turned, the rumble and squeaks of the cart itself. A heavyset man wearing a battered felt held the reins. Lawrence Kraymer sat next to him, his face ghostly white, his bloodshot eyes filled with disbelief and a pain too terrible to imagine.

TWENTY-EIGHT

The two men got down from the wagon and Lawrence then just stood there, adrift. He gazed at the bound man as if no longer trusting what he saw or how he felt about it, and the sheriff joined him, placing his hand on Lawrence's back. McDonall couldn't face either one of them. His good eye flinched and he had to turn away.

"Looks like someone gave him a good lickin'," the sheriff said, to no one in particular. He turned to Pierre, who stood nearby. "To tell you the truth, I expected worse. Most men, thinking what you did about this here fella, would have gone ahead and killed him. Then I would've had to make a decision about what to do about it. It's serious business, taking the law into your own hands. That's what people like me're for—so men like you don't have to pursue your own dirty work."

Pierre was looking at Lawrence, pitying him and regretting he had not been at the farm upon the poor soul's return. Pierre and his sons had ridden off thinking they had no time to delay. They couldn't have known Lawrence would show up soon after they had left.

"Whatever we did that was wrong, it was all my fault," Pierre said to the sheriff, but still looking at Lawrence and addressing his son-in-law as well.

"Hmmm . . ." the sheriff said, gazing at Georgie, who still leaned against his father, and then turning to take in the other two brothers. Anyone could see that grim business had been afoot. The boys looked chastened. They had come to their senses, but not before discovering what it means to be driven beyond the bounds of reason.

The sheriff turned to Pierre.

"I'm just the sheriff. I'm no judge and I'm certainly no jury. All I have to do is my part and the rest is up to others. My part is to secure someone and put him or her in safekeeping. I can't say that figuring out what happened isn't part of the job, but it's not as big a part as you might think. Figuring out what happened and what to do about it is thankfully something that I don't have to worry about."

He turned, stiffly, to look at McDonall.

"You look a mess," he said.

"Arrest them!" McDonall said, his good eye straining.

The sheriff turned to Jean.

"Untie this man from the tree," he said.

Jean looked to his father, who nodded. Taking his knife from his belt, he circled the tree and cut McDonall loose. McDonall no doubt thought the sheriff was sympathetic to his plight. He crawled toward him, grunting and moaning, but the sheriff placed a boot on his shoulder, holding him at bay.

"That's close enough," the sheriff said. He turned to Pierre. "You caught me at a bad time. Normally, I would have brought a couple of men with me, but my one man was down with the same grippe I have and the other was off somewhere hunting. I doubt this man has any friends, but you never know. People are close in this neck of the woods. They don't much like strangers poking around and I could use a couple of deputies, just to play it safe. I don't suppose you have any recommendations?"

"My boys would serve you well."

The sheriff ran his eyes over them.

"It would be kind of irregular, given their involvement up to this point." He gave it some thought and his mouth twisted with grim humor. Whatever decision he came to, it was good enough for him. "Consider yourselves deputized," he said, giving the boys a solemn nod.

He still had his foot on McDonall's shoulder and looked down at the man, giving him a shove that sent McDonall back onto his hip. He sniffed and turned away in disgust. For a moment, it appeared he might make a comment on the gruesome injuries to McDonall's face. But the swollen gash and scratches were several days old, which boldly bespoke how he might have gotten them, and the sheriff's countenance showed the abhorrence he must have felt.

"Here," he said to Jean and his brothers, holding out a pair of iron handcuffs. "Now that you're deputies, put these on him with his hands behind his back. The length of chain between the cuffs should be easier on his circulation than your rope. We don't want his hands falling off before the jury decides his fate."

"What? I'm innocent!" McDonall cried. "Them's the ones that committed a crime, terrorizing me and my family. Them's the ones should be arrested!"

"Put him in the back of the cart," the sheriff said.

The boys looked at each other to make sure they understood. Jean took the handcuffs and approached McDonall, who crossed his arms and hugged them to his chest. Georgie got on one side of the man and Andrew on the other. They each grabbed an arm at the elbow and tried to straighten them out. Jean grabbed the man's injured leg and raised it up suddenly and the man screamed. Then Jean twisted the leg to make the man roll over on his belly. McDonall held his arms straight out, but the boys managed to swing them behind his back and clip on the cuffs.

The sheriff then gestured to Pierre, taking him to the side for a private talk.

"You okay? You don't look so good."

"Aren't you going to arrest me, too?"

"You should think about your actions and ask yourself if they were right. Probably you should have just let me handle things. Not every fire is murder, you know, and crimes like this are needful of investigation."

He took a breath.

"The truth is, I don't know what happened, in spite of the evidence, and neither do you in the eyes of the law. It's up to a jury to look at what happened, decide who, if anyone, is to blame, and pass judgment. That said, I do have a role to play and no, in answer to your question, I'm not arresting you. A decent woman and her baby died sorry deaths, and that's more than a family should have to bear. I couldn't tell you exactly what happened, like I said, but I've common sense, too, and as far as I'm concerned you are free to go—and go with God, I might add."

"Help me!" McDonall bellowed, from the back of the wagon.

Ignoring the outcries, the sheriff approached Lawrence, holding out his hand.

"You have my sincere condolences," he said. "Nothing can change what was done and I'm sorry. What I can promise is that this man will get a trial and it will be as fair as it can be. I pray there will come a day when you say justice has been served and put your sorrows to rest."

Lawrence just gazed at the hand as if he didn't know what to do with it, and the sheriff nodded, as if he well understood, dropping the hand back to his side. Lawrence's face was drained of color. His eyes looked raw. He said he needed time and that the others should go on without him. At first, no one moved. Then Georgie stepped forward. He handed the reins of his horse to Lawrence.

It was a simple act and yet profound. But Lawrence looked at the boy as if he had never seen him before. Georgie stepped back and Lawrence just stared at the reins that lay across his palm. "Are you sure you don't want to tag along with us" the sheriff said, gently, giving Lawrence the opportunity to change his mind. But Lawrence just stood there, staring at him, and the sheriff finally shrugged and turned aside.

◆　◆　◆

PIERRE HAD A LOT TO think about on the ride back home. He hated to leave Lawrence behind, but there was a gulf between them now, caused not only by tragedy but by Pierre's own thoughtless deeds. There was a new distance with his sons, as well. They had gone through a crisis that affected them all deeply, and in their vulnerable state, he had let them down. They had looked up to him and relied upon him, and he had failed them.

Reining his horse, he turned in the saddle and looked back at Lawrence, still standing in the clearing in front of McDonell's cabin, and Pierre did not know what to do. Not hours earlier, he had been so sure of himself and of what needed to be done. Now he felt like a child again, back in France, waiting for the return of a father he would never see again.

What a man his father had been, when seen from a child's

vantage. He wore silks and fine leathers and had the powerful, erect posture of a chevalier. Traveling with a retinue, he would sweep into the manoir grounds after his long absences and Pierre would find it hard to breathe. Everything changed when his father was home. Manoir life buzzed. In retrospect, the amazing thing to Pierre was the depth of honor and homage his father gave to his wife, Eleanor. Whatever his feelings about her becoming what the French called a Cathar Perfect, or *parfaite*, he always treated her with an astonishing dignity and respect. Pierre had an image of his father kneeling before his mother after a particularly long time away. His mother sat in a chair and his father kneeled before her with his head in her lap, one of her hands lying gently on his head.

Later that same day, his father took him outside the manoir. On the other side of the courtyard was a rock wall that had been built as a defense several hundred years earlier, and Pierre's father led him across the courtyard and through the door in the wall, up a dark, narrow stone staircase. A footpath ran atop the wall, offset from the outer perimeter by several feet, so a body would not be exposed to whomever might be on the ground below, and the seigneur stood there gazing out over the countryside. To the east, the land sloped down and they could see treelines and cultivated fields, lavender that looked like the purple sheets of a bed with the coverlet thrown back, and in the distance, the rooftops of a village.

"Take a good look, son."

Pierre tried to see what his father saw, not quite understanding, waiting for more words.

"This land, the manoir, everything you can see from here. It will all become yours someday," Seigneur du Laux said. "Do you understand me? Do you hear what I'm saying?"

"What will I do with it?" Pierre said.

It was a question that made the seigneur pause, and he gave his son a long, searching look.

"Ah, yes—that's the question, isn't it?" the seigneur said, and while Pierre had felt only confusion and wonder at the time, it all made perfect sense to him now. His father was long gone and the estate was gone with him. Pierre was no longer a child gazing out over the lands he should by rights have inherited. He was a man on the new frontier who had carved out a new life all his own. He had a family that needed his guidance, in spite of his shortcomings, and his father had come through for him, after all, these many years later, a whisper from the past, the voice of reason. Pierre knew what he had to do.

CHAPTER
TWENTY-NINE

———————◆———————

Lawrence sat on a fallen birch log that lay alongside the road, his mind wrapped in a thick, ropey fog. A wagon had appeared, and at first, he thought the sheriff was back to nettle him. When the wagon neared, however, he saw it was a man with a florid face and white hair that winged out in feathery strands, narrow eyes and a long chin covered with white whiskers. His cotton shirt looked a size too big for him. His canvas pants had patches on the knees and he carried his right arm in a sling. Using his one good hand, he pulled the wagon to a stop.

"Seems to be a lot of activity in this neck of the woods of late," the newcomer said. His eyes drifted toward the log cabin not far away, with the hole in the wall and the pile of debris to the side. "A man can go months with nary a soul to goad him, and then come upon all kinds of curious mischief. You wouldn't happen to know what happened yonder, would you?" he said, pointing with his chin.

Lawrence didn't respond. He looked down at his hands—very capable hands that could have come to the aid of a mother and her child, if only he had known. If only he had seen what had apparently been so obvious to everybody else. If only he had done what he had promised to do. The hands wavered and the faces of his wife and child became lost in the fog.

"Say—are you all right?" the stranger said.

When Lawrence didn't answer, the stranger studied him, as if weighing his options. His eyes narrowed, shrewdly.

"A man who doesn't have much to say for himself might be grateful that a man like me came along," he said. "The missus calls me Morris and you can do the same. She might be happy to see you if you cared to stop over for a bit of supper. Unless you have more important things to do, of course."

Morris squinted at the nearby horse.

"That yours?" he said. But he didn't wait for an answer, perhaps accepting the obvious, but just as likely distrusting anything one as questionable as Lawrence had to say. "You can tie it to the wagon and ride on the bench with me, if you'd like."

"Do we know each other?" Lawrence spoke at last.

Morris gave a crooked little smile, showing a set of tea-colored teeth.

"What's to know, here at the edge of the world, where a man could go wanting for the company of a fellow human that he didn't happen to be married to? You're not a criminal, are you?"

"A criminal?"

Morris gave a hissing laugh.

"Rest easy, my friend," he said. "Anybody can see you're a gentleman, and anyway, you wouldn't admit to being a criminal, if you were one. If I can make another point, most criminals have more survival instinct than to sit by the side of the road with night coming on the way it is. Without proper shelter, the wild can put a man down quick."

But Lawrence had taken the man's question seriously and still pondered it. He had come back from Philadelphia with a bill of sale in his pocket, only to find the unimaginable. The blackened château walls still stood, but the roof had caved in, making a pile of rubble, and he ran the horse hard, swinging from the saddle and charging through the debris in search of his wife and child. They had to be safe. He couldn't believe otherwise, and when he had searched the house and barn to no avail, he got back on the horse and whipped it with the tail ends of the reins, heading to the only other place that Catharine and little Peter could be.

When he got to the farm and saw the coffin, he knew the awful truth. At first, he couldn't approach it, as if Catharine's family had taken her back and hidden her from him, and he sat on a three-legged stool at the back of the smithy with his face in his hands. He knew, instinctively, that the coffin contained two bodies, because mother and child were inseparable and the fire had been too extensive. He raised his eyes, hoping to find that the wooden box had disappeared and that he had imagined everything. But it was still there, sitting across two wooden supports, and Lawrence felt out of place. The smithy smelled of perspiration and charcoal, the presence of another man. The unpainted wood of the three walls, with the hook and nail where the leather apron and lantern hung, the bench with its hammer and tongs and other tools laid neatly in a row, the bellows and the immersion bucket where the red-hot irons were plunged. They had nothing to do with him, and he wondered why he had failed to understand this when he first rode onto the farm over two years ago. He should have known better than to insert himself where he didn't belong and a beautiful woman would be alive for it. A child would have remained unborn, perhaps, but would never have suffered so tragic a death because of a father who was too far away to save him.

Standing up and reaching out with his arms, he took a step, but could go no further. His mind slipped. He remembered Beatrice confirming his worst fears, that both Catharine and the baby were in the wooden box in the smithy, but he didn't recall her putting her arms around him and hugging him tight. The sheriff had already been at the farm. He was in the house, with Beatrice, and Lawrence remembered him accompanying her into the smithy. But by then his mind had started playing tricks on him and nothing made much sense anymore. A *criminal*? How would he know—maybe . . .

◆　◆　◆

THE WARDEN HOMESTEAD TURNED OUT to be little more than a log cabin, with its barn and the usual cluster of outbuildings. The pasturage was modest but the fences were well tended. A cornfield had already yellowed, ready for harvest. The table Mrs. Warden set would have been small enough for even two people with any appetites at all. Three meant they all got scant portions.

Mrs. Warden appeared to be one of those people suspicious by nature. She wanted to know who he was, which was a question sensible enough, and Lawrence knew the answer was there, somewhere in the fog. But it eluded him. Mrs. Warden waited on him, but he couldn't answer.

"Well," she said, as if his silence spoke volumes. She glared at him. "My husband is good at picking up strays," she allowed. Her eyes drifted to Morris's arm. "Here we are barely able to feed ourselves and have but a meager fare to offer. And yet we have the corn to harvest. He's hardly got a day's work in him even in the best of times."

Her voice trailed.

"Now, Martha, I'm sure our guest has problems of his own and can't be bothered by ours," Morris said, in an overly solicitous manner, shooting a cagey glance at their guest.

"We'll manage somehow," Mrs. Warden said. "My arm's not broke and I will do what I can."

Lawrence hadn't touched his food. No one had actually asked him a question, but he felt the need to respond.

"I've got nowhere to go . . ." he ventured.

Morris gave his wife a triumphant look.

"There—do you hear that, Mrs. Warden?" he said.

He turned back to face Lawrence with his eyes dancing.

"I knew when I first laid eyes on you that there was something different about you," he said. "I knew you to be a man of substance."

Later, Morris carried the lantern and Mrs. Warden an arm-load of bedding as they ushered him into the barn, and Lawrence lay long into the night with his eyes wide open, waiting, so close to the wild that he could feel its breath upon him. The barn reminded him of something, though he couldn't for the life of him think of what it was. Then the image became clearer. There was another barn in another place, the first barn he had ever slept in. His heart raced, unaccountably. He seemed to recall there was a dragon who lived in the other barn and that it would go out at night, spreading wings of darkness across the sky. In his present state of mind, Lawrence didn't question the existence of such a creature, though he did find it odd that a dragon would find common bedfellows with horses and cows. Then, somewhere off in the dark, a wolf howled, making a long, low sound mournful enough to break a grown man's heart, and Lawrence waited as he lay awake and waited as he dozed, waited long into the creeping chill of dawn.

◆　◆　◆

In the days that followed, Morris drove the horse and wagon, his broken arm clamped against his chest. Martha and Lawrence followed, off to the side, winging the wagon, stripping the ears of corn from their withered stalks, pulling back the yellowed husks and breaking the ears free, tossing them into the wagon. At night, the couple invited him to join them at the kitchen table, but he declined, feeling resolutely unfit for human company. He sat on the porch, where the farm curs hunched over their bowls of scraps. When the dogs finished pressing their pink tongues against the inner curves of the earthenware, they would sit and watch Lawrence with hard, unfriendly eyes, as if resenting the meager portions on his plate and daring him to set the plate aside and relax his vigilance for just one moment. Now and then he would flick them a tidbit, watching them snap it from the air.

On washing day, Martha came for his clothes, exchanging them for a blanket that he wrapped around his frame while his single set of clothes were washed and hung on a piece of rope to dry. When she came back to the barn with the clean, folded clothes in her arms, Martha regarded Lawrence warily.

"I found this in your shirt pocket," she said, holding out a folded piece of paper.

Lawrence took the document and looked down at it.

"It's a bill of sale," Martha said.

Lawrence read the words.

"Is that you?" the woman demanded.

Lawrence shook his head.

"I don't know," he said.

"How can you not know something like that? You either are the Lawrence Kraymer that it says on the paper or you aren't. I just need to know what's going on, that's all."

"So do I," Lawrence said.

Martha grew angry.

"I don't mind givin' out charity, but I'd like to know who I'm giving it to," she said.

Lawrence wished he could be more forthcoming. In fact, some of his memories had started to return. He recalled an old man in a brewer's apron, the smell of yeast, and a boy who was whipped if he didn't work hard enough. But there were other memories that still eluded him, and he wasn't so sure that he wanted to recover these. He had to consider that a criminal might not always care to be reminded of some of the things he had done. It certainly explained why a place to hide could have so much appeal and why he had come to expect so little from the path he now found himself on.

CHAPTER
THIRTY

———————●———————

Lawrence had a hard time shaking off Martha's misgivings. It occurred to him that with the corn harvest ending, she wanted to be rid of him, which made sense, given the Wardens' strained resources. In any case, he folded his blanket and cleaned up his part of the barn, and presented himself at the house to say goodbye. Morris was no fool and gazed at him shrewdly. The old man stood on the porch, struck by the morning sun. His white hair looked like a halo around his rough, red face.

"You have to forgive my wife for a bout of trepidation now and then," he said. "I'm not her first husband, you know, and she has her suspicions of men. Her first husband ran off on her. She thinks it was the Indians that got him when he was out collecting kindling, but I imagine he just had enough. Not everyone can live under the scrutiny of a suspicious person, day in and day out. Be that as it may, I have more work, if you're interested."

Catching Lawrence's eye, Morris stepped down off the porch, paused to get his footing, and then continued around the corner of the house. He limped more than usual, shifting from side to side, as if one leg were much shorter than the other. Behind the house, he gazed solemnly at a pile of hardwood logs lying next to the wood-shed. The shed was open to the front and nearly empty, with scattered woodchips on the earthen floor.

Turning a little to the side, he gave Lawrence a sly look.

"There's a lot of work here, for a man who's up to the task," he said. "This is our winter wood, you know, and we can't burn logs. Someone has to section them and split the rounds into cordwood."

"Your arm is much improved now," Lawrence ventured. Morris no longer wore the sling, though he still held the arm bent protectively against his side.

"Yes, thank God. The bracing is off and I don't need the sling anymore, though I'd gotten kind of used to it and could still want for it, I suppose." He held his arm out and inspected it, wincing as if the sight of it caused him pain. "It's not much good, after such a long rest. Amazing how quickly a limb weakens after falling out of use."

Lawrence looked at the arm and had to admit to himself that it made a puny comparison to the other one. Still, he hesitated. Much as he had nowhere to go, he didn't want to remain in a place where he didn't belong. Sometimes, he thought he heard a woman's voice, speaking in a language he didn't understand. He heard her at night when he was alone in the barn and sometimes in the open places, during quiet moments, such as when a breeze gusted and then got suddenly still.

"What d'you say, pilgrim?" Morris said.

Lawrence opened his fingers and the blanket dropped to the ground.

"You're a crafty old man," he said.

◆　◆　◆

LATER THAT EVENING, MORRIS SHOWED up at the loft carrying a glass jar with a clear liquid in it. He found Lawrence sitting with his back against a wall, his knees drawn up and his hands hanging between them, wrapped in whatever dark thoughts the mysterious man had, and Morris pitied him. He truly felt sorry for the tortured soul. The wild could do a lot to a man, the way Morris saw it, and sometimes it plain stripped someone of his reason. Morris had heard of such cases. They tended to linger somewhere until they wandered on and then you just didn't hear about them anymore.

"Thought maybe you could use a little bit of the Dutch courage, but don't tell the missus on me—it'll be our secret."

While he spoke, he looked around the loft.

"We have to do something about your living arrangements. We'll put you in the granary, where you can have a little more privacy. Not that there's any grain this year to compete for the space. I was under the weather at seeding time and never got the damn stuff planted. Could've been an issue, but the meat cow had twin calves and we can use the second one for trade." He gave a bark of laughter. "Funny how manna from Heaven sometimes comes from the ground up."

Lawrence accepted the jar and sniffed it, putting his nose up to it and then jerking his head back.

"You keeping secrets from your wife?" he said.

"Why, yes, of course," Morris said, adopting a serious tone. He dropped to his knees and then twisted sideways to sit with his back to the wall next to Lawrence. "I know it goes against conventional wisdom and I don't recommend it in all cases, but for me it suits just fine. You see, Mrs. Warden's an unhappy person, and that's the God's truth of it. There's not much I can do except live with it the best I can."

"You don't talk like a farmer," Lawrence observed.

The old man snorted.

"You noticed that, eh? Well, I'm not much of a farmer, as I'm sure Mrs. Warden would be glad to tell you, given half a chance. I was a schoolteacher once, up in Massachusetts. Truth be told, I wasn't a very good one of those, either, but that's what I was and there it is. Then my first wife died, and I didn't know what to do with myself. I wasn't ready to just fade away, if you know what I mean. Probably I should've stayed put in the town where I lived, but I always wanted to live on the edge of things. I can't expect you to know what I mean though I have to allow that you might. I always wanted to live on the frontier—the whole idea of building a domestic life in the wild places, you see. But New England was too cold. And what was so new about it, anyway? Then I heard of this widow who had a farm down in Penn's colony and, well, one thing led to another."

He held the jar at a distance, admiring it, then took a sip. His words had already started to slur.

"What I didn't know at the time was just how unhappy she was. That's the way it is, you know—human nature—to keep our secrets until we are forced to expose them, and her secret is the secret of unhappiness. If she finds any magic or discovers something that has some sparkle, she takes it to heart but very briefly, suspiciously, and then sets about tarnishing and smudging it and making it conform to her unhappy view of things. Soon there is no magic left. There is only what she ever thought there was, which for her is a comfortably unhappy place. I, on the other hand, need a little sparkle, so yes, I do keep secrets, small ones now and then, because if I shared them, she would ruin them for me. There, it's said. You can plainly see how pathetic I am!"

"What's your wife going to say when you walk in drunk?"

Morris looked at him with astonishment.

"Why, she'll blame you, of course."

"Why would she do that?"

"Because it's who she is and the way she thinks. She's got to blame someone for my shortcomings."

"But I'm innocent."

"We're all guilty of something," the old farmer assured him, giving him a knowing look.

"Guilty of what?"

"Human nature!" the farmer exclaimed, delighted with himself.

◆ ◆ ◆

AN EARLY SNOW STARTED TO fall, the flakes coating the logs and driving into the spaces between them, slanting in on a wind that carried them along, driving into Lawrence's eyes and down the collar of the heavy wool shirt Morris had gotten for him on one of his trips away from the farm. He raised the axe in a wide arc and brought the blunt end down with force, and the iron wedge inched into the round of wood on the chopping block in front of him.

He had the sudden odd feeling that he was not alone, and turning around, saw Martha standing behind him, watching. She wore one of her husband's cocked hats pulled down over her ears and a long canvas coat that reached to her knees. The coat was knotted with a belt. She held a basket with the handle hooked over one arm and in the opposite hand a steaming mug of tea.

"You know we can't afford to pay you anything," Martha said.

Lawrence accepted the tea and held the mug with both hands, warming them.

"I don't want your money," he said.

She gave her head a small twist.

"Aye, and I don't understand it, either. Why would someone work as hard as you do and not expect to get anything for it? Morris does seem to have the touch. He's got a real knack for getting people to drop their own chores and do his for him, and everybody knows we got no money. We hardly have enough food to put on the table, and yet we get by. Don't ask me how."

Lawrence raised the mug and blew on the dark liquid.

"Morris says you're a lost soul," the woman said, without malice or sympathy.

It was a statement Lawrence didn't wish to dwell on.

"I told him about the bill of sale I found in your pocket and he scoffed. He said if you were the man named in the bill of sale, he would be working for you and not the other way around. He has this crazy notion that lost souls are lost for a reason and looking for something they'll never find. He seems to think they're doomed to wander."

"Where is he, anyway?" Lawrence asked, trying to change the subject.

"Does it matter?" she said.

Her eyes drifted to the firewood Lawrence had stacked, and she gave her head a small, reluctant shake.

"I have to admit that without you, we'd be struggling to make cordwood day to day," she said. "I imagine I would have had to do most of the splitting myself. We'd have been sawing and splitting all the way through spring, trying to make wood just in time for the burning of it."

But Lawrence was not done talking about Morris.

"I thought I might have a word with your husband," he said.

"Well, you can't, because he went to Kinderville."

Kinderville. The word penetrated Lawrence and curled like a viper.

"He heard news there's a trial over in the next county, and you know Morris—or you should by now—when it comes to news like that. He was so excited he came near to hopping out of his skin. You would've known if you'd had supper with us, but you seem to prefer the company of the dogs on the porch. If you're going to eat our food, I don't know why you won't join us at the table."

"A trial?" Lawrence said, cautiously.

He felt the snake moving, sliding and recoiling.

"One of our more good-for-nothing neighbors went and burned some rich man's house down with a woman in it—the rich man's wife, her and her baby. Everybody's talking about it. They say the sheriff and his deputies dragged the murderer out of his house, right past his wife and children. Can you imagine that? The murderer's name is McDonall and I've never met his wife—some people just stay in their houses, you know. But I met McDonall a time or two. He isn't much to look at, but who'd've thought he'd turn out to be a murderer?"

She grimaced as she mulled the thought over.

"They say the house that burned was a castle. Can you imagine that? I should think that's just asking for it, if you want to know my thoughts on the matter. A castle's got no business in the colonies. That's what we came away from and left behind us—that kind of thing. Morris seems to think it was some kind of hubris, whatever that is. Me, I don't care what you say. It's just wrong. Anybody building a castle around here is just asking to get what's coming to 'im."

Lawrence's head had started to spin. Some of the fog that had plagued him these past several weeks began to thin.

"Are you all right?" Martha said.

His knees went weak, and he sat down on the chopping block. His head and shoulders sagged. He assumed Martha's prying eyes were those of accusation, as if whatever crime he had committed had left a brand on him that she was in the process of ferreting out, and he wished she would look someplace else.

◆   ◆   ◆

OVER THE COURSE OF THE next several days, more of Lawrence's memories returned. While some things still remained vague, he accepted that he must indeed be the man who had owned the brewery that Martha had spoken of. He remembered riding out of the city thinking he was finally done with the business at last and that a new and exciting life lay ahead of him. But why was he leaving, and where was he going? He exhaled in frustration.

"You know, there was a time in the Old Country when people— good people and smart people, not fools, mind you—thought the Earth was flat," Morris said. The two men sat in the granary, which was a small room adjoining the loft, and Morris looked particularly small and frail in the lamplight. A checkers board sat on a little wooden table between them. Outside, the night was as deep and dark as swamp water.

Morris moved a checker forward, paused, and then moved it back, speaking as if thinking out loud. "The reason they thought what they did had nothing to do with intelligence, nor even ignorance, per se. It was because of the natural limitations of observation."

Lawrence's head hurt, and he wished the old farmer would hold his tongue.

"Imagine, if you will, looking out at the ocean and all you see is water, and then, in the distance, a line that looks like the edge of the world. Is it any wonder they thought what they did?"

"You think too much about things," Lawrence said.

"Do I?" Morris said, with a chuckle. "Perhaps you're right. But give it some thought of your own. Put yourself in their position."

"Any sailor could have told them otherwise," Lawrence said, focusing on the playing board and making a move. He jumped one of his checkers over one of Morris's.

"Ah, but you see, the sailors stayed close to land," Morris said. "They didn't go out where the edge was. They liked to stay within sight of the shoreline."

"So what you're saying is that someone had to be either brave or foolish for us to get to where we are now," Lawrence said, testily.

"Good point, but no, not exactly." Morris raised a finger and gave it a wag for emphasis. "I'm making an analogy, of sorts, to our present situation here on the edge of the wild. When you get to the edge of things and all you can see is trees, you might be tempted to think that's all there is and that it goes on forever, until you either reached the edge and fell off of it or else found something unexpected. You'd be tempted to think there was just wildness and savagery out there, and you might be wrong on two counts. First of all, the point needs to be made that there's mother's milk in every wigwam. And second?" He paused, leaning forward a little. "The thing that we fear—and rightly so—is already with us. It's right here."

He tapped a long, bony finger on his chest.

"So, what you're really talking about is the trial," Lawrence said.

"Exactly right," Morris said, appreciatively. "I wish my students had been half as quick as you, my friend. Maybe I'd still be teaching."

He gave his hissing laugh.

"You see, a man gets to thinking, doesn't he?" Morris persisted. "Why would someone like McDonall, who had a wife and children to provide for, why would he do what he did? I heard that when they hanged him, they put a sack over his head and all he did was blubber and sob inside the bag. They tried to wait for him to quiet down, because who wants to hang someone while they're blubbering? But he wouldn't stop and they finally went and hanged him anyway. He begged for mercy up until the moment the rope cut him short."

"They hanged him?"

"That they did and for good reason. What he did was an act of wildness and savagery at its worst, to the point I was making a minute ago." The finger snaked up again and wagged forward and back. "But to my other point, that wildness and savagery are part of human nature, who would have thought what happened next?"

Lawrence couldn't get the hanged man out of his mind. He imagined the bulk of him suspended from the end of a rope and wanted to think the man had it coming. But Lawrence wasn't sure. He wasn't sure of anything. The world was full of heart-break, and if everyone got what was coming to them, who would be left unscathed?

"Are you interested in playing checkers or not?" he said, weakly, trying fend off the images that seemed to feint and jab.

"Oh, bugger the checkers. I'm talking about something import-ant. The very family belonging to the woman and the child that were murdered, the very ones McDonall so grievously wronged, what do they do? By rights, they were entitled to a full plate of revenge, but what do they do? They buy McDonall's widow's farm and let her live there rent-free, that's what," Morris said, slapping the table with the palm of his hand in an unbridled bout of enthu-siasm and shaking his head in wonder.

Lawrence just stared at him. He knew it wouldn't be long now. His mind was slowly settling, turning, and moving in on him. He saw images of a large house, maybe even the one Mrs. Warden had called a castle, and rather than make him happy, the images filled him with dread.

◆　◆　◆

LAWRENCE PACED THE GRANARY FLOOR, like an animal in a cage, at the mercy of his grandfather. The old man had come back from the grave with a triumphant roar, sneering at him and reminding him that he was a bastard, that the brewery had never been his to begin with, and that all of his success changed nothing. That having been born a bastard, that was his lot. It was all he would ever be.

Outside, the weather was changing, as if indecision was endemic to existence, and Lawrence paused at the granary window, where the snowflakes of a sudden spring blizzard flattened against the glass. From his vantage point, he could see the farmhouse far below, where he watched a stranger dismount from a big roan and stand at the gate with his hat pulled low and his collar up, hunching against the storm. The stranger seemed familiar, something about him, something Lawrence couldn't put his finger on.

Morris walked out of the farmhouse, pulling on a coat as he limped toward the gate where the man waited. The men talked. Then Morris lowered his head and turned it to the side, as if uttering an oath. Raising a hand, he pointed toward the barn— seemed to point to the very window where Lawrence stood— and the visitor turned to face in his direction. The man was Pierre Laux. He seemed to see right through the granary window, peering straight into Lawrence's eyes and through them, into his heart.

The last pieces of memory fell into place, and Lawrence stumbled as he backed away from the pane. Grabbing his coat, he shoved his arms into the sleeves. Bending down, he grabbed his blanket from the bed and ran through the granary door and toward the outer door of the loft. The snow struck him in the face and thickened around him, coming down in a sudden squall and filling his tracks as he ran. Driven by shame and horror, he ran, bending his knees and driving his feet through the snow. The flurries hit him in the face and collected in his beard, and he ran until he was in the woods and continued to run as the woods deepened, zigzagging his way around deadfalls and skipping over rocks and rotting logs.

He ran until he hit a road and then stopped, wondering which road it was and where it might lead. The snow swept around him in a swirling curtain, and he knew that he stood on a road only because the ground was flat and there were shouldering trees on each side that were barely visible through the storm. Roads in the settlements were relatively few, and Lawrence stood still, listening for sounds of pursuit behind him and trying to get his bearings.

That was when the first horse loomed out of the swirling curtain. The rider wore a long buffalo robe that had been fashioned into a coat. He hunched in the saddle, holding onto a length of rope. A boy of about ten followed the horse, the rope tied around his neck. Lawrence could see he was a native boy and that as the rope jerked him along, he plodded barefooted in the springtime snow.

A red rage filled Lawrence and he let out a roar, standing to his full height and throwing his hands up into the air. The horse snorted and shied, rearing, and the man in the buffalo coat swore loudly, releasing the rope and gripping the saddle horn with one hand while the other flailed. The horse bucked and the man's big body left the saddle and hit the ground hard. He landed on his head and did not move.

Lawrence grabbed the horse's bridle and steadied the animal as another horse came charging out of the wall of falling snow. The rider yanked on the reins and pulled the horse up hard, spinning it around in the clumsy, rough manner of a man used to beating an animal to make it cooperate. The man spun around again, the horse bucking and nearly sitting back on its haunches, the man's head jerking one way and then the other as he tried to ascertain what had happened, and then, seeing his fallen comrade, he spun the horse a third time and drove it off the road and through the trees, branches snapping and breaking under the horse's pounding hooves.

It didn't occur to Lawrence to ride the fallen man's horse, perhaps because the beast seemed too forceful a conveyance for a man who had nowhere to go. In any case, he just stood there, holding onto the bridle. The fallen man lay in a mound on the ground, the snow already covering the shaggy hair of his coat. The native boy was nowhere to be found.

Still holding the horse's bridle, Lawrence began to walk. The snow was in his eyes and his ears, down his neck, and at some point, he no longer held the bridle. The horse was gone and Lawrence continued to put one foot in front of the other, his head down and shoulders hunched. The snow deepened and Lawrence's legs fatigued. He had to pull his feet up before placing them down again.

His nose and ears numbed, and as his body tired, he started to feel sluggish and warm. He saw a deadfall alongside the road and sought shelter next to the fallen trunk, tucking his feet and wrapping the blanket around his legs. He heard a woman's voice in his ear, telling him he shouldn't stop, not now. It was the voice of Catharine, the mother of his child, and he wanted to die. Realizing what he had had and what he had lost, and the role he, himself, had played, he couldn't bear the thought of living. His wet clothes chilled his body. Icy fingers crept down his neck as the snow that matted his head melted past the collar of his coat, and his befuddled mind railed that freezing to death was far better than he deserved.

THIRTY-ONE

He awoke feeling very cold, his clothing damp and heavy on him, his arms and legs wooden and numb. A boy crouched in front of him, peering intently into his eyes. The boy had a red rope burn around his neck. Behind him stood several men, carrying muskets and wearing face paint, feathers in their crested hair. The boy pushed at Lawrence's chest with his finger and said something, the sounds stabbing at the air. He turned and said something over his shoulder to the men who stood behind him.

Standing back, the boy pointed at Lawrence and said, "*Generââ.*"

The men glanced at each other solemnly, then two of them stepped around the boy and helped Lawrence to his feet. They all turned and started to move, slow enough that Lawrence could keep up but fast enough to cover ground quickly. The snow had slowed to an occasional flurry and there were patches of blue sky. Already, the snow had started to melt, turning soft and slippery underfoot. Lawrence had trouble making his legs work and the first few steps sent jolts of pain up into his thighs. But as the group moved through the woods, he loosened up and walked with a freer gait.

One of the men wore a buffalo coat, and Lawrence recalled the man who had fallen from his horse back in the storm. It occurred to him that the natives had most likely been in pursuit of the men who had abducted one of their children, and that the previous owner of the buffalo coat no longer had any need of it. The boy, who had been barefooted previously, now wore a pair of moccasins that laced halfway up his legs. He also wore a deerskin tunic that belted at the waist and nearly dragged on the ground. Over the tunic, he wore a vest of thick brown fur.

They traveled for three days and arrived at a palisade that had bark longhouses inside. The boy ran on ahead and was greeted by a group of children. He pointed back toward Lawrence and then rose high up on the balls of his feet, raising his hands over his head in the threatening manner of a bear, and the children sucked in their breaths, looking at Lawrence with rounded eyes. One of them ran up to Lawrence and pressed a finger against Lawrence's leg, then ran off shrieking, and the others jostled each other in excitement.

The men walked to one of the longhouses and motioned for Lawrence to wait outside. One of the men went in while the others waited with Lawrence, and after what seemed a long time, the man came back out, accompanied by a very old man with a long face and a long nose, a nest of wrinkles around his eyes and mouth. The man wore a pale deerskin robe and walked with a staff.

He watched Lawrence closely, listening to what the men had to say. The boy with the rope burn kept his distance, but sidled as close as he dared, turning sideways the best to hear. The men spoke without emotion, nodding toward the boy and then nodding toward Lawrence, and one of the men performed the same pantomime as the boy had earlier, standing tall and raising his hands above his head, though without the enthusiastic abandon the boy had shown. Pointing at Lawrence, he uttered the same word the boy had earlier used. "Generââ," he said and the old man listened.

Then the old man spoke, and did so at length, his words breaking the air like the wingbeats of little birds. Lawrence could not understand what was being said, but listened quietly, and the old man went on and on, his words taking brief flight. When he had finished at last, he turned around and shuffled back into the long-house, and the other men took this as their sign to disperse. They simply drifted apart, leaving Lawrence standing alone.

Then one of the men turned around and came back, gesturing for Lawrence to accompany him, and Lawrence followed him into one of the longhouses, where the smoke from the fires burned his eyes and made his lungs itch. The longhouse was divided into partitions by screens made of deerskins. Each partition had its cooking fire, and the women who crouched in front of these fires stopped what they were doing to watch Lawrence as he passed. The younger men tried to appear uninterested, but the older ones showed as much curiosity as the women, turning their faces toward him and watching intently. Lawrence's host took him to one of the partitions, where a woman tended a small metal pot that hung from a tripod. She looked up at Lawrence and sucked in her breath, then looked at the man, who nodded reassurance. A bearskin rug lay on the floor, and the man pointed toward it and gestured kindly for Lawrence to sit down.

Much conversation ensued, none of which Lawrence understood. The woman served him a delicious broth in a wooden bowl, and at night, the man and woman slept on one side of a partition while Lawrence slept on the other. The boy with the rope burn on his neck curled up at Lawrence's feet, and the night passed long and deep, punctuated by snores from the other partitions and the popping of fireplace embers as they cooled, the hoot of an owl, and the occasional yap of an encampment dog. The night rolled on like a silent river, a deep and forceful current that flowed as smoothly as glass, and Lawrence sank deep into its waters, carried along, holding his breath as long as he could and then giving in, drawing in the silent darkness and pushing it back out again.

Now that his memories had returned, sleep was the only escape he had left from the sharp teeth of reality, and the next time he fell on his side and curled into oblivion, he didn't want to wake ever again. The woman prepared food for him, and he heard her voice as a distant thing, directing questions at him. The man's voice was silent but the boy prodded him with a constant string of sounds, words ending on rising notes that he knew deserved a response, if only he could figure out what was being asked. The days turned into weeks and all he wanted to do was sleep, and then, at last, the nightmares sniffed him out and even his sleep failed to protect him. The nightmares set upon him like a pack of dogs. A mob of human misfits chased him, grasping at him with bony fingers, and he took refuge in a rowboat and pulled hard on the oars, trying to escape. He rowed as hard as he could out toward the edge of the world, and the horde followed in wooden ships, flanking him, bearing down on him, until he was too tired to row, too fatigued to move, and all he could do was sit there as the wooden ships plowed the water toward him, overtaking him, and towering above him at last.

When the other dream finally came, he couldn't say. The weeks had turned into more than a month, and he woke in the mornings exhausted from the conflict of the night. He always found food waiting for him in a bowl or small basket, dried meat or corn cakes, gourds of wild tea, and he would stand in the sun outside the longhouse, like a tree that waited through an everlasting winter to be awakened to something else. He felt he had reached the end of the world, with truly nowhere to go, and closed his eyes. Unable to open them again, he felt the bathing warmth of sunlight as an island in a surrounding sea of darkness, and he fell into it, the darkness, drifting away from the island of warmth, waking to dreams and dreaming he was awake.

He realized he couldn't see and held his hands out in the darkness. There were no voices, no laughter, no barking dogs. No smoke from the cooking fires, no stream of talk from the native boy. He was in a dark place, somewhere on a dark water, sitting in a rowboat, alone, far beyond the edge of anything he had ever known.

And in the dream, he saw a foreign shore and as his boat drifted toward it, he saw a woman standing on the bank, a tall, thin woman wearing a white robe. She had long red hair and bone-white skin. As the rowboat neared the bank, she looked at him, and he wondered if he should be afraid. His enemies were behind him and on both sides. He would never make the shore in time. Their ships bore down on him and were about to crush him, when the figure on the shore began to glow. She got brighter and brighter, emanating a white light that swept across the waters, enveloping him and moving on past, and his enemies disappeared. Their ships vanished. Only the mysterious woman remained, her visage ebbing to a soft radiance. His boat drifted toward the shore, but the shore receded, and the image of the woman receded, too, until finally he awakened, opened his eyes, and gasped for breath.

◆　◆　◆

IN SPITE OF THE FACT that he had done nothing but sleep for over a fortnight, Lawrence was exhausted. In his weakened state, the world nevertheless spilled into him, the scintillating brightness of light, the wondrous smells of cooking fires, the distant barking of dogs, and the melodious laughter of children. Something had changed. The image of the woman on the foreign shore had been burned into his consciousness. She had been frightening in the execution of her judgment. But his recollection of her triggered an afterglow of love, and he felt something he thought he would never experience again. He felt forgiven, and the onrush of sensations that filled him carried him away. Even breathing felt new.

His wife and child were in the ether, waiting for him, and he grieved for them. He saw them in the clouds. He saw them in the shadows of the forest. He saw them in the myriad reflections on water, and he mourned, not through a mad flight from reality, as he had recently experienced, but through the fully engaged sorrow of a man who has lost the two loves of his life in an abrupt and brutal manner. He knew he couldn't stay with the natives much longer, though he had much to thank them for. He had another life to which he needed to return. But after many weeks of minimal use, his body was weak. He had to build his strength back, and while he now remembered who he was and had finally come to grips with this fact, he had no sense of his location. The Indian village was somewhere deep in the wilderness, and he had no inkling of where that was. Finding his way back to the settlement would be a challenge. He didn't even know which direction to take.

When he approached some of the other men in the village and tried to present his dilemma, with the few words of their language that he had learned, they listened patiently but then smiled as if they had no idea of what he said. One of the men pointed at the sky and gave Lawrence a questioning look. Another pointed at the ground. A third offered him some pemmican, as if the easing of hunger would solve whatever problems he had. They had accepted him as one of them and simply didn't understand why he would want to be anywhere other than where he already was.

But he persisted in these attempts and was speaking to yet another, when the boy he had saved came to get him. The boy had become as a little brother to him and often sought him out and tagged along with him. This time, he took Lawrence by the arm and pulled, using a word Lawrence had not yet heard. Lawrence gave the man he had been talking to a look that begged his indulgence, and followed the boy, not knowing what he would find and totally unprepared when he found it. His Indian friend, John, stood in front of the lodge where Lawrence's native family lived. Pierre Laux stood at his side, dressed in the garb of a frontier farmer. For his part, Lawrence had the European beard. He didn't wear a stiff crest of hair on an otherwise shaved scalp, like the native men, but he wore a deerskin tunic, along with leggings and moccasins, and must have been a sight to behold.

"Hello, John," Lawrence said, reaching out and warmly grasping his friend's hand.

His greeting of Pierre was far more tentative. He had assumed the Lauxes would rightly want nothing to do with him, now that Catharine and her baby were gone. The family had had to do the hardest part of the grieving without him, and he fully expected they would never want to see him again.

But Pierre took his proffered hand without reservation.

"Hello, Lawrence," Pierre said, regarding him with kind eyes.

In the conversation that ensued, John explained that he'd heard the Susquehannock had adopted a white man who was very ill with a sleeping sickness, and John had wondered if it was he. Lawrence admitted he had been in a bad way, but that he seemed to have turned a corner. He apologized to Pierre for the confusion and additional pain his absence must have caused. In response, Pierre said the family missed him. They were sorry for what Lawrence had gone through. They all had suffered but Pierre allowed that it was perhaps he, Lawrence, who had suffered the most, because the rest of the family at least had the comfort of each other. Pierre said the family was impatient to have him back home where he belonged. If that was what he wanted. If such a thing were agreeable to him.

Lawrence was at a loss for words. It all made sense to him now, more than he ever thought it would. There really was evil in the world and no one could fully prepare for it. But there were veritable angels, as well, along every step of the way. In the face of daunting challenges and, at times, unspeakable sorrows, they were always there—the grandfather who'd been cruel and mean-spirited in some ways but who had taken him in and given him a trade, the Lenape who gave the word friendship poignant meaning, again and again, the beautiful French woman and her astonishing family, an old farmer and his bitter wife who'd shared with him what little they had, the Susquehannock who fed him and tended him and gave him time to mend. All his life, the healing hands had been there when he most needed them, and as horrendously difficult as life could be, a person had a choice. He did not have to be alone. The angels were there to help him.

"Would you like to come home?" Pierre persisted.

The native boy must have sensed what was going on and gave Lawrence a look that nearly broke his heart. By now, Lawrence knew that the name the Susquehannock called him—Generâá—meant "good friend," and he hoped there would come a day when he could meaningfully return the love of this boy and his people. But for now, Lawrence had only one response to the question that Pierre had posed, and he prayed the boy would understand.

"Yes, sir. I'd like that very much," he said, bowed with humility.

⚜ ⚜ ⚜

EPILOGUE

The ruined château was waiting for Lawrence upon his return. Having missed the burial of his wife and son, he spent many long hours at the gravesite. The minister of the Reformed Church in Watertown had wanted the burial to be at the church, which had a growing cemetery. But Pierre had insisted, in no uncertain terms, that Catharine and Peter would reside at the Laux farm, where they belonged, and that was where Lawrence found them, in a single grave, resting together in a small copse of young oaks. The oak leaves made a green canopy overhead, and a fresh breeze blew from the meadow.

On this particular day, as he stood there, a hand slipped into his. Magdalena was only seven, but was growing at an astonishing rate, and her head was already fast approaching Lawrence's shoulder. She held his hand and leaned her head against his arm.

"Do you ever wonder if God is really love, like they say he is?" Lawrence said, gazing at the small cluster of white flowers Beatrice had planted in front of the stone.

He didn't really expect a response. It certainly wasn't a question he would have asked a child, given a moment's reflection. But Magdalena was far from typical. In spite of her youth, she already comported herself like an adult and took herself very seriously.

"I've always been afraid of the dark," she admitted, as if this were the answer to the question he had posed. "Papa says there are no such things as monsters. But I think he says that just to make me feel better."

"So, you're suggesting that without love, we just live in darkness?" Lawrence said.

Magdalena's body stiffened, as if she thought he might be mocking her.

"I'm saying that if I didn't know the sun would rise in the morning, I'd want to pull the covers over my head and never get out of bed. You should understand that better than anybody."

She started to disengage from him but he held onto her, fearing he had offended her and regretting it. But, still, he persisted.

"So, you're saying that God is the light," he said, and she turned her searing blue eyes upon him. So tall for her age, so straight and pale, she reminded him of the woman in the dream he had had while at the Susquehannock village. It was more than a little unnerving.

"All I said was that I am afraid of the dark. Those other words are yours," she said, bluntly.

Lawrence decided to leave well enough alone. He wished he could share his dream with her, because he suspected she might have a meaningful insight to offer. But that day would have to wait. It would come in due time, when the both of them were better prepared

◆　◆　◆

THE DECISION TO REBUILD THE château was one the family made, together, though the family had altered considerably during the several months of Lawrence's absence. Jean had sailed for England, where Pierre had a cousin whose circle of friends included a British general, and the cousin had offered to make an introduction. The second son, Andrew, had begun to build a house close to the sawmill. Even when he'd lived at the farm with his parents, Andrew had often absented himself, and once the house he was building advanced enough for him to move in, his family rarely saw him anymore. There were still the younger siblings, of course, Georgie and Magdalena. But although Georgie lived and worked on the farm, he had taken a liking to a girl in Watertown, and spent a lot of time there.

As for Magdalena, the red hair that had once wreathed her face like a campfire lengthened. Her eyes still riveted in their unwavering clarity and she was a force to be reckoned with, as the repair masons and carpenters soon learned. Lawrence helped with the reconstruction, making decisions as necessary and otherwise helping out by doing as he was told. Pierre and Georgie pitched in as well, from time to time, when their responsibilities at the farm permitted. But it was Magdalena who seemed to be everywhere at once, in her relentless fashion, and the men had to get used to being bossed around by a girl they started to call "missy", as if she were the woman of the house. By the time she was nine, she was tall enough to look a man in the eye, and not a one among them could hold her gaze without losing his nerve.

While the reconstruction of the château continued apace, the sawmill had more work than it could handle, and Lawrence opened two additional mills. At the same time, he started a drayage company, hauling lumber for the shipbuilding trade in Philadelphia, as well as rye and flaxseed for export. But the château was closest to his heart, and when the reconstruction was finished, he built a fire-pit in front of it, fully aware of the irony. The aroma of roasting pork soon lay like a blanket on the surrounding countryside, and the horses and wagons started to arrive, coming off the nearby farms, the village of Watertown, and from as far off as Philadelphia, the numbers gathering and swelling. The people brought food to share, jars of pickled vegetables and deviled eggs, bean dishes and baskets of bread, cakes and pies and molasses cakes in pie shells. There were fiddles and country drums and the music began to swell.

An old farmer named Morris Warden cornered anyone who would lend him an ear. He had done very well, raising corn that Lawrence now hauled to market for free. Marshaling his skills as a former schoolteacher, Morris held a bony finger in the air and regaled Pierre with what he called the principle of elusive inevitability, which was the notion that what a person thought he knew was premised on so many variables that the only thing truly inevitable was something he had most likely never considered in the first place. It was no doubt his attempt to rationalize how a young man who'd once slept in his barn could turn out to be such a person of worth, and Pierre listened patiently, nodding from time to time, as if what the farmer said made perfect sense.

Lawrence excused himself and wandered aside, where he could get a good look at the house. Although the building had been handsomely restored, he still saw the blackened walls, and the vision haunted him. Pierre joined him and placed a hand on his shoulder.

"I can't shake the feeling that she's still in there," Lawrence said, sadly.

"Great houses come at a price," Pierre responded. "Back where I came from, my family lived for hundreds of years in the same house, and don't think for a minute it didn't have its ghosts. That's what happens when you live in houses that outlive you. The ghosts pile up with the memories, and our Catharine will not be the only one to walk these halls. We had a great family in the Languedoc and there's no reason it can't continue to thrive here in the new land.

Having a great family takes courage. It takes effort. I have high expectations of my children . . . every one of you."

"I've been thinking . . ." Lawrence said, after a pause. He gave Pierre a look that begged forgiveness ahead of time. "Remember that little architect—LeBlanc? He was a wealth of information and one of the things he said was that a proper château should have a name."

Pierre's head gave a little wobble.

"What do you want to name it?" he said. "It should be something important. Something meaningful to you."

Lawrence paused, marshaling his thoughts and the courage to express them.

He closed his eyes.

"Respectfully, I would like to name it Château Laux . . . With your permission . . ."

Pierre gave the matter careful thought, his face long and sober. His gaze drifted to the reconstructed edifice, towering against the backdrop of the New World landscape. No doubt he saw the past, for the past is always there. But perhaps he saw a future as well, a way forward for one and all, together.

"We'd be honored," he said.

◆　◆　◆

MEANWHILE, NOT TO BE OUTDONE, the Laux farm had some drama of its own. One of Pierre's horses had gone into labor, which was not an unusual thing in spring, when miracles are known to happen. But the labor didn't stop when the first foal dropped. The labor continued. A second foal followed, and soon, both foals stood on wobbly legs, looking just a little astonished at the world they had tumbled into. Their mother nosed them and licked them and they knew just what to do as they raised their chins to nurse, and before long, they were too rambunctious to stand still. They bounced into the air and kicked their heels, irrepressible in their vim and vigor, just brimming with the joy of being alive.

By the PRESIDENT *and the* SUPREME EXECUTIVE COUNCIL *of the Commonwealth*
of Pennſylvania,

A PROCLAMATION.

WHEREAS it appears to us, that Catharine the wife of Lawrence Kraymer, jun. of the townſhip of Bedminſter in the County of Bucks, and Peter Kraymer, his ſon, were killed and murdered in the night of the twenty-firſt inſt. in the dwelling houſe of the ſaid Lawrence Kraymer, by a certain John M'Donall, and that he afterwards ſet fire to the dwelling houſe aforeſaid, by which the ſame was deſtroyed : And Whereas it is of the utmoſt importance to the lives of the good people of this ſtate, and a due execution of the laws, that the perpetrator of a crime ſo horrid, ſhould be brought to condign and examplary puniſhment : We have therefore thought proper to iſſue this proclamation, hereby engaging, that the public reward of *Fifty Pounds*, in Specie, ſhall be paid to any perſon or perſons who ſhall apprehend and ſecure the ſaid John M'Donall, to be paid on conviction for the ſame : And we do hereby charge and require an Judges, juſtices, ſheriffs and conſtables, to make diligent ſearch and enquiry after, and to uſe their utmoſt endeavours to apprehend and ſecure the ſaid John M'Donall his aiders, abettors and comforters, and every of them, ſo that they may be dealt with according to law.

GIVEN in Council, under the the hand of the Preſident, and the ſeal of the ſtate, at ' Philadelphia, this thirtieth day of June in the year of our Lord one thouſand ſeven hundred and eighty five.

JOHN DICKINSON.

ATTEST.
JOHN ARMSTRONG, Jun. SECRETARY. }

GOD SAVE THE COMMONWEALTH !

The ſaid John M'Donall is an Iriſhman, about twenty five years old, and five feet high, very thick ſet, much marked in the face by the ſmall pox, with ſhort curled brown hair, and walks ſlow and wide, had with him when he left Bedminſter, a double barrel'd piſtol the ſtock of which is inlaid with ſilver.

HISTORICAL NOTE

CHATEAU LAUX WAS INSPIRED BY a horrific event in 1785, which is referenced in the proclamation. The woman referred to in the proclamation as Catharine Kraymer was born Catharine Laux, and was a member of the author's family. Her name was preserved, as well as that of her husband, Lawrence, and their child, Peter. McDonall's name was also preserved. Some of the other names, however, were changed to avoid confusion.

Where the narrative took a major departure from the historical record was the setting, placing the tragedy at the much earlier date of 1715, so that the Laux family's provenance in France could be more closely tied with its first-generation experience in what later became known as the Commonwealth of Pennsylvania.

Lawrence's brewery in Philadelphia is fictitious. The château in the novel is also fictitious, and those who seek to find it will have to look inward. It is a monument to the spirit, which will hopefully endure, in one way or another, for a very long time.

⚜ ⚜ ⚜

ACKOWLEDGMENTS

---•---

IN *CHATEAU LAUX*, I RELIED on research into the Laux family surname that began in 2005. The results were presented in a paper titled "Laux Name Origins and Historical Context," which was delivered at the Laux family's 300-year reunion in 2010 in York, Pennsylvania. The high point of my research was the opportunity to meet Marquis Henri du Lau d'Allemans at Montardy, and I will be forever grateful for his warm welcome and the introductions he provided to his family. His sister, Madame Hélène Ustinov called me "cousin," which meant more to me than she could have known.

Along the writer's path, I have received invaluable help from others, and must first of all thank my wife, Lynn Crosbie Loux, who read the manuscript so many times I am sure she has memorized it. I am grateful for her support and helpful critique. To get a wide range of editorial opinion, I worked with three professionals, and would like to thank Erik Hane for giving me the gift of confidence in my voice; Laurie Chittenden, who not only helped me restructure the book, but gave me many valuable insights into the publishing world; and Constance Renfrow, who provided intensive editorial review and then went on to do the formidable job of copyediting the work. Throughout, Constance displayed an amazing ability to grasp the nuances of the book, and her subsequent copyediting displayed a truly remarkable attention to detail.

In addition to the content of a book, design plays a critical role as well, and I would like to thank Annie Reid, who produced the image for the cover; and Kat Georges, who did the overall cover and interior design. Kat made a challenging process look effortless as she guided me through the myriad steps of ushering the book into print.

Finally, I would like to acknowledge Thomas Campanius Holm, author of *A Description of the province of New Sweden, now called, by the English, Pennsylvania* (Philadelphia: M'Carty and Davis, 1834), which was subsequently republished as *A Vocabulary of Susquehannock* (Merchantville: Evolution Publishing, 2007). Holm published the notes of his grandfather, Johannes Campanius, who was a chaplain in the Swedish colonies on the Lower Delaware River, thereby recording some of the few Susquehannock words that have survived, including Generââ, which means "good friend."

ABOUT THE AUTHOR

DAVID LOUX IS A SHORT story writer, who has published under a pseudonym and served as past board member of California Poets in the Schools. *Chateau Laux* is his first novel. He lives in the Eastern Sierra with his wife, Lynn.

⚜ ⚜ ⚜